HIDDEN IN PARADISE

CARA KENT

Hidden in Paradise
Copyright © 2024 by Cara Kent

All rights reserved. Without limiting the rights under copyright reserved above, no part of this publication may be reproduced, stored in or introduced into retrieval system, or transmitted, in any form, or by any means (electronic, mechanical, photocopying, recording, or otherwise) without the prior written permission of both the copyright owner and the above publisher of this book.

This is a work of fiction. Names, characters, places, brands, media, and incidents are either the products of the author's imagination or are used fictitiously. The author acknowledges the trademarked status and trademark owners of various products referenced in this work of fiction, which have been used without permission. The publication/use of these trademarks is not authorized, associated with, or sponsored by the trademark owners.

PROLOGUE

Day 15
Leave your worries on the doorstep...
Just direct your feet on the sunny side of the street...
"Shut up, Weisman!"
I used to walk in the shade...
"Someone shut him up!"

Bruce Weisman rolled his eyes at the onslaught of insults being hurled his way from the other prisoners. What did they expect him to do? He was losing his mind. They were used to being stuck inside a cell, being told what to do day in and day out, but not him. He was used to his freedom. He missed it. He missed being able to take a slow deep breath without choking on the stench of shit and urine. He missed being able to take a shower without a dozen eyes watching him.

He missed being able to stretch without touching a wall. That was nice.

And if I never have a cent...

"I swear I will come in there..."

I'd be rich as...

Singing was all he had. It was all he could do. That or read, but the books left a lot to be desired. He needed to speak with his lawyer again and go over the best course of action to get him out of this cell. There had to be something he could do.

A shadow passed over his cot. Bruce rolled over and propped himself up on his elbow. A guard leaned against the bars, a grin pressed onto his lips.

"I just wanted to tell you that you will be released into gen pop tomorrow. You should get some sleep instead of doing all that singing. Might be the last bit of sleep you have for a while."

On the sunny side of the street.

Day 20

Bruce rubbed his bruised chin. The throbbing pain brought tears to his eyes. He was so tired. So tired of everything. How mundane prison was, for starters. It was nothing like he had imagined. And he had imagined every possible scenario. He knew getting caught was a possibility, but he never thought it would happen. He was too good. Too well trained. But here he was.

He sat in the yard under the shade of a tree, in view of the guards that stood near the gate but far enough away from everyone he didn't want to have contact with.

He couldn't take another beating. His ribs were on fire every time he breathed, let alone moved.

"Did I tell you about my case?" Sully walked over to Bruce and sat on the bench next to him. This had become one of their rituals every day. The men, along with their friend Kingston, sat on the bench and talked.

"I don't know why they care about this case now," said Sully. "It was years ago."

Kingston shrugged. "I don't think there is a statute of limitations on murder. They can arrest you at any time for murder, no matter how long it takes."

Sully shook his head. "I still don't know how they even found out about it. I mean, she's dead. It ain't like she's going to tell nobody."

Bruce laughed. His ribs screamed at the movement.

"You alright, Bruce?" Sully leaned over his shoulder. "They kick the shit out of you again?"

He nodded slowly. "Don't think I can take much more of this."

"If you can get out," said Kingston, "then get out. Whatever you have to do. Or at least get yourself transferred."

"You'll die here if you don't," added Sully.

Their words percolated in his brain for the rest of the day. He had to get out. He had to find a way out.

He knew how this whole thing was going to end with his death. They'd beat him to death. They were well on their way.

He was surprised he didn't have a collapsed lung by now.

After dinner, he found an unoccupied phone and called his lawyer.

"Yeah, I want to speak with the FBI agent that arrested me. The pretty woman. I want to see her and only her. Tell her I have something important to tell her. It's about a case."

His lawyer sounded confused on the other line, but he said he would get the message to her. Bruce smiled. He had found his way out, if not out of prison, out of this prison.

His life sentence might get better once he was sent somewhere else. He sat in his bunk at first and then laid down. He knew what was coming. He knew what was about to happen.

Leave your worries on the doorstep… Life can be so sweet on the sunny side of the street.

He heard the door to his cell slide open, and the familiar heavy footsteps walk in. But Bruce didn't move. This happened every night and would until he figured a way out. He stayed completely still.

He would give no one the satisfaction of seeing him scared. He would take whatever they threw his way.

He would take all of it, and he would smile.

And he would plan.

CHAPTER ONE

There was something about seeing Tony in a hospital bed, bruised and broken, that pulled at my heartstrings. Tugged on them relentlessly every time I looked at him. I had held his hand every day he was in the hospital. Stroked his forefinger with my thumb, coaxing him out of his sleep and talking to him until sleep called to him again.

When his mother was in the room, I kept our conversations light. When she wasn't, I talked about the case and what we had found. Tony's brother, King, was intrigued. He leaned forward and hung on my every word. Tony nodded through most of it and spoke when he could.

I had to repeat myself as the days went on, and he became more himself. He didn't remember our earlier conversations, so I told him what I could, and King filled in the rest. He was extra excited to tell his brother about the case that was closed while he was unconscious, laughably giddy at knowing something Tony didn't. It was cute, even though Tony found it annoying.

"Are you sure about this?" I asked for the millionth time since we had left the hospital. He was tired of answering the same question, and, truthfully, I was tired of asking. Tired of hearing my voice over and over. But I needed to ask. I needed to hear the words fall from his lips. The answer soothed my nerves. I had found that in his time at the hospital, I could not relax until I heard him say he was okay. That everything was okay. Only then did my shoulders fall, and could my mind drift to other things outside of his mangled body.

I found myself having to talk to him before I went to bed to make sure nothing had happened to him on my way home. Only then could I lull myself to sleep. These days, my dreams consisted of Tony in a casket and children in cages. Children calling for their mothers, begging to be set free. Faceless children. It was unnerving and confusing.

I couldn't see who the children were, and yet every night, they were there, begging me to find them but offering no clues as to who or where they were. I shook the thought out of my mind and focused on him.

"I'm tired of being in that hospital bed. And I'm fine. Even the doctor said so."

"What does he know?" I closed the front door behind me.

Tony glanced at me, his eyebrow raised slightly.

"You know what I mean." Gingerly, I guided him to the living room. "I just think I'd feel better if you were still in the hospital."

I slumped into the chair across from the sofa. He had spent a couple of weeks in the hospital, which canceled everyone's Christmas plans. We made do with a small dinner with my family and his together. Our mothers cooked and then took food to the hospital. The nurse was against the idea at first, but his mother was persuasive, and she relented.

My family left soon after. Tony had been cleared to leave the hospital, but I still didn't think he was ready. There was no bleeding on the brain or any lasting damage. He would just be sore for a while. He was lucky.

"I'm okay, Mia."

I smiled weakly. He didn't look okay. He looked broken, his bruises still prominent on his visible patches of skin. A tear stung the corner of my eyes, and I blinked them away. I had cried enough over him. And now was not the time for him to see me crying. Not when he was better. The doctor said he would be fine, but something like dread bloomed within me. He was okay now, but what about the next time? I shook the thought from my mind. I needed to focus on today. He was here. He was alive. And my parents had finally gone home.

I loved my family, but their hovering was too much. In the weeks that followed Tony's assault, my parents had looked at me differently. I saw it. Their long looks were laced with concern. Worry. My father wanted me to quit the Bureau. He had always wanted me to quit, even before I went to Quantico. But seeing Tony, my partner, bruised and broken in a hospital bed renewed my father's objection.

"This job is too dangerous. What are you going to do when it's you in that hospital bed? What are you going to do if help comes too late?" My father asked just before they left to go back home.

I didn't have an answer for him. I didn't know what I would do. I also didn't mention that I had previously been beaten or that I had been shot. It didn't seem like the best time to bring that up. My parents had enough to worry about on their plane ride home.

I looked at Tony and sighed. "I know. I worry, but I know."

"Good." A smirk danced across Tony's lips. "I like you worrying about me. I appreciate you worrying about me, but I have my mother for that. And she is great at it. Believe me."

"You worry about me. And I can worry about you. It's an even trade, although you do seem to end up in the hospital more than I do."

He rolled his eyes. His shoulders softened as he leaned back. Silence stretched between us like a comfortable blanket. The weight of it wrapped around me and tucked me in.

I woke with a start. The sound of metal pans hitting the tile floor had me on my feet before my brain could register I was up and wake.

"What are you doing?"

Tony smiled tentatively from the kitchen. "I was going to make you something to eat."

"Dude!" My heart pounded in my chest. I shook my head. "You shouldn't be up."

He sighed. Before he could offer a retort, I threw my hands up. "Sorry. Don't mean to treat you like an invalid. I know you're not. But now you know how I felt when I was hurt, and you were all over me."

"I wasn't all over you. I just helped out... a lot."

I cocked my head to the side and stared at him until a ghost of a smile kissed his lips. He was all over me. I could barely take a step into his condo without him asking me if I was okay or needed something. It was sweet and mildly annoying.

"You don't have to make me anything. I'm not hungry," he insisted.

"You are always hungry." I smiled, and his features softened. "We can order something. Neither of us should cook tonight. You need to rest." I inched closer to the counter.

"Fine."

I smiled and gestured to the sofa for him to sit down. "I'll order something."

"I think I'm going to take a bath." He glanced back at the doorway.

"Holler if you need help getting out of the tub."

His back went rigid. "I'm kidding. Go, and I'll order something." A long moment passed before he started walking again. When he rounded the corner, I sighed. I was kidding. Partially.

I ordered from our favorite taco place and waited on the sofa. I listened for the door, and I listened for him in case he needed me.

Moving into my new place and constantly checking up on him had been draining. I was ready for a bath myself and a nap.

Tony emerged from his room a few minutes after the food arrived. He smelled of sage and amber. His limp was less noticeable.

"You feel better?"

He nodded as he opened the fridge and grabbed two bottles of water. "A lot better. Hot water really helped ease my muscles."

"Good."

"You don't have to stay here and take care of me. You just moved into the building. You need to get to know your neighbors." He sat on the stool in front of the counter while I dished out the food.

"I am getting to know my neighbors."

"You already know me. I mean, your other neighbors."

I laughed. I knew what he meant, but I had gotten to know my neighbors. I met Harrison and Delia the first few days I moved in. Tony had still been in the hospital. Harrison had helped me move some of my things in. Just the smaller stuff the movers didn't have.

I met Delia the day after I moved in. She was about my age with a five-year-old daughter named Divine. We had gotten together and talked a few times since I moved in. They were nice enough. But I didn't really know them.

I was trying to get to know new people and break away from the work crowd. Well, maybe not break away, but find new friends to add to my old ones. Delia seemed like a good friend to have. She was easy to talk to. On the few occasions we spoke, words tumbled from my mouth uncontrollably. I felt like I could tell her anything.

I didn't, though. Whenever I spoke with her, I had to make sure that I reined in my tongue.

"I'm taking care of you today. So shut up and eat your food."

"Thank you."

We ate our burritos and drank our water in comfortable silence. After we were done, I threw away the trash and wiped down the counter.

"You want to talk about it?" His tone was flat and calm.

I scrubbed the counter and ignored the question. "What do you want to do now?"

"Talk."

I rolled my eyes. "I don't want to talk about her. I don't want to talk about any of it.

"It wasn't your fault, Mia. You couldn't have known that she was who she was."

I sighed.

I should have—I knew something was wrong. I knew it. I knew something was off about Yumi. Maybe not that she procured people for other people to kill. I didn't know that. I couldn't have known that. But I felt there was something wrong with her when I had dinner at her house. As soon as I walked in, I felt something was off. Something seemed wrong, missing.

At first, I thought it was because she had just broken up with her abusive boyfriend, and he took everything to be spiteful. Her house was so bare. It seemed like only one person lived there. Like there were just enough dishes and so on for one person.

I knew there was something off about her place. I should have trusted my gut, but I didn't.

Tony's hand rested on my fist on the counter. "None of this was your fault. You couldn't have stopped her even if you had put it together then. By then, the Reapers already had their victims. There was nothing you could do. Is she talking?"

I shook my head. Yumi hadn't said a word since the agents brought her in. "She asked for a lawyer, and that was it. Nothing else."

"She's smart. You think they can make her talk?"

"I think I could, but Davies doesn't want me to talk to her. She says I'm too close to it. Whatever that means."

"It means she knows that you are angry and that you feel like she made a fool of you, and that is going to cloud your judgment if you do talk to her. That's what that means, and she's right. I've done interrogations when I was angry, and I—I shouldn't have. They never ended well."

"And I understand that. But we need her to talk, and maybe I could rattle her. That's what we need. We need to know who she works for, and so far, no one can tell us that but her."

"Maybe I can help you with that when I get back to work."

"When is that, by the way?" I leaned forward, resting my elbows on the counter. I missed working with Tony. Working cases on my own wasn't the same.

"I'm not sure. I might be on light duty for a little while. I have a doctor's appointment at the end of the week to see."

"I hope it is soon."

"You miss me?" He wiggled his eyebrows. The wavy motion made me laugh.

"Maybe a little. I didn't like searching the house without you."

He tapped the counter. "Yeah, I'm sorry I missed that. Well, I am, but I'm not, you know. I heard you guys found some pretty messed up things there."

"Yeah? Who'd you hear that from?"

"Hattie kept me abreast of all the goings-on in the office."

"Did she now?"

He nodded. "Yeah. I couldn't stop thinking about all the bodies that we didn't find. All the ones on the bottom of the ocean or in a shark's stomach by now. Everything we don't know. And probably never will."

I sighed. That had been on my mind a lot lately, too. Mrs. Blackstone told me about her organization, but I still felt like she didn't tell me everything. I couldn't prove it, but there was something she wasn't telling us. Something her husband didn't know.

"I think her husband told us everything he knew. He doesn't think he did anything wrong, so he has no reason to lie. She, on the other hand, had a lot to hide."

"She probably ran things. He knew what he needed to know, but she controlled everything else. You think we found everything in the house?"

I took a moment to mull that over. The Blackstone house had so many hidden rooms and hidden compartments. The only people who knew where everything was were the Blackstones. I shook my head. I doubted we'd ever be able to find everything they had hidden in that house. One day, it would be sold, and the new owners would start renovations and find body parts and skeletons behind walls.

"I didn't think so. The way Hattie talked about the house... she sounded afraid to go there by herself. I think everyone was unnerved by it."

"I wish you could have seen it when we first got there. I don't think I could ever do it justice. I don't think I could ever describe to you what I saw, what I felt, what I smelled. It was... is definitely a scene that haunts me. It lingers. In a way, I'm glad you didn't see it. It was a lot. So much death. The house smelled like death."

"Makes sense. House for the dead."

"They need to tear it down."

"Once we finish with it, they might. It's been all over the news, and pretty soon, people will try to break into the house and summon the ghost of the victims and whatnot."

"Is that something that happens often here?"

"We did it a few times when I was a kid."

I barked out a laugh. "What kind of kid were you?"

He shrugged. "The kind that wanted to know if ghosts were real."

"And?"

He shrugged again. "Still not sure. But if they were, they would be in that house. It will be very popular next Halloween."

CHAPTER TWO

After a long conversation about how Tony was ready to go back to work, I put him to bed and then went to my apartment one floor below him. He said I made him feel like a toddler, and I told him I didn't care.

I set his cell phone on his nightstand and told him to call me if he needed something. Deep down, I knew he probably wouldn't call me if he needed anything. I should have gotten a baby monitor and put it on his nightstand, but that would have been a little too invasive, I guess.

"Hey!"

Delia's voice made me jump.

"Oh, sorry." She held up her empty hands.

"No, I'm sorry. What are you doing up so late?" I shoved my key into the door, unlocked it, and then pushed it open.

"Well, I'm a bit of a night owl. Drives Divine crazy. I try to keep the TV low so it doesn't keep her up. What are you doing?" She winked. I wasn't sure what that was supposed to mean, but I just smiled.

"I was just checking on Tony. He's home from the hospital finally."

"Oh! That's great! How is he?"

I gestured for her to come and then closed the door behind her. "He's good. Already talking about coming back to work."

"Is that wise? I mean, shouldn't he take more time to rest?"

"He should, and he is. I doubt our boss will let him come back this soon. Not until he's cleared."

She followed me through the foyer into the living room. I loved the open floor plan, which was the thing that initially attracted me to the place. It was a little smaller and more basic than Tony's more extensive suite on the top floor, but that was fine. I didn't even know what I would do with that much space. This was perfectly fine for me. Delia sat on the sofa.

"Hopefully he'll listen to her."

"She is the kind of person you listen to whether you want to or not." I sat in the large off-white chair across from her. "So, he'll have to listen to her. Or to his mother."

Delia laughed. She knew Tony, so I wasn't telling her anything she didn't already know. They had known each other since high school, and she was still friends with one of his sisters. She tucked a clump of black hair behind her ear.

"His mother ain't nobody to play with. I think she's gotten scarier as she's aged."

"She's so sweet, though."

"Don't let it fool you."

I laughed.

"So, how do you like the building so far?" She leaned forward, resting her elbows on her thighs. Her black curls bounced forward, shielding her face. "Meet anyone?"

"I just got here. It's only been a couple of weeks, and I spent most of that time in the hospital. I've met you, Harrison, and Keisha."

She leaned back, her arms folded across her chest. "You've already met Harrison? He's hot."

"I know, right?" Harrison lived across the hall, and he was *very* hot. With chiseled features, light green eyes, and dark hair, he was something to marvel at. Something to behold. I ran into him while carrying a box of books up to my condo. We both entered the elevator at the same time.

"You're new. That's cool," he'd said in his deep voice.

My tongue felt thick and heavy in my mouth. All I could do was smile and nod like an idiot. Delia got a kick out of that. She laughed a little too hard for my liking.

"I think everyone who has ever met him in this building had that same reaction. He's so cool and laid back and gorgeous. The same thing with Tony. All the women fawned all over him when he first got here."

"Yeah, I could see that."

"Really?" She rested her chin in her hand. "Tell me more."

"There's nothing else to say."

"Mhmm. Right."

I rolled my eyes. "Stop it. We are just partners. That's all." I swallowed the words, ready to bounce off my tongue. There was nothing else. Nothing left to say about my relationship with Tony. He was my friend. My partner. Nothing more. And he would probably never be anything more.

I didn't mention how beautiful I thought he was or how heat pooled at the base of my spine when he looked at me. Or how my heart fluttered when he called me Mia. Or how seeing him broken on the ground knocked something loose in me.

I swallowed my words. They weren't necessary, not now. I doubted they ever would be. "What's going on with you?"

Delia shrugged. "Nothing new. Trying to keep it together for Divine. My ex isn't making it easy."

"What's he doing?"

She shook her head. "Just little things. He spoils her when he has her. He never tells her no, so when I have to, it makes her hate me. I have heard 'I wanna go back to Daddy's house, he's fun' six times this week."

"It might take her a while, but she'll see it for what it is. A tactic to manipulate the both of you. She'll see it when she gets older. Just keep doing what you're doing."

"I'm trying. I want to be the fun parent, too, but I can't because he won't do what he's supposed to do as a parent. And now he has a new girlfriend."

"Have you met her?"

Delia laughed. It wasn't a genuine laugh, more forced than anything. "She's my cousin, believe it or not."

"I'm sorry, what?" I leaned forward. "He did what?"

"Her, apparently."

"No! While you were together?" I tried to strip some of the intrigue out of my voice. I wanted to know more. I wanted to know how it happened. Why it happened. Everything. I relaxed my face and leaned back. Let the information come to me.

"He says it was after. They only got together after we separated."

My eyebrow raised slightly.

"I know. I know. I was thinking the same thing. There's something about that not sitting right with me. I mean, it could be possible, but I'm still not sure. I feel like it was during. I just don't know when exactly."

"Does it matter? I mean, at this point, does it matter when they started seeing each other?"

She shrugged.

"Were you and your cousin close?"

She shook her head. "Not really. Her family's from Louisiana. Didn't get there much except during the summer when I was in elementary. But still."

"Yeah, that is shitty on both their parts. But it is what it is. You want to know how, when, and why, but none of that really matters. It doesn't change anything. You're still divorced, and he's still the kind of guy who would sleep with your cousin."

"Good point. Yeah, you're right. When and all that makes no difference. It is what it is." She gave a curt nod and took a deep breath. "Hopefully, it will get easier."

"It will, I think. I hope."

She smiled.

"What does your family say?"

She waved a hand dismissively. "My mother says she's staying out of it. But I think she is more pissed than I am. She called her sister and cussed her out. I had nothing to do with it, and yet I was still a little proud. It caused a lot of problems at first. I think now... I guess we've all gotten used to it. Or... I don't know. I just try to stay away from them best I can."

There was a soft knock at the door. Delia and I both exchanged a look. My first thought was Tony had made his way down to my apartment. He still hadn't seen it. I took my phone out of my pocket and glanced at the screen.

He hadn't called.

I jumped up and hurried to the door.

"Hey, are you busy? I'm bored." Keisha leaned on the door frame. "So very bored, and I don't feel like leaving the building." She extended the arm behind her back and wiggled a bottle of tequila.

I grinned. "Come on in."

She giggled as she walked through the threshold. I closed the door behind her. Keisha was around my age with no children. She liked to have fun but didn't like leaving the building. She worked from home and didn't have to go anywhere if she didn't want to.

I went into the kitchen and got three glasses. I sat down beside Keisha on the couch and held the glasses as she poured the tequila. It was a heavy-handed pour. All her pours were a bit heavy.

"How was your day?" asked Delia.

Keisha sucked her teeth at the questions. "I do the same shit every day. Nothing new. I want to know more about this case Mia was working on."

I blinked. I sipped my tequila slowly before I said anything. Talking about the case didn't sit right with me for a variety of reasons. The Blackstones took a deal, but the case still didn't feel over. It wasn't settled. There were still so many things that I didn't know. So many questions I didn't have the answers to, and maybe that was what irked me so much.

I swallowed hard. Keisha and Delia watched me expectantly. I chose my words carefully. Leaving out most of the details. The gruesome ones, anyway. Keisha's jaw dropped, and Delia leaned forward like she was trying to catch all the details, all the information falling from my mouth. She listened greedily, but I kept the details to a minimum. Broad strokes of what happened.

"I heard there was something in the suitcases. Something etched into the suitcase."

I stared at Keisha.

She shrugged. "I have nothing better to do than to read blogs and conspiracy theories posted on Reddit."

"Do that a lot, do you?" I sipped my tequila slowly. The heat bloomed in my chest.

She shrugged again. "I do. People are crazy, and I like to be informed on how crazy they can be. But back to the thing in the suitcase. Is there any truth to that?"

"I cannot confirm or deny any parts of an ongoing investigation." I needed to spend some time on Reddit. I wondered for a moment if they knew more about my case than I did.

"Well, that was what I read," said Keisha as she lifted her glass to her lips. "The red reaper."

I blinked. The smooth tequila caught in my throat. I coughed violently. "What?"

"I guess that part is true." Delia leaned back on the sofa. "I saw something like that downtown. Or at least I thought I did. I went back last week, and it's gone."

"What's gone?" I asked after I gulped in cool air. "What are you talking about?"

Delia recounted how she saw a drawing of a grim reaper outlined in red on a building downtown. She didn't know the name of the building, but the graffiti was on the back.

"What were you doing that allowed you to see this?" I set my glass on the coffee table.

"I was on my lunch break downtown, and I just saw it. I thought it was weird, but I didn't think anything else of it. And then I started talking to Keisha and her conspiracy theories, and now…" She shrugged. "I don't know. Maybe there's nothing to it."

I cocked my head and regarded her comment thoughtfully. She wasn't the first person to say that. I thought back to the investigation when we spoke to an officer who said he had seen something like it before. So did Tony. But neither of them could remember where they had seen it. Could it have been the same building?

"That's interesting." I swallowed the words bubbling up my throat. They weren't words meant for them. I needed to save them for Hattie or Tony, or someone else who was part of the investigation. Keisha and Delia watched me expectantly.

"I told you I can't talk about the case." I threw my hands up. I wasn't giving in to them and their peer pressure. I told them what I could. I held back the rest.

I had become used to doing that. I did it all the time with my parents. Swallowed my words, my thoughts on my cases. They didn't need to know details, and I couldn't tell them, anyway. It was difficult, especially when I was still working on a case and needed to figure out how the pieces fit together. Talking it through helped, so I spoke to Tony, Hattie, or myself in the mirror.

"Fine." Keisha rolled her eyes. "How's T?"

"He's fine. Back home, already talking about coming back to work."

Keisha's eyes went wide. "He better sit his ass down somewhere. He needs to rest. You don't take a beating like that and just get up and go to work."

"Exactly! I told him if he tried anything, I was going to tell his mom."

"Now she will shut that down," said Keisha. "Mrs. Walker don't play about her boys."

"She's like that with King, too?" I noticed King seemed a little annoyed with how their mother doted on Tony. It made me think she didn't treat him the same way.

"Definitely. She's protective of them both. You know, mothers and sons."

We spent the rest of the night talking about the building's politics. Keisha and Delia informed me about who I needed to stay away from and who I shouldn't tell my secrets to.

"Mrs. Williams on the floor above you can't hold water. She tells everybody's business. Don't tell her yours, but if you want to know what's going on in the building, she's the person to listen to," said Delia.

"Right. Mrs. Lee, down the hall, pretends to be blind. She ain't. She sees everything and is always watching."

The building was filled with older people who were retired. Apparently, they were nosy but kind. The women left a little after one in the morning. I placed the empty glasses in the sink and went straight to bed. A few hours later, I woke, grabbed the notepad I kept on my nightstand, and made notes of all the things I still wanted to know about the Blackstones and their murder club. Six things, starting with the symbol in the suitcases.

I rolled over to go back to sleep, but sleep never came. My eyes felt like there were rocks underneath my eyelids. It had been so many nights since I'd had a good night's sleep. Between moving and worrying about Tony and the Blackstones and the faceless children in my dreams, sleep was as elusive as ever.

I got out of bed and headed to the living room. After pouring a glass of water, I sat on the sofa and pulled the giant puzzle from underneath the coffee table. I worked on it whenever I couldn't sleep. It was over a thousand pieces. A picturesque scene of the French countryside.

When I finished it, which would probably happen in a couple more days, I would frame it and hang it up in the office I hadn't decorated yet. It was an empty room with a chair. I hadn't gotten around to getting a desk or a file cabinet or putting anything on the walls. Part of me wondered if I needed an office. It could be another guest room. I usually didn't bring work home with me, which was probably for the best.

My mind wandered to the Blackstones and their house of horrors. We were missing something. My forefinger tapped against the lavender fields. Fatima Blackstone had an ace up her sleeve. What was it? Why was she so sure she could walk away unscathed after all she had done? When I interrogated her, she agreed to the deal. What changed her mind? Who changed her mind?

Who made her think she could get away with it, or was it just as simple as Tony said? She knew her husband would say nothing against her, so she had nothing to worry about. She must trust him. And he must love her. What could we do to turn him against her?

Fatima was guarded when I interrogated her. But her husband was not. He believed in what they were doing. He believed that it was the right thing. When I started to question him, he was open and honest. He was at peace with his actions. She was not.

I chewed on my bottom lip. There was something we were missing. Something. I needed to speak with Corey Blackstone and hear what else he knew. Ask him if he planned on testifying on behalf of his wife. This was why I shouldn't have an office, why I shouldn't bring my cases home with me.

If I brought my cases home with me, I would never be able to let them go. And I was barely getting any sleep as it was. I worked through the puzzle until four in the morning. Only then did my eyes finally feel heavy. I relaxed on the sofa, leaning back. I allowed my eyes to drift closed and prayed I would stay asleep until the sun came up.

CHAPTER THREE

"LIGHT DUTY!" DAVIES HAD REPEATED THE WORD several times since we walked into her office. She stared at Tony and only Tony. "Only. I better not catch you running into buildings or apprehending suspects. Light duty only!"

Tony threw his hands up. "Yes, ma'am. I understand. Light duty."

"Now, I'm not going to tie you to your desk, but I will keep my eye on you. I mean it, Walker."

"Yes, ma'am."

I tried not to grin while pushing down my surprise. I didn't think he would be back so soon, light duty or otherwise. I figured he would have to take a few more weeks off. But apparently, he was a fast healer. The doctor saw no reason for him not to return to work, but he couldn't do anything too strenuous.

"While I have you… can we talk about Yumi?" I held up my finger as she rolled her eyes.

"Storm!"

"Hear me out. Has she said anything yet? Said who she works for?"

Davies rolled her eyes and leaned back in her chair. Her reaction told me everything I needed to know. Yumi hadn't said anything since she had been arrested.

She sighed, a deep, heavy, I'm-not-in-the-mood-for-your-bullshit kind of sigh.

"Let me talk to her, please. I need to know why she moved across the street from me. If everything was just a ruse to get close to me. I need to know why. Who she works for?"

"And we will get that information without you. I'm not repeating this. You are too close to this. I can tell from how personal your questions are. This case isn't about you."

That stung. She was right. It wasn't about me, but there was something else going on. Yumi moving in across the street was not a coincidence. There was a reason. A plan, and I needed to know what it was and why.

"I know what I'm doing. I've been doing it a lot longer than you. We will get her to talk."

I sighed. My fists clenched at my sides. She wasn't going to talk to them. She probably wouldn't speak to me either, but I had to try.

My shoulders dropped. "What about her house?"

"Looking through it would be light duty," said Tony. "Especially since we don't have another case to work yet." He clasped his hands in front and rocked back on his heels.

The movement brought a smile to my lips. He had a point. "That's true. It's nothing really."

Davies crossed her arms across her chest. "If you find anything, you call. You don't look into it yourself. I mean it. I'm only letting you go because you two have a knack for finding things and stumbling into cases. Maybe you'll find something we missed."

"Thank you." I grabbed Tony by the wrist and dragged him out of the office before she could add another stipulation. I closed the door behind us swiftly and gently.

"Ow."

"Oh, I'm sorry." I let go of his wrist. He brought it up to his chest and hugged it like it was an injured baby bird or something. "I'm sorry. I forgot for a second."

"I see." He shook his arm out. "Let's get to the house before she changes her mind."

I nodded. We pulled into the empty driveway. I glanced across the street to my old place. The driveway was empty now, but someone had moved in. The people who bought my house were a lovely family with twin girls and a large dog. They were a friendly, happy family looking for a new start after the father had gotten out of the military.

"Okay, what are we looking for?" Tony asked when he slammed the car door.

I shrugged. I wasn't sure what I was looking for. I didn't know what Yumi was hiding, but she was hiding something. And I needed to find it.

I broke the tape on the door that told people to keep out. I pushed my shoulder against the door and turned the knob. The wood groaned and then relented.

Inside, the house was stuffy and dark.

"The last time I was here, there wasn't much to find."

Tony closed the door. "Well, you said you were only in the kitchen. Let's have a look upstairs."

I headed for the stairs. It was clear someone had been here looking for something. The place had been tossed. FBI agents weren't neat when they searched a house.

We didn't purposely try to break or mess things up, but we weren't careful either. Suspects hid things in the strangest of places. If you were too cautious, you might miss something.

I caught a glimpse of the living room on my way up the stairs. The couch cushions had been thrown across the room. Bookcase cleared, and books and knickknacks were piled on the floor.

Upstairs was much of the same. I wanted to get a feel for the kind of person she was. Who she was when no one was looking.

I stood in her bedroom.

"There's nothing here. So, either she didn't sleep here, or this was part of her cover. Like she wanted to make me think she didn't have anything."

In the main bedroom, there was a bed, a dresser, and a wicker chair in the far corner of the room. Nothing else. No pictures of family or even books. It was like a fake house that had been staged for pictures online to rent out.

Tony looked in the walk-in closet while I checked the dresser and the one nightstand. Nothing. The drawers in the dresser had a couple of shirts and two pairs of pants. In the nightstand, there was an empty notebook, a flashlight, and a pair of tweezers.

"You think they took a lot of from the scene?" Tony emerged from the closet, hands empty.

"I heard from Hattie there wasn't much to take. They found some notebooks downstairs, but other than that, the house was just like this."

"How could she live like this? Even if her goal was to get close to you, how could she stay here like this? I mean, she didn't have anything. No clothes. Nothing. She couldn't have been staying here."

"Yeah, that's what I was thinking. The house was to keep up appearances, but she had to actually live somewhere." All the time I spent with Yumi came flashing back. "I took her to stay with a friend once, but I can't remember the address. Didn't think I'd need to. I should have written it down."

"You didn't know. What about when she filed a restraining order against her boyfriend?"

I had remembered that and then forgotten and then remembered again. Things had gotten so crazy that I forgot to ask what was going on with it.

If we had really been friends, I would have felt bad about it.

I shrugged. "Hattie looked into it since I wasn't allowed to. She said Yumi gave them a fake name. Not hers, but the guy. They could not find someone by that name, and when they tried to contact her, she had given them the wrong phone number."

"Damn. So that whole thing was a ruse."

Every time I thought about it, it made my blood boil. She used me, and now it was so clear. She and her boyfriend fought a lot. The fights always seemed to take place when I was home. They would leave the door open like they wanted me to hear. They did. They wanted me to hear them fighting.

She wanted me to sympathize with her. And I did. I fell for it. I didn't know who I was more pissed at, her or me. Me. Definitely me. I was a Special Agent with the FBI. I knew better. I should have put it together sooner. I should have figured it out.

How could I be good at my job if I didn't notice she was conning me? And why? That was the most infuriating thing in all of this. I still didn't know why she went through the trouble. Who was she working for?

"Stop beating yourself up."

Tony's voice shook me from my thoughts. Tethered me back to reality. I blinked.

"You are not the first FBI agent to fall for a con artist. To become friends with a criminal. And you won't be the last. No one wants to look at the people in their lives and figure out if they are hiding something or doing something they shouldn't be doing. That's a hard way to live. And you shouldn't. If you live your life like every person you come in contact with could be a criminal or wants something from you, it's going to burn you out."

"I should have been more cautious." I slumped to the bed.

"I met her. I didn't think anything was wrong either."

"I went to her house. I came here and saw this bare-bones home and thought nothing of it."

"You said you did think it was weird."

"I did. But I should have investigated. I should have been…"

Tony leaned against the door frame to the closet. "I think what's bothering you is that you don't know why. You don't know how things are connected. I get that. That would drive me crazy, too. But worrying and fixating on it is not going to help. She played you. Whatever her reasoning, it happened. Be more cautious next time. Trust your gut when it tells you something is wrong. That's the best you can do. You've got to move on."

He was right. I had to let it go. I couldn't become fixated on her and the why. My shoulders dropped a little as my body relaxed.

"I know. I just. It's so infuriating."

"I know." I stood and glanced around the room one last time. "Okay."

I left the room. I was headed toward the door but stopped and spun around. I hadn't been in the living room before.

There was nothing there. She did have a sofa and a coffee table. There was a bookcase across from the couch and a TV stand. Surprisingly, the TV was not on the ground. But everything else was. I searched the pile of knickknacks and found nothing.

"Staying here would have driven me insane." Tony stood in the doorway. "There's nothing here."

"I know." I finished my search before following him out the front door. "I wonder where she lived. Full time."

My phone vibrated in my back pocket. My body tensed when I saw Davies' number.

"Storm."

"You find anything?"

"No, we didn't. We are on our way back."

"Good. Bruce Weisman wants to speak with you."

I hung up the phone. My jaw twitched. I didn't like Bruce. I didn't like him as a person. I didn't like talking to him.

There was something about interviewing someone who has no problem or remorse about killing people. He was so cold. His presence had no warmth. It was scary, creepy, and something I never wanted to do again.

"Bruce Weisman wants to speak with me," I announced on our way back to the car.

"You must have made a lasting impression."

"I guess. Wish I could undo that."

"Did she say what he wanted?"

I shrugged. "I didn't think to ask. She didn't say I had to speak with him. But it wasn't a question either. But, why now?"

Tony shrugged. "Maybe he has more he wants to confess."

Bruce Weisman had already confessed to murdering multiple women, over twenty, on his own. He had also killed women alongside his father-in-law. They were both serial killers and while more than one serial killer in a family was rare, it did happen.

Tony had been hurt, so I had to get Bruce's confession by myself. And I had been scared. Perhaps more nervous than scared, but there was a slither of fear. He was a serial killer. He enjoyed killing women and felt no shame or remorse for it.

It was clear from the way he talked about the victims and what he had done to them. The grin on his face. The light in his eyes. His face lit up when he spoke about the women he hurt, and that was something I didn't want to see again if I didn't have to.

"I hope I can say no."

Tony eased the car out of the driveway. "Well, I'll be there with you if you can't."

CHAPTER FOUR

A SAC Davies rocked in her chair with her hands resting on her stomach. She shook her head several times and sighed. A heavy, irritated-sounding sigh. She wasn't in the mood for this or any other kind of conversation.

"Ultimately, the choice is yours." Davies sat back in her chair. "I've talked to the USA, and she doesn't think he has any pertinent information on anything."

"He just wants someone to listen to him. He wants some attention." My arms folded across my chest as I leaned against the door. I didn't want to talk to him, and yet I was curious. What did he think he could tell me that would pique my interest?

"But she is in the conference room. She wants to talk to both of you."

I glanced at Tony, who cocked his head. I nodded and opened the door. I hadn't really had any dealings with the new

US Attorney, Aisha Taylor. Now seemed like as good a time as any to meet her.

I walked into the conference room. Aisha Taylor was beautiful. Cinnamon-colored skin, dark hair with caramel highlights. Her red pantsuit was expertly tailored, cinched in at the waist just enough to show off her hourglass figure without being too tight.

"Finally," she said when she looked up. Her eyes were hazel, more green than brown. Her lips pressed into a hard line when she looked behind me. Something passed over her face for a brief second, and then she smiled.

"Nice to meet you, finally, Mia Storm." She held out her hand, and I took it. Her hands were soft and smooth like silk.

"Nice to meet you, too."

Her eyes passed over Tony, and he didn't make a move to introduce himself. The air pulsed with something. Not anger, but it wasn't a happy feeling either.

Instead of making a smart-ass comment to ease the tension, I tried to fill the void of silence.

"Have you spoken to Bruce Weisman?"

She nodded. "I have, and he is an arrogant asshole who wants everything to be about him. The only reason he wants to talk now is," she threw her hands up in the air, "prison wasn't what he thought it would be. I'm told he's not making a lot of friends."

"He's a rapist. They don't usually do well in prison," said Tony. He moved from behind me and sat at the table.

"I guess he didn't get the memo. I honestly don't believe he has any new information on anything. You can still speak with him but leave me out of it. I am not making that monster any deals. He will stay in prison for the rest of his life as he should. But that is not why I am here."

I glanced at Tony, who straightened in his seat. I sat next to him.

"Is this about the Blackstones?"

She gave a curt nod. Aisha wasn't one for conversation. She opened a folder and slid it across the table.

"I thought they were taking a deal." I stared at the folder.

"The husband is taking a deal. Fatima changed her mind. She refuses to take the deal we offered her, and I'm not giving her less than life in prison."

I was surprised, but I wasn't surprised. Mrs. Blackstone didn't seem like the type of woman to give in. She would want her day in court. No matter how wrong… how depraved what she did was, she would like us to prove it in court.

I sighed. Tony placed a hand on my shoulder, squeezed, and then let go.

"I shouldn't be surprised. But in a way, I am."

"Me too," said Aisha. "It tells me, for some reason, she believes that she can get off. And that is what worries me. So, I need to know what you did."

I blinked. "Excuse me? What I did?"

"Yes. What did you do? What corners did you cut that makes her think she can get acquitted? I need to know so I can prepare my case."

"What are you talking about?" The edge to Tony's voice was sharp. "What are you accusing her of?"

"I'm just trying to figure out why Fatima wouldn't take the deal. It was a good deal, which tells me she knows something I don't. What is it?" She turned her stare to me.

"I didn't do anything. I did my job."

"If you did your job, I wouldn't have this problem. She would have taken the deal."

"I can't make deals! I followed the evidence and got you what I could."

I jumped to my feet. Heat bloomed in my chest and pulsed in my veins. How dare she suggest that I did something wrong? I wasn't the one killing people in a murder club.

"That's not fair. She's rich. She probably believes she'll get away with it like she has in the past. And that her husband won't testify against her." Tony slowly rose to his feet.

Her eyes narrowed. "I guess I'll have to take your word for it. But if anything comes up during the trial that proves you overstepped your bounds or did something you said you didn't, I will hang you out to dry."

She pointed to the door. "You can leave now." She closed the folder. I inched toward the door. When I looked back, Tony and Aisha stared at each other.

Well, Tony glared at her, and she didn't look away. Her gaze was defiant like she was daring him to say something. Do something. I opened the door and stepped out of the room. I didn't wait for Tony in case they wanted to have a private conversation. Instead, I went to my desk and sat down.

Tony emerged from the room a few minutes later, face red, brows furrowed, lips pressed into a hard line.

"Come on."

He grabbed his keys off his desk and headed to the elevator without breaking his stride. I jumped up to join him.

We didn't say anything until we got into the car. The engine roared to life, and Tony leaned back.

"You okay?"

He turned to face me. "Are you?" He cocked his head to the side. "I'm sorry about what she said. I know you didn't do anything to tank to the case."

I shook my head. "It felt like I was being attacked. What is her problem? Why isn't Fatima taking the deal?"

He sighed as he leaned back in his seat. "She doesn't think she will be convicted. I mean, when I look at them, I would swear he was the mastermind, not her. And the jury might think the same thing. I think that is what she's counting on."

"He won't testify against her. That's what she's banking on. And if he doesn't, she can say that it was all him. She had nothing to do with it. She was his prisoner or something. He forced her to do everything. And with nothing to refute that... she'll walk."

"That's the worst-case scenario. We don't know that will happen, and it will be a while before she goes to trial. Gives Aisha time to build a case against her. There has to be someone, somewhere, that knows something."

My thumbnail wiggled its way between my teeth. I wanted to believe what he was saying, but my optimism was waning. It didn't seem fair that her husband would spend the rest of his life behind bars, and she would walk away.

Did I do something? I replayed the case over and over in my mind. Picking it apart. Had I done something that could have been misconstrued? Something that would help her case? I couldn't think of anything. We did everything by the book, even though there were times I didn't want to. It would have been easier if I didn't.

"What do you think about Bruce?" My voice sounded so foreign in my ears, far away and distant.

"I'm curious. I know you don't like talking to him, and I completely understand. But I am curious about what he knows or what he thinks he knows that would get him a deal. And why is he coming to us now? I'm also curious if he worked with Yumi to get some of his victims."

Gooseflesh broke out along my arms, and the hairs on the back of my neck stood up. I hadn't thought about that. I was so focused on never wanting to hear his voice again that I forgot about how he got his victims. Bruce and his father-in-law killed so many women. Quite a few that worked with them. But there were others they had to get from somewhere. If Yumi was supplying murder victims to the Blackstones, she could have done the same for Bruce.

"If you do go, let him talk. He's the kind of guy that likes to hear the sound of his own voice."

"He's definitely that."

"Let's go to lunch."

After lunch, we sat in the car for several minutes. Silence enveloped us. Surrounded us. It wasn't the uncomfortable silence filled with unsaid words or the electric charge of emotions not yet processed. It was a comfortable silence. I did want to ask him about Aisha, but I knew it was none of my business. It might come up later. Tony was the kind of person you didn't probe.

You had to let him come to you. He was a quiet man but spoke when he wanted to when it was called for. When he was relaxed, words spilled from him like water from a faucet. You just had to wait. And so, I would. It was none of my business, after all.

I leaned back in my seat and weighed my options. We didn't have a case we were working on at the moment. And Tony was on light duty. Talking to a prisoner would fall into the parameters Davies set for him. Did my curiosity outweigh my disdain for the man? It did. And I hated that. I hated being curious about him.

I want to know more about his life and why he did what he did. There never seemed to be a reason for it. He did it because he wanted to. Because he had found someone early in life who shared his dark desires. A father figure. And instead of squelching his desires, Charles Tanaka stoked the murderous flames. Cultivated the desire to match his own, and then he let him loose on the world and sat back.

I wondered what their conversations were like. If they, at the end of a long day at work, came together and talked about their kills. Reminisced about their murders and laughed as they spoke about the palpable fear they felt from the women they tortured moments before they killed them.

I sighed. "I'll talk to him."

"I knew your curiosity would get the best of you," he said with a smirk.

"Don't act like you know me so well."

"Like the back of my hand."

I rolled my eyes as a smile crept across my lips. My curiosity was going to be a problem one day. Instead of driving back to the field office, we went ahead to the prison. Bruce should have been held in confinement. He should have stayed in a cell twenty-three hours a day and never had any interaction with anyone but the guards.

That was what he deserved. But now he was in the general population, and I couldn't help but think that was a bad idea. He had an audience. And sure, he was a rapist, and men in prison probably hated him, but he could still find a way to make friends. He was annoyingly charming, and if he found the right weak mind...

I shuddered at the thought.

"Detectives?" The guard at the gate cocked his head as he stared at us.

I chuckled as I took out my badge.

"Oh! It's the fancy police." His voice dripped with sarcasm. He pressed a button, and the gate opened. Another guard walked up.

"Who are you here for?" The older man stared at Tony and me like we didn't belong. Or like we were about to ruin his day.

"Bruce Weisman," I answered.

The two guards rolled their eyes. The one who sat at the security desk sucked his teeth. "Can't believe, after talking about it for weeks, he actually got the FBI here. You are about to be disappointed."

"Yeah, I figured as much, but right now, I'm not doing anything else. So here we are." I forced a smile.

CHAPTER FIVE

We were led to a room with a metal table and four metal chairs. I sat in one of the chairs facing the door. Tony stood in the back corner, watching the door. I wasn't afraid. I didn't think Bruce would try anything. My pulse quickened, but it was less fear and more anticipation.

What did he have to say? What information did he have to give? Was there another serial killer out there? One he worked with? Charles Tanaka took in a lot of young boys, and while we didn't know for certain whether he groomed them all to be killers like Bruce, it would have made sense.

He trained Bruce. Validated his killer instincts. And Charles took in boys who had behavioral problems. It would make sense that Bruce wasn't the only killer in the bunch. He might have been able to tell us if there were more and if he knew where they were. I was sure they would have kept in touch.

A few minutes later, the door opened, and chains rattled through the door. Bruce entered the room. His eyes went wide when he saw me. His smile was bright and welcoming, but it wavered for a moment when he saw Tony. He was expecting me but not him. When we were told Bruce wanted to speak with me, Tony was not mentioned.

He shuffled into the room behind the guard, grinning. The guard cuffed him to the table and then left the room without another word. He seemed annoyed. Bruce could have that effect on people.

"You came. I knew you would. You like puzzles. I get that about you."

"You don't know me."

His head tilted slightly. Prison had not been kind to Bruce. His face was covered in purple patches outlined in blue. His arms and hands were covered in bruises. He winced as he adjusted himself in his seat. When he leaned back, he sighed.

"Looks like someone doesn't like you." I pointed to the bruises on his face.

He shrugged. "Doesn't matter. I've made a few friends, but that's not why I'm here."

"You're right. You're not here to make friends. You're here because you are a murderer and a rapist."

He waved a hand dismissively. "I was never one for labels. And whatever I am, you still came to see me." His grin was bloody and missing a few teeth.

Bruce had looked so well put together. Designer suits and shoes. Now, he was a mess.

"Why am I here, Bruce?" I kept my voice low and measured. Careful not to give away my true feelings. Talking to him made me sick to my stomach.

"Don't rush me, Agent Storm. I want to catch up. How have you been?" He glanced at Tony. "I see your partner is doing well. I heard a lot has happened since the last time we spoke. I heard he got the ever-loving shit beat out of him." he smiled. "Good to see he is healed and moving around again. He needs to be more careful."

"Apparently, so do you."

Bruce winced at the comment. He recovered and smiled at me. Tony didn't say anything. I glanced at the corner he was occupying. He was so still, eyes fixed on Bruce.

"Now that we've caught up, I need to know why I'm here. What information do you have to tell me?"

I wanted to get to the point. The sooner he told me what he wanted to tell me, the sooner I could go. Aisha already made it clear he was not a priority, and she would not be making any deals with him. Not now, not ever. I doubted he could tell me anything that would change her mind. And yet I was still here. I still wanted to know. Needed to know. Needed to make sure I hadn't overlooked anything.

"It's an open case." He stroked his thumb with his forefinger.

I leaned back. "I don't have any open cases." I glanced at Tony to make sure. He nodded slowly.

Bruce smiled. His smile was unnerving. It made my skin crawl that he could still be so happy.

"I didn't say it was yours."

I blinked. He brought me here to screw with me. I knew it. I should have known it. Deep down, I did. He just wanted someone to talk to who was not beating the shit out of him. That was all this was. A distraction.

"If you have something to say about an open case, then you need to speak with the agent over that case. I have nothing to do with it."

I started to stand. Bruce cleared his throat.

"I won't talk to anyone but you, Mia."

My name in his mouth sounded disgusting. The way he said it, slowly. Careful to pronounce every syllable.

"I like you."

"No offense, but I don't think that is a compliment."

His smile widened. "That's why I like you. I feel like we have an understanding. You get me."

"I don't get you. I don't understand why you did any of the shit you did."

"But you want to. Like I said, you like puzzles, and I am a puzzle to you. And you are more interesting than I initially gave you credit for. You're definitely smarter."

"Thanks." I heard the sarcasm in my voice. Before I said my next words, I had to check myself. I didn't want him to see or hear how he was getting to me. Irritating me. "I can't infringe on a case I am not working on. You need to speak with the agent in charge."

"Here's what we'll do... I'll tell you about the case. I won't tell you everything I know, just general information. If it piques your interest, then you can go to the special agent in charge and sort it out between the two of you. Trust me... you are going to want to hear what I have to say."

I glanced back at Tony, who shrugged.

"Fine."

"Good to hear." He leaned back in his chair again, wincing at the motion. His fingers drummed against the table for a long moment. Seconds ticked by. "The Dale and Ortega families were killed in their beds, and their murderer has never been found."

"Is that it? That's all you can tell me?"

He smiled. "So impatient... I can tell you that the scenes were a mess. The families were tortured. Played with. Especially the little girls." His smile widened. "It was horrible. That's really all I can say. Go see if it is an open case, and once you know that I am right, come back, and we can talk." He cocked his head to the side. "I look forward to seeing you again. CO!."

The guard hurried into the room just as Bruce rose to his feet. He winked at me as he was led out. I shuddered.

"Still disgusting," I said as I stood up.

"He really likes you." Tony stared at me. "I don't like that."

My brow rose slightly as a smirk kissed my lips. "Jealous."

"It's not funny, Mia. He might be obsessed with you."

"He is also in prison." I gestured to the room we were in. Bruce was not a worry. He was under lock and key, and judging by his face, he had other things to worry about. I wasn't worried in the slightest.

Tony's eyebrows drew together as he stared at the door. Tension pulsed in the air between us. He was worried.

"Just don't become attached to or obsessed with him."

"I won't. He's not that interesting." I headed toward the door. "You think he's right about the case?"

"He is. I remember hearing about it earlier this year. Or maybe last year. It was a while ago. I don't remember if it was solved or if they even had any suspects."

"Okay. He wasn't lying about that, at least. Now we need to see if the agent will talk to us."

Tony sighed. "Agents are territorial about their cases. I know I am."

"Hopefully, they don't feel the same way."

On our way back to the field office, Tony suggested we speak with the agent before we researched the case. I wanted to look up the case first, but he advised against it.

"Think about it. How would you feel if someone went behind your back and looked up one of your cases so they could try to solve it without you? You would be pissed, and so would I."

"We aren't trying to solve it without them. We just want to see if there is any truth to what Bruce said. And we can do that much without them."

"We can. But just because you can do something doesn't mean you should. It's about respect, and if you do this the wrong way, other agents aren't going to trust you around their cases. It's a reputation neither of us need."

I sighed and relented to his viewpoint of the situation. I didn't want to start any shit with any of the other agents. To be a good FBI agent, you had to be able to work with others and not overstep. So, I would do that the best I could. I just hoped the agent shared our views on working together. Well, Tony's views.

I got to my desk just as Hattie stepped out of Davies' office. When she saw me, she rushed over.

"Did you go?"

I nodded. "Do you know anything about the Dale and Ortega family murders?"

Hattie turned over her tablet and started typing. "Oh, right. I do remember this. Vaguely. I don't think it's been solved."

"Who is the agent working the case?"

"Ayanna Yagher. She's in the building somewhere. Here is her number."

I wrote it down. Tony walked over to his desk just as Hattie walked away.

"So, what do I say?"

He smiled. "Just ask her if she has a moment to talk about one of her cold cases. Try to sound helpful and nice."

"I am helpful and nice," I said as I picked up the phone. I repeated what he said, and she said she did. She was on the third floor in the conference room going over notes for a trial she was testifying in. I told her we would meet her there.

Special Agent Ayanna Yagher looked how she sounded. Rough and like she didn't take any shit. She looked like she could fight and did so often. And won. Her long black hair was pulled up in a tight ponytail, and she had on minimal makeup and jewelry, just one gold necklace. Her nails were painted a neutral color, and she wore a long-sleeved, dark-blue shirt and light gray pants.

When I walked in, she was hovering over a piece of paper, talking to herself.

"Agent Yagher?"

She looked up and gave a quick nod. "Special Agents Storm and Walker. I've heard a lot about you two." She shook both our hands. "Should you be up and about?" she pointed at Tony.

"Light duty."

She nodded slowly. "Well"—she gestured to the other chairs at the table—"I only have a handful of open cases. Which one is this about?"

"The Dale and Ortega case."

She blinked. "Those are two separate cases."

"Well, we might have information that they are not separate."

"Information from whom? Leave me their information, and I'll get back to them." Her voice was not an invitation to talk about the case. It was more 'this is my case, and I will sort it out.'

I glanced at Tony. "About that... do you know... have you heard about Bruce Weisman?"

She leaned back. "The serial killer you lot put in prison. I did. It was good work."

"Thanks. He says he has information on those two cases. He isn't claiming he did the murders himself, although I wouldn't be surprised if he did. He says he will only talk to me about it, but I wanted to see if the cases were even real and unsolved and if the little bit he has said is true." The words spilled from me. I wanted to get everything out and in the open.

Her eyes narrowed immediately. "It's my case."

Tony stepped in. "And we understand that. We could work it together. It's just he said he has information, and he's made it clear that he won't talk to anyone but her. Not even me."

She stared at me for a long moment. "You are not taking over my case."

"To be honest, I absolutely do not want to." I leaned forward, resting my elbows on the table. "We just want to look at it and then maybe try to solve it without his help."

"I don't need your help. I can solve it myself."

"And I understand. But it's been a cold case for months. How long has there been no movement on it? Be honest."

She sucked her teeth. "It's been a few months. But I can only work with what I have, and I am not using a serial killer."

I waved my hand dismissively. "I do not want him to be anywhere near this case. I want to see if we can solve it without him. I'd hate for him to think he was helpful, and that somehow wipes away what he's done. I don't want to use him if we don't have to."

She leaned back, her hands resting behind her head. "I guess another set of eyes could be helpful in solving both cases. I still don't see what they had in common, but... fine. I will accept your help."

"It looks like it hurt you to say that, so thank you for allowing us to help you solve your case," I said with a smile.

"Well—"

"Okay. So now that we have agreed to work together, how about we get started? What can you tell us about the case?" Tony cut his eyes at me and then shook his head.

I mouthed sorry before he looked away. He was right. We were supposed to be playing nice, but her attitude was annoying. We were here trying to help her solve her case. She could have been nicer about it.

"I'll go grab the files."

CHAPTER SIX

AYANNA RETURNED WITH A SMILE A FEW MINUTES later.

"You didn't have to go far," I said as she slid the folders across the table.

"I keep all of my cold cases in my desk. That's why they stay fresh in my mind."

"How many cold cases do you have?" I asked as I flipped through one of the folders.

"Five. What about you?"

"None." I handed the Ortega folder to Tony. He sighed next to me.

"Lucky you. I guess it makes it easier when you have a partner."

"You don't have a partner?" I stared at her. I thought all agents had to have partners. I didn't know anyone could work alone.

She shrugged. "My last partner was killed in the line of duty. I just haven't gotten around to getting another one. I don't really need one. But I guess some people do." She gestured to me and Tony. "You two look that over while I get back to my testimony."

Tony squeezed my thigh. I knew what that meant. Swallow your retort. So, I did. I swallowed my words and my attitude and started examining the Dale file.

The Dale family consisted of a mother, a father, and three children. The family of five was murdered in the middle of the night. The mother and father were found in their beds. The son was found under his bed. One of the daughters was found on the sofa in the living room, and the other girl was found in the hallway that led to the bedrooms at the back of the house.

Attached to the file were several crime scene photos of the bodies and the blood splatter. The house was a mess. Bruce had been right about that. The killer or killers seemed to have killed the parents first in their beds. I stared at the picture. It was like they didn't have a chance to get up. The killer snuck in and caught them while they were sleeping.

As for the children, from the pictures, it looked like they took their time with them. The boy was under the bed, but there was blood splatter on the sheets and all over the walls. He probably started stabbing him while he was in bed, and the boy tried to hide under the bed and get away from the killer.

One girl was on the sofa. Blood covered the walls and the carpet. The sofa was soaked. The nine-year-old girl was naked from the waist down. Bile caught in my throat. I swallowed hard. Her eyes were wide open. Like she was staring straight at me.

I flipped the page. It didn't get any better. The older daughter, thirteen, was in the hallway that led to her parents' room. To me, it looked like she heard something or saw something and was trying to get to their room. In the hallway, her head was pointed toward the kitchen and her legs toward the bedroom door.

She was also naked from the waist down. Her legs were spread, and there was blood everywhere. She was soaking in blood. Steeping in it. There was so much blood I could barely make out the color of her nightshirt underneath. I closed the folder. Tony was still looking through his. I leaned into him to get a better look.

"Seems to really hate the children," he said. He held up pictures of their bodies. I shook my head.

"Yeah, this would be something Bruce would know about. Right up his alley."

"What did he do?" asked Ayanna.

I recounted the murders and everything we found. When I started, she was flipping through one of her folders. By the time I finished, her eyes were fixed on me. Her mouth a thin, hard line.

"Yeah, I guess this crime is his wheelhouse. Sure he didn't do it?"

"No!"

"No!"

She smiled then. I didn't put anything past Bruce, and it was good to hear Tony didn't either. However, why would he bring our attention to a crime he committed? No one was looking at him for the murders. Why bring it up now?

"I'm pretty sure he just wants attention. Wants someone to talk to that isn't trying to beat the crap out of him."

"Is he getting beat up a lot?"

I nodded. "It looked like it the last time we saw him. His face was practically purple, and he was missing a few teeth."

"Good."

"What can you tell us about the case that isn't in the folders?" asked Tony.

Ayanna finished writing something and then closed her notepad. "Well, the scenes were as bad as you would think they were. Horrible. My first child murders, and those stay with you for a long time."

"Who was killed first?"

She glanced at me. "The Dale family were killed first, and then a few days later, the Ortega family were killed."

I sighed. "Was there anything that made you think the two were related?"

Her head tilted slightly. "Well, they happened so close together that initially, it seemed like they were related. I was never a hundred percent sure either way. The families were killed, and that was how they were similar. But in the Dale family, the young girls were raped and then killed. The oldest daughter was raped as she was dying. We could tell by the movement of the knife stuck in her chest. But with the Ortega family, yes, they were tortured, but there were no signs of rape. So that made me think they were separate."

"Yeah, that makes sense. The Ortegas were tortured. It seemed like with the Dale family, the children were the focus of the murders."

"Yeah, that's what I thought. The Ortegas went through a lot. In fact, the way they were targeted also made me think that there were two separate killers. And there may have been more than one in the Ortega household because they were such a large family. Eight in all. To wrangle them all together and no one got away... had to be more than one killer."

"Were they killed in their sleep?"

"That's another difference. To me, it looked like they were woken up, taken out of their beds, and corralled into the dining room. They were forced to sit at the table. Once there, they were tortured. One by one. I mean, those pictures were gruesome, but they don't do it justice. They had their teeth pulled out and their ears sliced off. Tongues cut out. It was horrible."

"What happened to the parts removed from them?"

Tony opened the folder and pulled out one of the pictures. He handed it to me. "I see. They just left them on the table. What were they trying to get from them?"

"I definitely thought they were trying to get information from the parents and were torturing the children to get them to talk. Either the parents didn't know or wouldn't say because the children's bodies had the most damage. All of them. They tortured all of them. Three of the kids had all their teeth pulled out, their fingers broken, and their nails ripped off."

I shuddered. "Jesus. What about noise?"

"Now, that's the strange part. The neighbors on either side of the Ortegas just happened to be out of town. Why? Because they both won some kind of free vacation to Maui. So, no one was home when the family were being tortured."

"That was planned."

"Right. I tried to trace down who made the reservations, but it was a dead end. The company that paid for it led to a shell company, and that was the end of that. But it made me think the Ortegas were killed by someone else."

"Did they know each other?"

She tapped her pen. "I never thought to ask. To me, the murders weren't related, so why would that matter."

"To me, it seems like the killer of the Dales was trying to prove a point. They were a warning, 'Look what I can do to your children.' Mr. or Mrs. Ortega didn't listen. There is something that connects them. We just need to find it."

Ayanna snatched the folders back across the table. "I'm still not sure about you working on the case. As I said, I have exhausted all leads. I've looked at all the evidence several times." She stood up, folders pulled tight to her chest. "I'll talk to Davies and see what she says."

Before I could utter another word, she left the room. That was a quick turnaround.

"What was that about? At first, she seemed on board, and now nothing."

"Well, to be honest, she wasn't on board at first. More like at second."

I rolled my eyes. He was right. She didn't want to at first, but then she changed her mind. I guess she changed it back. I shook my head. "There's something about this case or cases. There's something there."

Tony stood up, and I followed. "Yeah. It doesn't seem like a coincidence."

"Because you don't believe in them."

He chuckled. "Exactly."

We spent the rest of the day waiting. I didn't want to go back to Bruce if we didn't have to. And if Ayanna allowed us to help her close the case, we wouldn't have to.

"It'll work out," Tony said a little after five. "It will work out. She'll come back. She's just not used to working with someone after her partner died. The whole bouncing ideas off of someone and the back and forth probably got to her."

"What happened to her partner?"

"She was shot and killed while hunting down a drug ring. They cornered a drug dealer who worked for the cartel, and she was shot in the head. Ayanna was shot in the ribs and the leg."

"Damn. Hopefully, she comes around." Before going home, we stopped at a restaurant to get something to eat.

It was a new place that neither of us had been before. An Indian place that just opened up downtown. Tony's brother talked about it the last time they were together and told him the food was amazing. King acted like Tony's mere presence annoyed him, but while he was in the hospital, King visited him every day. He checked up on him and brought him snacks he knew Tony liked. He even slept there a few nights.

It was clear he loved his brother, but he didn't want Tony to figure that out, so every day before he left, he made a smart-ass remark to set him off. It was cute.

"Did he say what we should order?" I asked as I glanced over the menu.

The smell of spices and roasting meat was intoxicating. My mouth watered as soon as we walked through the door. The place was packed. Once we sat down, there were only two empty tables in the building.

"The food must be good," said Tony as he glanced around the room. "No, he said he got something about butter chicken and that it was amazing."

"Alright. Looking for something called butter chicken."

I had heard of it before in passing. I didn't know what it was or what was in it other than chicken and butter. But it always looked good on TV. After reading the menu twice, Tony and I settled on what we wanted. I was hungry, and he was starving, so we ordered a lot after agreeing to share the dishes.

Samosas, butter chicken, dal makhani laddu, and garlic naan. We didn't know what half of it was, but we were willing to try something new tonight.

"How are you feeling?"

The waitress walked away from our table, and Tony leaned back with a wince. I eyed him carefully. We hadn't really done anything today, but he was still sore and bruised.

He shrugged. "I feel better. I mean, I don't feel like I've been hit by a truck anymore."

"Well, that's something. You still need to take it easy."

"I will."

"You could let me drive."

"If..." he cocked his head, "sure. You can drive us home. I'll sit in the back."

"I am not driving Miss Daisy."

He laughed. "I'm surprised you're old enough to know that movie."

"I know things." I gave him my biggest smile. My mother liked the movie and watched it a lot when I was younger.

It took a while for the food to come, but when it did, it all came at once. Steaming hot dishes flooded the table. My favorite was the butter chicken, which was rich and creamy and perfect with the naan. The samosas were good, too, and so was the dal makhani, which reminded me of a curry with black lentils. It was amazingly flavorful and also went great with the naan. Tony would have liked it better if there had been meat in it, but all in all, the meal was delicious.

"We have to come back here," I said as we walked out.

"Definitely."

After we left the restaurant, we went to his parents' home because he wanted to check on them. His mother and I had worked together with his sister to clean up his place before he was released. While his mother and I cleaned, his sister went through his things.

She went through his nightstand and medicine cabinet, looked underneath his bed, and rummaged through his closet with such glee that she reminded me of my mother going through my things. She searched through drawers without actually cleaning and putting anything away.

At least until her mother kicked her out since she wasn't actually helping. When Tony was attacked, he fought them off as long as he could, causing damage all over the apartment.

Then, when we were looking for him and searching his place, we made the place an even bigger mess. I felt a little bad about it.

Tony wasn't a neatnik or anything, but he kept his place tidy, cleaning it at least once a week. We tried to get it back to how it was before. It took a while to get the blood out of the carpet, though.

His mother opened the door to her house before Tony even touched the doorknob.

"What are you doing upright?" She smacked him on both shoulders before pulling him into a tight hug.

Tony groaned, but his mother did not let him go. "If you can walk around, I can hug you. Shut up." Her embrace tightened for a moment, and then she let go.

We spent an hour talking to his mother and father before leaving and heading home. His mother pulled me to the side while he spoke to his father.

"How is he?"

"He's fine. I've been keeping an eye on him. He seems okay, just a little sore."

She nodded slowly. "Good. Let me know if that changes, even if he doesn't want you to. Tell me anyway."

I smiled and nodded. I would. Tony was afraid of his mother and would do anything she wanted him to do. She was my trump card.

He said he was okay, but toward the end of the night, his movements were slower, like he was moving through quicksand. And he winced more often than not. Every movement, every inhale, pained him. He gritted his teeth as I drove, even though I tried to be as careful as possible. However, there were a couple of potholes that were difficult to avoid. I apologized as he inhaled sharply.

I wanted to help him inside, but I stopped myself from saying or doing anything. I didn't want to make him feel like an invalid. I knew how annoying that could be. He wasn't sick or mortally wounded. He was a big boy and could take care of himself. I wanted to help him, though.

I wanted to help him into his apartment. Help him to bed. Soothe him to sleep and take his pain away. But I fought the urge. I wouldn't do anything unless he asked me to. So I walked

Tony to his door and then got back on the elevator and went down a floor to my apartment. I walked away, planning to go to bed myself.

I wasn't tired, but I would need the rest. It seemed we had another gruesome case to get involved in.

CHAPTER SEVEN

Harrison and Keisha were in the elevator when I got back on.

"Hey girly, what are up to?"

"Just getting home from work," I answered. "What are you two doing?"

"He's just gettin' in from work. I'm just getting back from a date," said Keisha.

"How did that go?"

"She said it sucked." Harrison's raspy voice sent a shiver down my spine. Keisha bit her lip.

"I said it wasn't fun. He was too into hearing himself speak. And it wasn't about me."

I rolled my eyes, and Harrison chuckled. Keisha asked me what I planned on doing the rest of the night. I sighed. I knew I wasn't going to bed right now. I wasn't tired, and even if I was, I would dream of faceless children and wake up again.

I shrugged. "I'm not sleepy. Think I'll just pour myself a drink and do a puzzle."

"Way to party hard," said Keisha.

"There's nothing wrong with a good puzzle," Harrison said.

"Thank you." It did sound boring, but I didn't have anything else to do.

"I guess we'll join you, then."

The doors dinged open, and the three of us stepped out onto the floor. I wasn't expecting them to really join me. But we all went to my door and into my apartment. Bourbon was the drink of the night for Keisha and me. Harrison settled on a beer. I took out the puzzle I had been working on.

Keisha's eyebrows raised. "Oh, you were really working on a puzzle."

"What did you think I meant?"

She shrugged. "I haven't done a puzzle since I was a kid."

"Most of the word puzzles I do are on my phone," said Harrison. He leaned back on the sofa next to me and sipped his beer. He looked comfortable, like he was at home. Keisha and I sat on the edge of our seats like we didn't know how to relax.

"I do puzzles all the time. I did them a lot when I was a kid. They help me think, especially now when I have to work through a case."

"Gives you something else to focus on," said Harrison.

"Exactly. And I could use that right now."

"Difficult case?" Keisha raised her eyebrows.

I told them about Bruce, but I left out most of the details.

"Feel like there is more that you aren't saying," said Harrison. He looked at me, eyebrow raised. "But I get why you would be upset. I wouldn't want to talk to him either."

"Yeah, I don't understand how you could do that and keep your cool. I mean, I saw that shit on the news, and it made my blood boil. Like how could someone do the shit he's done and then get the nerve to try to be helpful and solve another case. He's just bored. Better yet, he probably did it."

"That's what I was thinking!" I had thought originally that Bruce could have murdered the families. And the Dale girls were raped, and he loved raping women, although none of his victims had been that young. At least not that we knew of. "But then I thought, why would he confess to a crime now? No one is looking at him for these murders, so what is the point of that?"

"You," said Harrison. "He seems to like you."

Keisha nodded at the comment. "He might be doing it to talk to you. Or maybe he likes having an audience. You listened to his last confession."

I leaned back. She had a point. Bruce did seem to enjoy hearing himself speak. Maybe this was his way of opening up and trying to find the right words to unburden himself. The more I thought about it, the more that did not sound like him.

"There's a reason for it," I said. "He has a reason, and I know the reason is about him and him alone. I just don't know what it is. But anyway, that's enough about my work. What are you two up to?"

Keisha shrugged. She worked from home for an insurance company and was not happy about it. "If I didn't need the job, I would not be working. I wish I could just be a stay-at-home dog mom."

Harrison chuckled. "Dog mom?"

"Yeah! But I can't do that, so I have to get yelled at by people who are pissed they got in a car accident and the driver had no insurance. Or they just figured out their insurance lapsed, and now they've been in a car accident and don't have coverage. It's the same thing every day."

She let out a loud, heavy sigh. "What about you, Mr. Harrison?"

"I like my job. It's not as boring as an insurance agent or as exciting as an FBI agent, but it's something I love."

"What do you do?"

He smiled. "Psychiatrist."

"So, it's your job to get into people's heads?" Keisha sipped her bourbon slowly. Her eyes fixed on Harrison.

He smiled. "Something like that. I get to study human behavior, and that's what I like. People are just puzzles, and it is my job to figure out where the pieces go to fix them. I like that. I like understanding why people behave the way they do."

"Both of your jobs sound exhausting," said Keisha.

"It has its moments." Harrison finished his beer. "But there are some bright spots as well. It's not all bad."

"I guess that is true. I deal with serial killers most weeks, but there is something about bringing them to justice that makes me feel like all the sleepless nights are worth it."

"You work long hours?" asked Keisha. "I thought you guys were done by five and off on the weekends."

I had to laugh. That kind of schedule would have been nice. Perfect even. But alas, it wasn't meant to be.

"Nope. We are usually never home by five, and we are not off during the weekends. Especially not if we are working on a case and are still looking for leads. On a case, we are round the clock. I usually get home a little before midnight."

"Is that the reason for the sleepless nights?" Harrison set his beer on the table.

I sighed. "Sometimes. But sometimes the cases… they linger. Haunt. Makes it hard to go to sleep and get up in the morning. If I have one more dream about faceless children, I'm going to lose my mind."

Keisha stilled. "Faceless? Did you actually find faceless children?"

I waved my hand dismissively. "No. It's just a dream I keep having."

"Your brain is trying to figure out who the children are. It's trying to help them, but it can't do that. I'm assuming you don't know who the children are you are trying to save, hence the faceless," Harrison explained.

"So, my brain is trying to make sense of a case, and it's trying to put the pieces together, but because I don't know who the children are, they are faceless?"

He nodded. "Sometimes when we push things to the back of our mind for whatever reason, they have ways of snaking themselves through our subconscious."

That would make sense why I was having the dream now. The trafficked children came up in my first case as an FBI agent. And while I still thought about the case and the children, it had been pushed to the back of my mind. Cases and murders kept popping up and taking their place.

This dream might have been my brain's way of reminding me that it still needed my attention. We spent the rest of the night talking about our jobs and our families. Keisha was an only child, and Harrison grew up in an orphanage until he was ten. Then, he went to a really nice family.

"It was the happiest day of my life. The only thing I ever wanted was a family. And that was what I got, complete with brothers and sisters."

"Are you all still in touch?" Keisha finished her glass and gently placed it on the coffee table.

"Yeah. Holidays, we all get together. My parents passed away a little while ago in a car accident, but we still try to make sure we spend time together."

"That's good. My family came for Christmas, and it ended up being a disaster. We didn't really get to spend that much time together."

"Oh, right. Your partner was hurt," said Harrison.

"Yeah. Tony, He was hurt, and then I was working this big case, and time just kept getting away from me. We spent Christmas at the hospital. And Tony's getting hurt caused my dad to get on my case again about being an agent and how dangerous it is."

"Fathers and daughters," said Keisha. "No matter how old you get, you will always be their little girl, and they can never get past that. My father could never see me as a grown-up. It was why I had to move. So, I could grow up, and he could see me as a woman and not a five-year-old who needed him all the time."

"My dad gives me space, but this FBI thing, when it comes up, especially now.... Tony getting hurt shook him up. Which I guess I understand."

"He's not wrong, though. It is dangerous. Doesn't mean you have to quit, but still, it is dangerous," said Harrison.

"I know. But it's worth it. At least, it is to me. Being a psychiatrist is also dangerous."

He nodded slowly. "I am aware. I had a patient in the psych ward once that tried to strangle me. If the security guard had gotten there a minute later, I wouldn't be here."

"And you keep going?" Keisha stared at him, disbelief etched onto her face.

"It is my job. And he was having a psychotic episode. It wasn't completely his fault. He needed help. So, I helped him. Once we got his meds into him and talked him down, he was great. Perfectly fine and nonviolent."

I blinked. I didn't think I could see it that way. I would have been angry for a long while before and after we got him his meds and talked.

They left a little before eleven, which gave me plenty of time to wind down and fall asleep. I still dreamed of faceless children.

I woke the following day, still tired and foggy. I hadn't been on a run in a long while, but the building had a gym. One day, I would make it down to the basement. But not today. I wanted to roll over and go back to sleep, but it was almost seven. I needed to take a shower, get dressed, and make breakfast. It was almost eight when there was a knock on the door.

"Ugh, I was going to wrap up the food and bring it to you."

"Come on, Storm. I'm fine," Tony insisted. "I am fully capable of taking the elevator down one floor."

Closing the door behind him, I nudged him further into the room.

"I know. I know. Just wanted to make it easier on you." Making things easier on him was my primary goal until he could move around without wincing or gritting his teeth. He wasn't there yet.

"And I haven't seen your place yet."

I grinned. That was why he came over. He hadn't seen my apartment yet. I nudged him with my shoulder. "You just wanted to see the place. It looks exactly like yours." The floor plan was similar to Tony's, but with one less room than his.

He looked around the foyer. "Not exactly. I think your place is a little smaller." He eased down the hallway.

"Are you in pain?"

He shrugged. "No more than usual. And I took something, so I should be fine in a few minutes."

"Come on." I pulled him by the elbow into the kitchen. "Sit down." I helped him onto the stool at the breakfast bar. "You know, you could take it easy by staying home and actually getting some rest."

"I'd be too bored. And it's only light duty. I'll let you do all the heavy lifting."

"Well, thanks." I set a plate of eggs, bacon, and fruit in front of him, along with a piping hot cup of coffee.

"Oh, fruit."

"Instead of something starchy, fried or smothered in syrup."

He laughed. After breakfast, I placed the dishes in the sink, vowing to wash them before I went to bed. "Have you heard from Ayanna?"

He shook his head. "Might be a few days."

"You think she'll go to Bruce and try to force him to talk to her?" I sipped my coffee slowly.

"That's what I would do."

I nodded. "Me too. I hope it works out for her."

"It won't. Bruce has some kind of hard-on for you."

"Choose better words."

"I did. That's exactly what it is. He is fixated on you. I know he's in prison, but that worries me a little. He says he won't talk to anyone but you, and I believe him. She'll be back. She wants to solve her case, and if Bruce is the only thing standing in her way, she will bite the bullet and work with us."

"I guess we just wait."

CHAPTER EIGHT

Two days later, we finally got called into a conference room with Ayanna and Jill Pittman. Jill smiled when we walked in.

"How is he?" She pointed to Tony, but she didn't look at him.

"He says he's fine, but I've been keeping my eye on him. He seems to be moving around a little easier. Wincing less."

"Well, that's something."

"Please don't talk about me like I'm not in the room."

Jill glanced at him. "You hush and sit down before your ribs start screaming at you."

He opened his mouth like he was going to comment but walked over to a chair and sat down wordlessly.

"Now, can we get back to why we are here?" Ayanna sat at the head of the table. Her eyes narrowed at me. I tried to hide the smile blooming on my lips. She had gone to see Bruce. I saw the annoyed look on her face that only he could put there.

"How was Bruce?" I sat in the chair across from Tony. I swallowed my smile and my chipper attitude. I wanted to rub it in her face. Say 'I told you so.' I knew he wouldn't speak to her, and that both made me smile and cringe at the same time. I didn't want to speak to him either.

The plan, or at least my plan, was to solve the case and then go back to Bruce and rub his face in it. Remind him that we never needed him to do our jobs. Tell him there was nothing he could do or say that would ever help us. I couldn't wait to see the look on his face when he learned we solved it without him.

Ayanna rolled her eyes. "Can we get started, please?" I would have said meeting with him soured her mood, but she never seemed to be in a good mood. At least not where we were concerned.

"Sure." Jill flipped through one of her folders. "Okay, so I'm going to talk about the murders in the orders they happened, starting with the Dale family." Jill had a whole presentation prepared for us, complete with a video of the crime scene, autopsy photos, and all her notes, which were passed around between the four of us.

"You were very thorough."

Jill shrugged and smiled. "Well, since you two weren't at the crime scene to see it for yourselves, I wanted to set the scene for you as best I could."

Jill loved her job. She was passionate about it. She looked at dead bodies the way I looked at puzzles. Always trying to understand how the pieces fit together.

"Appreciate that," said Tony.

"First, we'll watch the video of the crime scene so you can see how the bodies were found," said Ayanna.

"Question. Are the houses still empty, or have they been sold already?" I asked. If the house were empty, chances were we could walk through them searching for missed clues. Granted, after all this time, we probably wouldn't find anything. But it was still worth a try.

But if the houses had been sold with the permission of the owners, we could have still done a walkthrough, but it would have been tainted. They would have already moved their stuff in and would have been moving throughout the house for months, slowly erasing any evidence we could have found. Not to mention what they threw out before they moved in.

"Both houses were sold a few months ago," answered Ayanna.

"I'm always amazed by people who buy houses that people have been murdered in. I wonder how they sleep at night," said Jill as she projected the video on the screen at the front of the room.

I wondered that, too. I didn't think I could sleep in a house I knew someone had died or been murdered in. I would stay up all night waiting for something to happen. It would probably be haunted. I would never be able to relax.

"Okay, so let's get started."

The video started playing. All crime scenes were documented before the medical examiner arrived on the scene. It was a way to preserve the scene before it was messed with. The camera entered the house and started in the living room after documenting the door and how the lock wasn't tampered with.

I held my questions in my mouth. I didn't want to constantly interrupt Jill while she tried to explain the scene to us. The cameraman documented the body on the sofa and the blood splatter. They zoomed in on the walls and the ceiling above the body. The cameraman scanned each room, following the agents and catching what they pointed to. Blood spatter, papers strewn across the room, and the chairs that had been kicked over.

Jill recounted everything that she remembered from that night.

"This was a scene that stays with you. I can still almost smell the bodies. They had been killed the night before. Mr. and Mrs. Dale were killed first in their beds. And then the son, Malcolm, was killed next. Now, he was in his bed when he was stabbed. At first." She pointed to the screen as the camera panned to Malcolm's bedroom.

"He must have jumped out of bed or fought off the killer and then ducked under his bed. Judging by the blood splatter on the back of the door, the door was closed, so maybe he didn't think he could get out."

"Jesus, how could a human being do this to a child?"

"No idea." Jill shrugged and shook her head.

"The two daughters, Maya and Maria, were not treated as gently. Both girls were raped and sodomized before they were stabbed to death. Maya was found on the sofa, half-naked. On a chair across from Maya's body, there were smears of blood belonging to Maria. It looks like the killer may have forced her to watch as he raped and brutalized her sister. There were remnants of tape residue on the arms and legs of the chair."

The camera panned from the sofa, down the hallway, and through the kitchen. "Maria was found in the hallway leading to her parents' bedroom. She was also half-naked. I thought she broke away from the chair and ran to tell her parents or maybe get a phone. Her cell phone was found smashed to pieces in her bedroom, and the phone in the kitchen had been yanked out of the wall. The door was open to the bedroom, and her mother's cell phone was just inside the room on the floor, and there was blood on it. Maria's blood."

The cameraman panned back through the house, making sure to document all the rooms. I watched as he panned over the overturned furniture. The kicked over chairs had to have been from the children being chased through the house. The parents were killed in their beds. The children would have barely had time to react to the murderer. Or maybe the killer was looking for something. But what could they have had that warranted this level of depravity?

I made a note in my notepad to look into Mr. Dale. He and Mr. Ortega might have had some connection. Even though Ayanna says the cases weren't related, I couldn't shake the feeling that they were. They had to be.

I was starting to side with Tony on coincidences. They weren't real. The Dale family's murder seemed like a warning. Like someone was saying they didn't care that Mr. Ortega had children. They would be next.

Jill turned off the video and slumped into a chair. "The irritating thing about this case that still bothers me is how little evidence was found at the scene. There was blood everywhere, but none of it was the killer's. And we tested all of it. It all belonged to the members of the family.

He stabbed them all to death, and yet he never cut himself or cut off a piece of glove or anything like that. I have worked so many stabbings, and that has almost never happened. Stabbings are always up close and personal, and once the person gets going with inflicting multiple stab wounds, they end up cutting themselves. This killer was careful. He cleaned up after himself. Left behind no semen, just lube. He took the tape with him, the knives, everything."

"He must have done it before," said Tony.

Ayanna shook her head. "He might have, but if he did, it wasn't the same way he killed the Dale family. I checked for any murders in the US that matched my crime scene, and nothing. Which I found hard to believe. I've checked several times since then. I figured he might have killed again after this, but nothing so far."

"Wow, that's... I don't know what to say to that," I said. Tony shook his head.

"Now, let's look at the Ortega family. This is where things get crazy," said Jill.

"Having examined both families, do you think it was possible for it to be the same killer?"

Jill stood up and turned the screen back on. "Yes, and no. Well, I—if I had to make a guess, I would have to say no. With the Dale family's murders, the killer was more focused on the children. It was like, see how I can torture them, see how I can hurt them. With the Ortega family… well, let's take a look."

Another video started to play, this time in a different house. This time, the foyer, the living room, and the hallways were all free from blood. There was no blood splatter on the walls or the ceilings. Only when the camera entered the dining room did we see images of the murder scene. All the carnage pooled there and nowhere else.

It was fascinating how the killer was able to keep the blood in that one room. How did he get them all there?

Jill walked us through the home and the scene. "I want to reiterate because I really need you to understand how amazing this is. There is no sign of forced entry and no blood or other fluids in any other part of the house. There is only blood in the dining room. Which begs the question, how did he get them all into that room? Now, I figured it was one by one, but there are so many of them that it doesn't really make sense. Also, Mr. Ortega had a broken nose. The killer probably punched him in the nose before he got him into the dining room. But there is no blood splatter from a nose or anything else outside of the room."

"How is that possible?"

Jill shrugged. "I have no idea. We never figured it out, and there were no signs of peroxide or any kind of cleaner. I'm telling you this is the strangest murder… well, one of the strangest that I have ever worked on. Each victim was tortured. Teeth pulled, ears sliced off, tongues cut out. Eyes cut out. It was gruesome. And all parts were on the table, just waiting for us to figure out who they belong to."

"And there was no forensic evidence left behind by the killer?" asked Tony.

"Nothing," answered Ayanna. "Absolutely nothing."

"Was anything taken from the house?" I asked.

"We had a friend of the family come in and look around, and they said it looked like everything was still there. Nothing was moved to any other part of the home. Nothing else disturbed. It was like they went in for the family and nothing else."

I swallowed my smile. This case was a puzzle. A true puzzle. So many pieces. Now we just needed to figure out how they all fit together.

CHAPTER NINE

THE REST OF THE DAY WAS SPENT WORKING OUT A PLAN of action. We sorted through all of Ayanna's notes from interrogations and interviews. Jill suggested we start from scratch, and I agreed. Which meant that we would interview the people she talked to without her. This way, we could come to our own conclusions and see if they matched hers or not.

"We need to work this case like we are seeing it for the first time." I wished I had thought of that before we looked at all of her notes and evidence, but that was done now. And here we were. We sat in the conference room across from Ayanna, sorting through the notes of her interviews.

She didn't seem too happy about us looking through her papers. That was something I understood. An agent keeps their notes close to the vest. Our notes were where we wrote down everything about the case. Who we spoke to, why, what they said, how they acted. It was our first thoughts on the case, the victims, and suspects. The notes weren't sacred, but showing them to people was like showing them our innermost thoughts, and I didn't think I would like that. So I understood the pained expression on her face as I turned the pages in her notepad.

She was thorough.

It was clear Ayanna cared about her job. The notes were detailed. She wrote down who she spoke to, what they said, their facial expressions, and what they wore that day. She was more detailed than Tony.

I continued flipping through the notebook while Tony made his own notes from Jill's autopsy reports. Jill was also thorough. She made notes not just about the bodies but also the wounds, placement of the bodies, and any other findings like blood splatter and other evidence.

Tony made the notes to look at later. There was something about the murders of both families that made me believe they were connected. But after searching through Jill's notes, there was no evidence proving it. Right now, it was just a gut feeling. A strong one.

"I don't think you two should be working this on your own. It is my case, after all." Ayanna's arms folded across her chest in one quick motion. "It doesn't seem right." Her eyes narrowed at me and then at Tony.

It was clear she felt like we were taking over her case, but that wasn't the plan. I didn't want to take over her case. I didn't even want to work her case. I wanted to work on my own. The goal was to solve these murders and see if they linked back to Bruce. Both Tony and I felt like it was a possibility. Bruce wouldn't have a problem killing an entire family. I needed to look for the link to Bruce. There had to be one.

"Like I said, we are not trying to take over your case, Ayanna. We would never do that. But the case needs a fresh set of eyes. and we are those eyes. All we are doing is going over the case and interviewing the same people you talked to. If there is an arrest to be made, we won't stand in your way."

Her shoulders softened for a beat. "Fine."

She didn't really have a choice at this point, but I kept my comments to myself. Davies had already signed off on Tony and me working the case, so we didn't need her approval. But it was nice to have, even though it was given begrudgingly.

As Tony kept pointing out to me, we needed to be as friendly as possible with other special agents. We couldn't make it seem like we were stealing other agents' cases or showing them up. We had to work together.

"Agents talk," he had said. "A lot. Especially if they have been drinking. And you know how we drink. If word gets around that an agent is difficult to work with or steals cases... it will be that much harder to get them to respect you, let alone like you, which will make it much more difficult moving up the ladder."

"I know. I know."

"I'm not saying don't stand your ground. You should if you really know your shit. But try to go about it the right way. For example, the way we went to Ayanna before we went to Davies and asked her about her case. That was the right thing to do. We asked her if we could help, and then once she agreed, she went to Davies. Agents should work things out amongst themselves before they bring the higher-ups into it."

After all the cases we had worked together, Tony was still teaching me things. I hadn't gotten the opportunity to work with other special agents outside of Hattie, Love, and Eli. Hattie didn't work her own cases. She was more of a floater. She floated from case to case, department to department, going where she was needed. In the IT department, Eli and Love had their own computer crime cases, but they also helped the rest of the agents with their cases as needed.

I met other agents in passing but not to work a case. With Ayanna, this was an okay start. She wasn't happy to have us, but maybe if we helped her solve the case and let her arrest the person responsible, she might soften toward us.

"Was there anyone you thought was holding something back?" I asked Ayanna, closing the notebook.

She shrugged. "All of them. Everyone I talked to knew more than they were telling. But I couldn't figure out what they were hiding and why. It's still a mystery to me. But there was something they weren't saying. Maybe you two can figure it out. Time has passed, and maybe someone feels guilty about it. Although I doubt it because they would have come forward by now."

"Maybe they are just waiting for someone to ask."

"Start with Mrs. Ortega's sister. She definitely knew more than what she was saying." Ayanna stood up and gathered her things. "Good luck." Her tone was flat. I glanced at Tony, who smiled.

"Starting with the sister, then."

He nodded. "Sure. Ready when you are."

Nallely was Mrs. Ortega's older sister. She lived in a modest-looking home with a black fence and a black door. The white wood and black trim made her house stand out among the dull, beige-colored houses on the block. It was a newer development filled with retirees from out of state and vacation homes with high price tags because of their proximity to the beach.

The ocean was so close I could smell the salt on the breeze. Tony knocked firmly on the black door. A long moment later, an older woman appeared in the window on the right side of the door. She looked from me to Tony, her hand resting on the doorknob. Her eyes narrowed at me as I took my badge out of my back pocket and held it to the glass.

Only then did she open the door. "How can I help you?"

"We are looking into your sister's case. Do you have a moment to answer a few questions?"

Her eyes softened as she stepped back. "Sure."

Her home smelled like freshly baked cookies. If I had to make a guess, I would have said oatmeal raisin. The air smelled sweet and buttery, with notes of brown sugar and vanilla.

"Come right on in." the door closed softly behind us. She led us into the living room. "Have a seat, and I'll be right back."

It was ten minutes before Nallely returned to the living room carrying a large tray.

"Fresh coffee and cookies. I just made them this morning."

I stared at the plate of cookies on the coffee table. I was right. It was a little late in the day for coffee, but I did take a cookie. It was still warm.

"So, what is this about exactly? I thought Special Agent Yagher was working on the case. She seemed really dedicated at the time. Haven't heard from her much, though."

"She's still on the case, and she's still dedicated. We just thought a fresh set of eyes would be helpful in closing the case.

A different perspective," I said. I bit into the cookie. It was soft but crispy around the edges.

"Oh, well, alright then. What do you need to know? Are you going to ask me the same questions she did?" She sat down in a chair with large yellow flowers that stood out against its orange fabric.

"Not quite." I finished my cookie. "What can you tell us about your sister and her family? What kind of people were they?"

I had noticed in Ayanna's notes that this was one of the questions she hadn't asked. And it was the one question I almost always asked. Asking a person what their loved one was like was a good way to get them to open up. To let their guard down. Usually, it worked. Unless they had something to hide. But Nallely looked relaxed, open. Like she had nothing to hide. She blinked at the question, her mouth slowly easing into a smile.

"Well, they were a lively bunch. They had six kids, you know. They were always getting into something. Going somewhere on the island. They liked the outdoors… loved the beach, especially. Marisol loved being their mother. She had so much energy and was involved in all their activities. Their oldest, Javier, had just gotten accepted at a *futbol* academy in Spain. He was really good. He would have gone pro."

Her voice faltered for a moment. The smile slowly slipped. And then there it was again. But her eyes were sad, dim. "They were a good family. They really loved each other. They really—" She choked back a sob.

"What can you tell us about the Dale family?" I asked in an attempt to change the topic. She looked on the verge of a breakdown, and I didn't want to see that. If she started crying, the interview would go nowhere.

"Who?"

"The Dale family. They were killed before your sister's family."

Her forefinger drifted up to her bottom lip. At that moment, I understood what made Ayanna believe she was holding something back. The way she looked at me. The way her finger tapped against her bottom lip. She had something to say, but it was like she was weighing her options. Trying to sort out whether she should say it or not. Hold it in or not. But whatever it was, she had been holding it in for months, and it was time to let it go.

"I believe the murders were connected. And I think you know something you aren't saying. And if we don't know everything, we can't solve the case. If you are hiding something or if there is something we should know that could help us, you need to speak up."

She glanced at Tony, who had been relatively silent up until now.

"He... I'm not sure. I don't know what I know and what I don't. The murders have me second-guessing everything. If I knew them at all."

"She was your sister. Is your sister. You knew her," said Tony.

"Did I? If you had told me last year that my sister and her entire family would be killed in their home, I would have told you it was impossible. That they could never do anything that would make someone want to kill them, but now... someone murdered all of them. I keep thinking they must have done something, but I can't for the life of me figure out why."

"So, what do you think you know?" I leaned forward, hoping to coax the words from her. She looked at me and sighed. Her shoulders relaxed, dropping away from her ears.

"I never told Yagher this. I didn't think it made a difference, and I was never really sure if Lloyd and Gabriel knew each other or not."

Tony took out his notepad. He never wrote everything down, just what he found interesting. And this was interesting.

"Why wouldn't you know? Gabriel was your brother-in-law. You two didn't spend much time together?"

She sighed. "We did plenty of times. But my sister was friends with Lloyd's wife. At first, I figured that was how they were connected. They weren't close friends, but they got together sometimes. My husband thinks I'm being paranoid. He thinks it was just a coincidence, and he might be right. But I was never sure."

"What makes you think they might have known each other, outside of their wives?" I leaned back and glanced at Tony scribbling in his notepad.

"The way they acted around each other. There was a familiarity there that seemed strange. Everyone was cagey about it... on whether they knew each other before they came to the island. Before the Dales moved here, they used to vacation on the island. That's when Marisol said she met Miranda. They always got together when the Dales visited. And when the Dales moved here, my sister was happy. But Gabriel seemed annoyed. Almost angry. I could never understand why."

"So, the way they acted with each other made you believe they knew each other before they got to the island. You never got anything concrete? You never asked your sister about it?"

Nallely shrugged. "She was cagey about that, too. She never wanted to talk about it and was very dismissive. She would just say, 'Oh, you know, they might have met years ago,' and that was that."

"That is interesting. Why would they hide that? Why keep that from you?" Tony asked.

"I don't know. I'm trying not to dwell on it, but it was strange. And I don't want to think that they were into something bad. Something dangerous or illegal. I don't know."

She let out a weighted sigh. "I don't know. When Lloyd and his family were killed, we heard about it. My sister was upset, naturally, but Gabriel... it was more than that. He looked... I remember we were sitting at their kitchen table. Marisol sat across from me, and I turned to face Gabriel. We were talking about how Lloyd and his family were found and the look on Gabriel's face. Marisol was crying, but he was... I think I saw fear in his face. He looked scared. And I remember thinking it was such a strange emotion to see from him."

"Because he didn't like Lloyd?" I asked.

She nodded, her hand resting underneath her chin. "I thought, 'you don't even like this guy. Why that look?' And that was the only look. There was no concern, and he didn't ask questions or anything like that. It was so odd. My husband said it was nothing."

"Might be. Might not be," I said. "But either way, thank you for speaking with us. Before we go, is there anyone else you think we should speak to?"

She leaned back in her oversized chair. She was so small the orange practically swallowed her.

"I don't know. Gabriel didn't have any other family. Umm... I would say his coworkers. That was all he did. Gabriel went to work, and then he came home and spent time with his family. He was all about his family."

"Okay. Thank you."

Tony and I stood up to leave.

"Please let me know when you find something—if you find something. I would like to put this to rest. It will be hard to move on until I know for sure. I just want them to find peace. I want our mother to be able to find peace."

I nodded slowly as we followed her to the door. "I understand. We will let you know as soon as we learn anything."

She smiled weakly.

Gabriel Ortega worked at a small, custom stationery company. He had been a supervisor, and from Ayanna's notes, he had been well-liked. Tony thought that was impossible.

"What supervisor is well-liked?"

I told him it was possible, which elicited an eye roll.

"Either he was a pushover and wasn't doing his job, or the employees didn't want to speak ill of the dead. And it's probably the latter."

"Or maybe he was a good supervisor. Maybe he knew how to keep everyone in line without being an ass. It can happen."

He shook his head, his black curls falling into his eyes. He quickly slicked his hair back into place.

"That hasn't been my experience. I'm just saying."

I wanted to ask him about his past job experience, but we pulled into the parking lot in front of Gabriel's workplace. Mentally, I ran through the questions I wanted to ask. Tony and I were both concerned being this late in the investigation. There was a chance that the people Yagher talked to no longer worked for the company. And the ones who were still there could have forgotten what they said to Ayanna or could have forgotten what transpired in the weeks before his death. All of those were possible.

After our talk with Nallely, one thing kept nagging at me. A question we would probably never have an answer to. If the two men knew each other before they came to the island, did Marisol know about it, and did she know why Gabriel didn't like Lloyd?

Did the men have a secret life that the women knew nothing about? Maybe Marisol didn't want her sister to know she had no idea why her husband disliked Lloyd or that they knew each other before they moved.

But it was also possible that one of Gabriel's coworkers could have remembered something or had a crisis of conscience and had been waiting for someone to come along and ask the right question.

Inside, the building smelled like paper and something floral that might have been someone's perfume. When we walked in, a woman in a light blue shirt stood next to a rack of cards.

"Excuse me, ma'am?"

The woman spun around. She pushed her bright, red-rimmed glasses up her nose. Her eyes flicked from me to Tony and back again. "Can I help you?"

I held up my badge, and Tony did the same. Her eyes went wide.

"Umm..." Her arms folded across her chest for a brief moment and then fell to her sides. "What is this about?" She clasped her hands behind her back.

"Gabriel Ortega."

She blinked. "Oh! I thought that case was closed or something. Well, no one came back around asking about him or his family. You never caught the guy?"

I shook my head. "We are reopening the case. Fresh set of eyes. Did you know him?"

Her lips quirked up into a smile. "He was nice. Well, I only worked under him for a couple of months before he died. But he was nice those two months. Very kind to everyone. That's why it was so shocking. I mean the whole family. I... never thought he, of all people, would have died like that. He didn't deserve it."

"Was he acting strange before he died?"

She shrugged. "Not that I noticed. But you know what, you should talk to Christopher Balor." She glanced around the store. "But he doesn't work here anymore. He quit a week after Mr. Ortega was killed. They were close. It hit him hard.

He looked like he hadn't been sleeping before he left. He might know something. And Miss Angie. She was here before me, and she knows a lot about what goes on here. Information just kind of falls into her lap."

"Is she here?"

She pointed down one of the aisles filled with card stock. "Straight back, you'll find the door to the breakroom."

"Thank you."

CHAPTER TEN

WE FOLLOWED THE PATH PAST COUNTLESS SHELVES filled with paper and cards to the back of the building, and stopped at a door labeled 'Break Room.' The door was wide open. Inside were two people. One was an older black woman with short hair. I admired the gray streak in the front of her black hair. It was beautiful. She looked up from her plate of food. While she was eating, the other worker, a young man with black glasses, sat at another table reading a book. He didn't pay us any attention as we walked in.

"You don't work here." Miss Angie's voice was flat and matter-of-fact. I didn't need her to tell me her name to know exactly who she was. She just seemed like a Miss Angie.

I held up my badge.

"What do you want?" she sighed.

"We wanted to speak with you about Gabriel Ortega." I sat down across from her at the table while Tony stood in the doorway, leaning against the door frame.

She glanced at him for a moment before turning her attention back to me.

"Didn't you catch the man that killed his family?"

I shook my head. "No, ma'am, we haven't."

"I could have sworn. Well, maybe that's because I hadn't heard anything about it in a long time."

"Right. It was a cold case, but now we have reopened it. We're looking for new leads wherever we can."

"I don't know anything about that." She took a napkin, wiped her hands, and then placed the top back onto the container holding her half-eaten chicken tacos.

"What can you tell us about Gabriel? Did you see him before he was killed?"

"Yeah. He came to work the day before." She leaned back in her seat. Miss Angie seemed like a no-nonsense kind of person. She folded her arms across her chest.

"Did he seem stressed or was he acting unusually?"

She looked at me, her head slowly tilting. "I don't think so. He..." She sighed heavily. "Well, I guess he was a little jumpy. But I know a friend of his wife had been killed before. Like a couple of weeks before, I believe."

"The Dale family."

She pointed at me. "Right. I know Marisol was shaken about it. She was devastated. She and the wife were friends. I don't think Gabriel got along with the husband, though."

"What makes you say that?" I leaned forward, resting my elbow on the table. "We've heard they didn't seem too friendly. Or rather, Gabriel didn't seem like he wanted to be friends with Lloyd Dale."

Her eyebrow raised slightly. "I remember one day, Lloyd came into the building. Gabe immediately, I mean mid-conversation with me, stopped talking and barreled toward him. He... I don't know what was said, but Lloyd turned around and walked out here real fast-like."

"Did you ask Gabriel what it was about?"

She shrugged. "Gabe liked to… he was a private person. He kept certain things to himself, which was understandable. But when he walked back over to me, he shook his head. He said that the guy kept following him. He made him sound like a stalker. I told him to call the police. I mean, if the guy is bothering you, then you need to take care of it, you know."

"Did he think Lloyd was dangerous? Like a dangerous stalker kind of situation?"

She took a long moment to stew on the question. "I don't think so. I don't think Gabriel thought he was dangerous. If anything, he was annoyed by him. He said once, 'I don't even know what he's doing here. Why here?' I asked him what he meant, but when he said it, I think he forgot I was there. And when he looked up and saw me, he kind of shook it off. He said nothing and walked away."

"Did you tell the last special agent this?"

She shrugged. "I don't think so. I didn't think anything of it. The Dale family was killed first, so it wasn't like Lloyd killed the Ortega family. I might have believed it if that had happened since Gabe didn't like him so much. But it happened the other way around. So, Lloyd didn't have anything to do with it. I still don't see a connection."

"So, you think the murders aren't related?"

She nodded. "And I'm not the only one that sees it that way. Just about everyone I know thinks the murders were separate, and no one understands why someone would kill the Ortegas. I didn't know Lloyd and his family, so I couldn't speak to his family. But the Ortegas were a good, kind family. And I don't understand it. I really don't."

I smiled. "Thank you for your time."

She shrugged as I got up from the table. I followed Tony back out of the building, waiting until we got back into the car before I said what I was thinking. Everything I had learned about the families up until this moment made me believe the murders were connected and the two men knew each other.

"So, they knew each other, right?" Tony shoved the key into the ignition.

"Right. They knew each other, but why hide it? Why shy away from it? That's what I don't understand."

He nodded slowly. "Unless how they knew each other was the problem. Maybe they were both into something illegal and moved here for a fresh start. People do it every day."

"That's true. We should find his friend, Christopher. Maybe he knows something."

§

Christopher was elusive. Not only had he quit his job, but he had virtually dropped out of sight. Deleted all social media and kept a small internet footprint.

"This is so annoying." Love sighed into her hands. Once Tony and I turned up nothing in our search for Christopher, we turned to her. If anyone could find him, she could.

"Why do people do this to themselves?"

I glanced at Tony, who shrugged. Neither of us knew what she was talking about. She wasn't really talking to us but rather her computer screen and her failed searches.

"He really doesn't want to be found. I find that interesting," said Love.

"Yeah, me too." I stared at the screen. He was hiding, but why? If he didn't know anything or hadn't seen anything, then why go into hiding a week after their murders? Unless he did it.

"He removed every trace of himself from the internet. I mean, there aren't even any Facebook posts. There was one a few years ago that was posted by a woman who might have been his mother or aunt. She posted a picture of the family together, but when you click on it, the picture is gone."

"Why would he do that?" asked Tony. He sat on the empty table behind Love, his hands in his pockets. "He's hiding something. Either he is hiding from us, or he knows who killed them, and he's hiding from them. He doesn't want the killer to know what he looks like."

I looked at Tony, a scenario unfurling in my mind. He had a point. If he knew the killer or had seen the murders, he would want to hide. Was he our killer, or was he a witness? We wouldn't know until we asked him, but first, we needed to find him.

Love promised us she would keep working on it. She seemed determined to figure out who he was, mostly out of annoyance. We left her to find Ayanna. She sat at her desk. When she saw us, she jumped to her feet.

"Did you find anything?"

We filled her in, her brows knitting together with every detail. Her frown was pronounced and unyielding. I understood her frustration.

"I wish someone had said something when I asked them months ago."

"Neither woman thought it was relevant. Nallely didn't think there was a connection because Gabriel denied knowing Lloyd. And Angie didn't think Lloyd had anything to do with the Ortega murders because he died first. She didn't see the connection, so she kept it to herself."

Ayanna sighed. "Sure. I guess that makes sense. What now?"

"Now we need to find Christopher Balor so we can talk to him about Gabriel," I answered.

Her brows pinched together. "Who is that?"

"We were told they were close when Gabriel worked there. I think he knows something because he essentially dropped off the map a week after Gabriel was killed."

"That's suspicious."

I nodded. "He's also erased all traces of himself online. Love is trying to find him as we speak. She said she will let us know when she does."

"Okay. Thanks for letting me know."

We left her and decided to go out to dinner while we waited. We might not be able to go to his house tonight, but we would wait for his whereabouts. We went to the same Indian restaurant as before. The food was amazing, and the atmosphere was relaxed, which was what we needed.

We ordered the same food as last time; neither of us was in the mood for something new.

"How are you feeling?" I dipped a piece of naan in the butter chicken sauce before shoving it into my mouth.

"I'm okay. A little tired but not as sore as I was before. What about you?" He rested his elbow on the table and his chin in his hand. "What you been up to… outside of work?"

I giggled. "Nothing. Met some people in the building." I told him about Keisha, Delia, and Harrison and how we talked in my apartment and had drinks. He smiled.

"Good. They are good people."

"Yeah, they talk about you a lot and how handsome you are."

He wiggled his eyebrows and laughed. "Yeah, they are just being kind."

"Sure."

We talked about people in the building and the ones he had met up until then. And then the conversation turned to his mother. His mother had come to check up on him and put food in his fridge. He rolled his eyes, unable to conceal his annoyance at the gesture.

"Why does that bother you? It's sweet that she does that for you."

He sighed. "She told me she wanted me to… there's a dinner at her place, and there's someone she wants me to meet."

"A blind date?" I leaned in. I was curious if he would go. Tony didn't seem interested in dating anyone right now. He hadn't said it explicitly, but that was how it seemed to me.

"Yeah. I don't want to go. I'm not in the mood to date right now. She keeps suggesting women for me to date, and I'm just tired of hearing it. And when I say it, I'm the bad guy. She even suggested you and Hattie."

I coughed. A piece of chicken went down the wrong pipe when I sucked in a breath of air. I gulped down some water. "Us?"

He nodded. "She keeps suggesting people from work, but I'm not doing that. Not again. It… dating people you work with ruins things. Ruins the work. It ruins the relationship. I don't want to fall into the trap again."

I nodded as my chest tightened. He was right it would ruin things. Make them more complicated than necessary.

"I understand that. You should talk to her alone. Let her know how you feel. You shouldn't have to go if you don't want to. Set some boundaries with her."

He sighed. "I know. It's hard, though, with her. I don't think she sees boundaries with people she pushed out of her body."

I chuckled. "Sounds like my mother, although she has been getting better about it."

He smiled. "I won't go, and when she asks why I didn't show up, I'll go to the house and talk to her."

"Sounds like a plan." The tightness in my chest eased a little. I should have known that was how he felt. I should have known better. Not that I had any inkling that we could have been in a relationship. I was fairly certain I wasn't his type, but he was nice to look at. That's all it was.

By the time we finished dinner, Love hadn't called us. I sent her a text as we left the restaurant.

"Love says she still hasn't found him. He has no bills or anything registered in his name. And there is no movement on his social security number. And there hasn't been since the Ortega family was killed."

Tony leaned on the car. "You think he's dead?"

I stopped in my tracks. I hadn't thought about that. I figured he had tried to make himself disappear. Him being dead never crossed my mind, but that might make sense.

"You might be on to something. But when did he die and how?"

Tony shrugged. "Text Love and ask her if she can find anyone else in his family. Maybe they know where he is or why he's hiding."

I sent the text, and Love said she would check. We wouldn't be able to interview them until morning. I glanced at the clock, and it was almost ten. It was time to call it a night and start fresh in the morning.

"You gettin' in later and later."

I recognized Delia's soft voice almost immediately. I spun around, and there she was, standing by her door. "Were you just standing there waiting for me?"

"Not for you exclusively. Anybody, really. I was bored, and here you are." She opened her door. "Come on in."

I shoved my key into my pocket. The only thing I wanted to do was go to bed. But Delia wanted to talk about something, and I guess I was the chosen one. I stepped into her apartment and closed the door behind me. Her apartment's layout was a lot like mine. I walked down the hallway that opened up to the living room.

Delia stood in the kitchen mixing a drink. "You want one?"

I shook my head. "No, I'm okay. So, what's wrong? Everything okay?"

I sat with her on the soft, black leather sofa. I looked at Delia for the first time in a few days. Her eyes were red, and she looked so tired.

"He wants full custody."

"Can he get it? Don't courts usually side with the mother?"

She shrugged. "Usually, but not all the time. He said he wouldn't go for full custody, but because my cousin is now pregnant, he wants the kids to grow up together, and he thinks the best way to do that is if they live in the same house."

"They can still grow up together and know each other without living in the same house. He's just trying to be spiteful." I sighed, my body relaxing against the cushions.

Delia's ex-husband was not a good man. Not because he was abusive. At least she hadn't mentioned that he was. But he had an affair with Delia's cousin, so to me, that made him a horrible person.

"The family… my family have been distant to my cousin lately. Not inviting her to family functions and all that. I think they think that if they have Divine, whenever they want her to come to something, they have to come too."

"They are trying to restore her reputation in your family?"

She downed the last of her drink, vodka, by the look of it. "I don't know. I think they believe they didn't do anything wrong, or they just want everyone to move on and get over it."

"They don't get to dictate how long it takes you to move on. They hurt you. You take all the time you need. Do you think he'll get custody?"

"I don't think so. I hope not. I have a more stable job and a stable living environment. I work from home, and he's a doctor, and he works long hours. I am the more hands-on parent. I don't see why they would give him custody, but it still irks me that he went back on his promise. However, I shouldn't have been surprised. That's kind of his thing."

I spent a few hours with Delia, mostly for moral support. She seemed like she really didn't want to be alone, but once she fell asleep, I took the glass she had clutched to her chest and set it in the sink before leaving. Her daughter was at her father's house for the weekend, so I didn't have to worry about the little girl finding her mother passed out on the sofa.

As soon as I closed the door to my apartment, I kicked off my shoes, bypassed the kitchen, and went straight to bed.

My first action when I woke up was to check my phone for a text from Love. I went to bed with her and Christopher on my mind. So much so that it took me a while to fall asleep. My mind drifted to Christopher every time I wasn't focused on going to sleep.

Where was he? Why go into hiding? He must have heard something or seen something. When I closed my eyes, I saw the crime scene photos that both Jill and Ayanna had let us look at. The Ortega crime scene was contained in the dining room. If someone had been there that night, would the techs have found DNA or blood from someone outside of the Ortega family? Was he the killer? But if he was, and he had gotten away with it, why remain in hiding? Someone was looking for him. We just needed to figure out why. When I finally fell asleep, it wasn't for long.

Love's message had been sent a little after two in the morning. The list consisted of Balor family members, three of whom lived on the island. I sent the message to Tony before I pulled myself out of bed and went to take a shower.

After breakfast, we went to the first name on the list, Christopher's sister Tami. First, we went by her house, but no one was there. Love had also given us a list of where his family members worked. Tami worked at an Asian market. She was the manager.

I definitely needed to write down the address to this place for future reference. It wasn't that far from my apartment, but I had never noticed it before. It was a pretty small store in a plaza next to a Chinese restaurant and an ice cream shop.

The shop had everything—kimchi, roasted duck, all different kinds of spices, and teas. I wanted to just walk through the shop to see everything they had, but I needed to focus. We were here to find Christopher. Tami stood behind the counter, identified by her black name tag with gold lettering. Yesterday, I had seen a picture of Christopher, and the two were clearly related. Christopher was a little wider and taller, but they shared the same bone structure, eyes, and mouth. She was the female version of her brother. I held up my badge as I walked toward the counter.

She gasped. "Umm... what's going on?"

"Are you Tami Balor?"

She nodded slightly. "What is this about?"

"We need to ask you a few questions about your brother, Christopher. Is there somewhere we can talk?" I gave her my best warm smile.

Her eyes narrowed at me. "No need. I haven't seen or talked to him in months. Not since he went crazy."

"Went crazy?" Tony inched closer to the counter.

"He became... paranoid, out of nowhere. He was afraid to stay home by himself. He was afraid to leave the house. He was always looking out the window, pulling the curtains, pacing back and forth. He never said why, but I couldn't take it anymore. He didn't want to get help, and he didn't want to tell us what was going on. My mother might know where he is, but I stay out of it."

"She was gonna be our next stop," said Tony.

Tami looked down at her watch. "She should still be home. She doesn't get out much these days. I have to do all her shopping for her, and sometimes I take her with me."

"Okay. Thank you for your time." I followed Tony out of the shop and to the car.

"You think it's weird she didn't ask us why we were looking for her brother."

"I guess when she said she didn't care, she meant it."

I shrugged. "I guess so." Maybe it's because I'm nosy, but I would have asked questions. Even if I didn't care about my brother anymore, I'd still want to know.

Our next stop was his mother, Sherry Balor. She lived in a modest home with a cow mailbox out front.

"That's adorable."

Tony shook his head as we walked up to the door. He knocked. A short moment later, the door opened slowly. I held up my badge to the elderly woman with white hair and thick glasses.

"FBI? I haven't done anything, I don't think."

I smiled. "Yes, Mrs. Balor, we are looking for your son Christopher. Have you seen him?"

She stepped back. "Well, I guess you better come in then so we can talk."

She stepped away from the door, allowing us to come in. Tony closed the door behind him. She led us through her house into the living room, where we sat on a soft leather sofa, and she sat in a rocking chair across from us. She watched us intently, rocking back and forth.

"Now, what is this about?"

CHAPTER ELEVEN

Her voice was monotone. Not an ounce of concern or worry. She stared at us expectantly, her eyes narrowing as seconds ticked by. I took a deep breath. There was something unnerving about the way she watched me… us. My spine straightened. She wasn't looking at me but *through* me.

Even Tony adjusted in his seat next to me. She had cold eyes. Nothing like Christopher or his sister Tami, although they did favor each other. They got her delicate bone structure, but that was it.

"We are looking for your son. Have you seen him? It's important that we speak with him." The words crawled out of my mouth, scraping against my tongue. My mouth was dry all of a sudden. Her eyes were fixed on me. I wanted to look away.

Look anywhere but at her but that felt wrong. I didn't want her to think she was making me uncomfortable.

There were family pictures all over the walls, mostly of Christopher and his mother. A few had Tami in them, but Christopher was definitely her favorite child, and it was clear. No father, though. Not that I could see. The house was nice and clean. It had a stale smell, like the windows hadn't been opened in a long time, but the house didn't stink. Behind her rocking chair, there was a bookcase with books on the bottom shelf. On the other shelves, there were dozens of small angel figurines.

It was creepy.

"Are you now? Why?"

I glanced at Tony, who leaned forward. "We think he has some information on the murder of a friend of his, Gabriel Ortega."

"My boy doesn't know anything about that. You don't need to talk to him."

"We need to hear that from him, not you," I said.

Her brown eyes glared at me. "My boy was not involved in that mess. He has nothing to say in the matter. You don't need to talk to him."

Her reaction told me she knew something. Or better yet, he knew something, and he had told her. Mrs. Balor had a cold, matter-of-fact demeanor that was a little intimidating. She cared about her son. The pictures made that clear. If she was afraid for him, the odds of her telling us what we needed to know were slim to none. I didn't want to arrest the old lady, but I would if it meant she would tell us where Christopher was.

It was my turn to lean forward. "Be that as it may, we need to hear this from him. Unless you want us to drag you down to the field office and arrest you for hindering an investigation, then you need to tell us where he is so we can speak with him. And just in case you are not aware, lying to an FBI agent is a federal offense."

Her eyes softened for a moment. "He didn't do anything wrong. I don't know why people keep picking on him. He's sick. He needs help."

"And that is probably true. But we still need to ask him our questions. And then we can get him the help he needs. What makes you think he needs help?"

She chewed on her bottom lip for a moment. "He just hasn't been in his right mind. He saw something that frightened him. I don't know what it was, but he wasn't right after. He's afraid to go out in public. He's afraid of people. He's afraid someone is looking for him. I don't know why they would be."

"Something made him paranoid, and he thought someone was out to get him," I said. "We can help him with that. We just need to know what he saw."

Her eyes softened, and she sighed. "Fine." She pulled herself out of the rocking chair and disappeared down the hall. She returned a long moment later with a scrap of paper. "Here."

I turned it over in my hand. "So, he's not dead." I glanced at Tony. He shook his head.

"Of course not." She blinked. "He's just scared."

"Why?" I still felt like she knew more than she was saying. How could she not know who he was afraid of? He had to tell someone, and he only seemed to speak with her. She knew more than she was saying, and even threatening her with prison time didn't loosen her tongue. Maybe she was afraid of the same thing, or she didn't believe we would actually take her in. Or he didn't tell her. I could only picture that scenario if he was afraid of putting her in danger.

She shrugged. "He wouldn't say, but he was awfully jumpy. He wasn't like himself. He still isn't. I don't get to see him anymore, but he calls occasionally. And I send him things when he asks. That's why I have the address."

"Okay."

"Don't hurt him," she said softly.

"We won't. We just want to ask him a few questions, that's all."

She smiled slightly. I could tell by the look on her face she was weighing whether to believe me or not. Her smile faltered for a brief second. I thought it was time for us to leave before she changed her mind about trusting us and decided to call and warn him. As we exited the home, I couldn't help but think we should have taken her phone away before we left.

We had no cause to do that, but I still felt like we should have. I sent the address to Hattie, who texted me back saying it was owned by Kenneth Balor, who was deceased. The house was in a remote area with few neighbors around. On paper, it sounded like the perfect place to hide out if you were so inclined. Surrounded by trees and nothing else. The closest neighbor was a mile away.

We walked up to the house, guns drawn, ready for whatever might happen. If he was hiding from someone, this was not the smartest place to go. The house was in his family's name. Easy enough to find him. And if we thought about it, so could the killer.

I banged on the door. "Open up! FBI!" There was rustling on the other side of the door. I glanced at Tony, who raised his gun again. The door opened. A half-naked man stood in the doorway, eyes wide. His hands shot up in the air.

"Please don't shoot!"

"Are you Christopher Balor?"

He nodded.

"Is there anyone else in the house with you?"

He shook his head. I looked at Tony, who slowly lowered his gun.

"Good because we need to talk to you." I pushed past him, and Tony followed. I pointed to the sofa in the living room and told him to sit while Tony checked the house. When he returned and shook his head, I relaxed. Twenty questions rested on my tongue, ready to be freed.

"What are you doing here?"

He looked at me, a question of his own forming on his face.

"Why did you make yourself disappear?"

He sat up straight. Christopher did not look the way I pictured him. When we started our search for him, we looked at his driver's license photo. He was once clean-shaven with short red curls and bright blue eyes. But now, he looked like one of the men from *Deliverance*. Wild red hair and a full beard that hadn't been brushed in months. A pungent smell emanated from him that made bile coat the back of my tongue. Something had him shaken up. He looked so happy in his driver's license photo. Bright and happy. "What happened to you?"

Christopher played with his fingernails.

"Christopher, we can't help you if you don't tell us what happened. Did it have something to do with Gabriel?"

He went completely still. his hand stopped moving. His chest stopped rising. He didn't move a muscle. "What did you see?"

Christopher rocked back and forth. "He's going to come and find me. You've led him right to me."

"No. No one knows we are here. And we can keep it that way. Or we can bring you down to the field office and protect you. Would you prefer that? Be surrounded by FBI agents?"

He jumped straight up, nodding fervently.

"Okay. We'll get you out of here and take you to our field office. We can talk there."

Christopher smiled slightly. "Thank you."

I looked at Tony, who shrugged. He seemed more worried about the smell on the way to the field office rather than Christopher's safety. Until we knew what he knew, it was difficult to say whether the killer was really after him or if he was just paranoid.

And we wouldn't get a sane answer from him until we made sure he felt safe, and that wasn't going to happen in this house. It was a cottage-style house. The wood paneling inside was beautifully made. It would have been a nice place to live if it wasn't for the smell.

"Okay. Let's go. But first, you might want to put on a shirt and maybe some shoes."

Christopher looked down at himself and then nodded. "Right."

We waited for Christopher to get changed. Tony stood by the door while I stood at the entrance to the hallway that led to the back of the house. It was a three-bedroom home with a small kitchen and a smaller living room. Christopher wasn't taking care of it. Dust coated the floor, the walls, the ceiling, and every other surface my eyes fell on. It was a surprise he could breathe in the house. He emerged from the back a moment later in a dingy black shirt and flip-flops.

"Better."

He smiled weakly. He looked drained. Like it took him enormous effort just to put his shirt and shoes on. He didn't comb his hair or detangle his beard.

Tony opened the door. Christopher followed behind him, and I brought up the rear, ready to take in the fresh air. Water sprayed my face the second I stepped into the sunlight. The forecast didn't say anything about it raining today, and the sun was so bright.

"Is it raining?" My eyes adjusted to the sunlight for a moment. A moment too long.

Without a sound, Christopher collapsed to the ground, a sharp crack sliced through the silence as his head hit the concrete. A gaping wet hole in the back of his skull. My mouth went dry and we immediately ducked for cover. My hand darted to my gun. I glanced at Tony, his gun drawn, scanning the area.

But there was no one there. The trees rustled in the breeze. Silence blanketed the area. My eyes darted to the tree line, scanning the leaves, looking for something that didn't belong. Sudden movement. The barrel of a gun. Something that explained why Christopher was bleeding on the ground.

"Tony!"

"I'm okay, Storm. You?"

"Yeah, I'm good."

"Back up into the house!"

I stepped back, and he followed. He closed the door as I took out my phone and called for backup and a coroner. When I told them to send the coroner, Tony looked at me surprised. But when he looked out of the front window, it was clear there was no helping Christopher. The back of his head was gone completely.

"Hey, Hattie, send a car to his mother's house. Whoever did this must have followed us from there."

I hung up the phone. "What are we going to tell his mom?"

Tony shook his head and opened the front door.

"What are you doing?"

He peered out the front door. "We weren't the target. The killer was only after Christopher."

"And we gave him what he wanted."

Tony walked outside and leaned against the car. "Technically, we didn't hurt him. Someone else did. That's what we tell his mother."

He was right, but it still felt wrong to say or think. Christopher lay at our feet, blood pooling, seeping into the concrete driveway. I shook my head. How did this happen? Was he just waiting for us to leave? Or was he going to come in and kill Christopher and us? We just gave him a better opportunity.

I leaned against the door. We were supposed to be getting him to safety. It wasn't supposed to end like this. "What happened?"

"I don't know. It happened so fast... I didn't realize it until it was too late. I didn't see anyone out here, but truthfully, I didn't think to look. I didn't think that anyone would have followed us out here. And now I'm not sure what that means. Did he follow us from Sherry's home? Or was the killer just watching and waiting for the right moment?"

Sirens blared in the background, rushing toward us.

"Exactly. Was he waiting outside her house?" My voice was quiet, distant. The sirens grew closer and closer. I couldn't take my eyes off Christopher. Blood pooled beneath his head, and it was only getting bigger. The coroner van pulled up behind three black cars.

Tony barked orders as soon as the agents got out of the car, telling them to comb the wooded area. We were still intact, so we weren't their target. That was partially reassuring.

"Well, at least you two aren't hurt." Dr. Pittman walked over with her black medical bag. She stopped short when she saw the pool of blood. The puddle had broken off into long slivers of blood like fingers reaching out to us. It was a little creepy. "What happened here? Did you shoot him?"

"Sniper in the trees, I think." I pointed to the trees. "I didn't see them. I didn't see anything."

"Me either. Whoever they are, they're good. I didn't see or hear the shot. I just heard him fall." Tony shook his head.

"Must have used a silenced sniper rifle or something," said Jill as she bent over the body. "Oh, wow. Look at the back of his head."

She didn't have to tell me to look. I hadn't been able to concentrate on anything else since it happened. Brain matter littered the ground next to his body.

I couldn't understand what had happened. My brain couldn't make sense of it. It was so fast. Everything happened so fast.

"How did they know?" I asked mostly to myself. Jill caught my eye, her frown deepening. "We need to go back and speak with his mother. See if anyone came to talk to her after we left."

Tony nodded and lifted himself off the car. "Right."

We left Jill bent over Christopher, examining the back of his head. On our way back to Sherry's home, my phone rang.

"Hey, Hattie, we're on our way back to Sherry's. Did agents get to her yet?"

"Yeah. But they are waiting for you."

I hung up. There was something in her voice. Something not said. A somberness misplaced. My heart sank. Something was wrong.

"Something's not right," I said as we pulled into the driveway. There were several cars framing the property. I jumped out of the car just as a man in a dark blue suit darkened the doorway.

"Special agents Walker and Storm?"

"Where's Mrs. Balor?"

He stepped back, allowing me to enter the house. Inside the house was busy. Agents walked from room to room with gloved hands. I wandered down the hall until I stepped into the living room. It was hard to say what led me there. I just had a feeling that was where she'd be. It was where we left here. And where someone else found her.

Mrs. Balor sat in her rocking chair, black eyes staring up at the ceiling. A large hole in the back of her head. Brain matter splattered across the wall behind her. I gasped when I saw her. I was expecting it. It explained Hattie's tone. It explained how the killer found us.

We led them to her and then to Christopher. A firm hand gripped my shoulder. I knew instantly who it was. The touch, familiar and warm, kneaded into my shoulder. I sighed.

"Can't help but feel like we got her killed," I said on the way back to the car. I needed fresh air.

"Technically, Christopher got her killed. Whatever he saw that night or whatever he knew, if he had come forward from the beginning, this might not have happened."

I leaned against the car, and he rested next to me. "You can feel bad, but don't linger there. Feeling sad won't help you solve her case or the others."

I nodded. The special agent from before walked out of the house. "So you two just saw her today?"

I nodded. "A few hours ago." It took us an hour to get to Christopher. "How long has she been dead?"

"Coroner is still looking at the body, but he says that maybe within the last thirty minutes to an hour. Her fingers were broken first, and three of her nails had been ripped off."

"Someone tortured her." It was more of a statement than a question. Why else would someone break her fingers and rip off her nails unless they were attempting to get her to talk? Talk about Christopher.

"That's what we were thinking. Nothing else in the house was disturbed, so they were here for one reason and one reason only. Also, the coroner said he wouldn't be surprised if the killer broke her fingers and all that, left, and then came back and killed her. He'll have to get her on the table to be sure. Said her hands were tied behind her back during the torture. There are restraint markings on her wrist. No blood on her wrist, though. So she was untied and then shot, and the restraints went with him."

"So, the killer might have tortured her right after we left, then went to kill Christopher, and then doubled back to kill her just in case she could identify him or she knew what Christopher knew."

The agent nodded. "That's what I was thinking."

"Please let us know what you find," said Tony.

"I wonder what he knew," said the agent. "I mean, taking the guy out and his mother... that's some mafia type shit."

"He was scared," I said. "He was terrified of something. He wouldn't speak until we got him to the field office so he could be safe. He saw something or heard something that rattled him."

"He didn't hint to what it was?"

I shook my head. "When I mentioned Gabriel Ortega, his body went completely still. He was afraid of something or someone. And now we will never know."

"You might. Just got work the case from another angle," said the agent. "Good luck." He backed away and headed back to the house. He was older than Tony but not by much, with wide shoulders and a small waist. He looked a little like a bodybuilder and not an agent.

"I guess we go back to the field office."

Tony nodded.

Hattie waited for us by our desk.

"That must have been scary." She held her tablet tight to her chest. "Someone getting their head blown off in front of you… Literally. You okay?"

"Yeah. We're good. Disappointed. Still trying to figure this shit out. And how they found us."

"Techs found a camera right above the door. Really small. She probably didn't even know it was there. Someone was watching her house to see who came by. They were probably expecting Christopher and not two FBI agents."

I sighed into my chair. My body melting until the chair and I became one. He was watching us. Watching her. Waiting for a hint as to his whereabouts.

"They were probably waiting to see what Christopher was going to do. If he just laid low everything would be fine. But when they saw us, they might have panicked. If we were looking for him, then he might tell us something they didn't want us to know. So, they decided to clean house."

"That's plausible," said Tony. He leaned back and rested his hands on his stomach. "Now, we need to come at this from another angle. I just wish we knew what he wanted to tell us. If it was something he saw or something he heard someone say."

"Yeah, that would have been perfect. But now we need to focus on what to do next." I sighed. I had no idea what that was, but we had the rest of the day to figure it out.

CHAPTER TWELVE

AFTER A TALK WITH AYANNA, WHO WAS JUST AS FRUStrated as we were, Tony and I went back to our desks to start over. Instead of looking for Christopher or looking for someone who might have seen something that night, we started looking for a link between Lloyd Dale and Gabriel Ortega. There had to be one.

Christopher hadn't left that house in months. He didn't even take out the trash. In one of the back bedrooms, there were several trash bags that probably contributed to the smell in the house. I doubted he talked to anyone outside of his mother.

His sister didn't speak to him. He had no one to confide in. I doubted there was a soul on this earth he would have told this secret to. And now that he was dead, his secret was dead too. So now we had to approach from another angle. And there were so many things that I wanted to know.

I was curious about why Gabriel acted like he didn't know Lloyd before and seemed annoyed by his presence. And I was even more curious as to why Lloyd didn't take the hint. If everyone else noticed that Gabriel didn't want him around, why didn't Lloyd stay away? It sounded like he got a kick out of annoying Gabriel.

"Hmm."

My eyes darted from my screen to Tony, who stared at his screen, eyebrows pinching together.

"Did you find a link?"

"I think I found something, but not a link. No proof they knew each other, but when I looked up their social security numbers, I found that they are only seven years old. Credit history, too. Nothing before that."

"How is that possible?" I leaned back in my chair. "We should dig up their bodies."

Tony blinked. "Is there a reason for that?"

"DNA? Maybe fingerprints." I fished my phone out of my pocket and called Jill to ask if she still had DNA from the Ortega and Dale murders.

"I did all that when the bodies were brought to the morgue. I never ran the DNA because I never had a reason to. Do you want me to do it now?"

"Please."

It made sense she hadn't run the DNA beforehand. There was no reason to. The men, the families, were the victims. Why would she run the DNA against the database? But now that we knew they might have known each other and might have been hiding something, it needed to be done. I thanked her for taking the time.

"She said she'll do it now with the samples she has."

"That's good. So now we don't have to get a warrant and go through all that to dig up the bodies."

"You know what I find strange?"

He shrugged.

"All this happened because Bruce told us about the case. If he hadn't, we would never have gone to Sherry, and she and Christopher would still be alive."

"Are you thinking he did it on purpose?"

I shrugged. "I was just saying a thought. It is strange, and I wouldn't put it past him."

"Yeah, me either. But we aren't going to see him, right?"

I waved my hand dismissively. "Of course not. I'm determined to work this case without him. I don't need him to finish this. Besides, going there will just give him what he wants. He wants us to need him. He wants the attention, and I won't give it to him if I don't need to."

"Okay. That'll work for now. Hopefully, we can find something."

My phone rang before I could comment. "That was fast. Did you get the DNA results back?"

Jill sighed. "I've looked through everything, and I can't find the samples. And they were here. I logged them myself. But they aren't here. And I wouldn't throw them away. The case wasn't solved. There's no reason it shouldn't still be here. I don't understand it, but I will get to the bottom of it."

Jill sounded motivated and annoyed before she hung up the phone.

"Jill says the DNA samples are gone. They are not where she left them, and she was the one who logged the samples. So that is a bust."

"We have to dig up then, I guess. Davies isn't going to like hearing this," he said as he stood up. "Which is why you are coming with me to tell her."

He was right. She wasn't happy about exhuming the bodies.

"Is that really necessary? Nothing else you can figure out by asking around?" She plopped down in her chair.

"Well, we tried that, and two people were killed. Asking around doesn't seem to be working."

Her eyes narrowed at me and then softened. "That wasn't your fault. How were you supposed to know someone was watching his mother? They didn't even know."

I shrugged. "But still. We asked around, and that led us to Christopher and only Christopher. And with him dead, we are out of leads. We don't know what he was hiding from or who he was so terrified of. Too terrified to bathe or shave or take care of himself. So, digging them up and getting their DNA is where we are right now. They knew each other, and they were trying to hide it. Well, Gabriel was."

"And their socials only go back seven years. Both of them. What are the odds of that?" added Tony.

Davies sighed. "Fine. I'll get it done. But you better find something. Who are we digging up?"

"Lloyd Dale and Gabriel Ortega," I answered.

"So, just the men?"

I glanced at Tony and shrugged. "Well, they were the two that seemed to have known each other before they came to the island. The wives met here and became fast friends. So, whatever this is, I think it starts and ends with the men."

"Okay. I can understand that. It'll be done in the morning. Now you two go home and get some rest. Especially you." She pointed to Tony.

He bowed slightly. The wince was brief. He pulled himself back upright and smiled as if to say he was okay. "I'll get him home right now."

"Good."

I dropped Tony at his apartment and then headed up to mine. It was quiet in the hallway. I checked my watch as I walked up to my door. It was almost eleven. Everyone was probably in bed by now. I closed the door behind me and sighed as I leaned against it. I was so tired. I was hungry, too, but more tired than hungry. I stuck my food, a burrito Tony and I got on the way home, into my fridge before heading to bed. I'd eat it in the morning for breakfast or dinner tomorrow when I got home.

I woke up the next morning and got ready for work. Instead of eating the burrito, I made a bacon, egg, and cheese sandwich for us.

Tony's face lit up when I welcomed him in. "I missed your sandwiches."

"You look like you're feeling better."

Tony looked like he had a little pep in his step. It looked like it was easier for him to get around.

"Yeah. I woke up this morning, and it didn't hurt to roll out of bed. I have a doctor's appointment today, so I'll have to leave around noon."

"You going by yourself?" I leaned into his shoulder.

"My brother is taking me."

"That's nice."

"Yeah, whatever."

I nudged him with my elbow. He didn't believe it, but King was worried about him when he was in the hospital. I saw it in his face. He was worried. Scared that Tony wasn't going to make it. No matter how many times I said it, he didn't believe me. Their brotherly relationship was a strange one. They seemed to care about each other, but neither brother wanted the other to know. It was weird.

"I guess I can survive without you for an hour or two."

"Good to hear. I guess."

I nudged him again. "I won't do anything interesting without you."

"That makes me feel a little better."

I chuckled. "They should be exhuming the bodies soon. You want to head to the graveyard and watch?"

"Watch someone be dug up? Interesting hobby you've got there, Storm." He shoved the rest of his sandwich into his mouth. "But, yeah, I would love to."

I laughed. I finished my sandwich and gathered my things before following Tony out of my apartment.

Oahu Mortuary was beautiful. Weird thing to say about a graveyard, but it was. And well kept. It was clear that families and the owners took care of the grave and the gravestones. The grass was cut, and there were no weeds.

"Looks like a nice place to be buried." I got out of the car and slammed the door.

"I'll remember that if something happens to you."

My lips quirked up into a smile. "I want to be cremated, just so you know."

"You want to be burned?"

"Not alive. I'm dead. What happens to my body is of no concern to me. I don't see the point in putting me in the ground."

"What if your parents want to come visit you?"

We walked along the path, not sure where we were going. A truck pulled up along with Jill and more agents on the other side of the graveyard. We figured they knew where they were going and followed. "If you want to see me, visit me while I'm alive and can enjoy my company. Once I'm dead, there's no point."

"Understood."

We joined Jill near one of the graves.

"Gabriel is buried here, and Lloyd is on the other side of the building. We'll start here. Now bear in mind he's been in the ground for a while, and we don't know what state he's in."

"Wouldn't he be mostly bones by now?" I asked.

"Hard to say. Depends on embalming and casket quality. There are a few factors. I've seen bodies exhumed, and they were relatively intact. Skin and all. And I've seen others with raggedy caskets that allowed moisture to seep in, and their bodies were a mess. A soppy mess. But I guess we'll see which one he is."

I took a giant step back. I didn't want to see anything, or more importantly, I didn't want to smell anything. A body in the ground that long could get pretty ripe. Tony followed me in moving upwind.

"You two wussies." Jill laughed. "It shouldn't smell that bad if he was embalmed, and he probably was."

"I understand you are good at what you do, but I'm still going to stand over here until we know better." I pointed to the ground beneath my feet.

She laughed even harder and shook her head. The bulldozer dug into the ground, breaking up the grass and the dirt. The sound of the metal scrapping against the coffin stopped everyone in their tracks. The truck backed away, and two men with shovels jumped into the hole and finished the process. Once the confine was clear of dirt, the men jumped out of the hole. The coffin was raised out of the hole and placed on the grass next to the headstone.

"Okay, give me a moment." With crowbar in hand, Jill walked over to the coffin and pried it open. "Uh-oh."

My legs jerked and rushed toward the coffin before I knew I was moving. There was no smell.

There was no smell because there was no body. Jill opened the coffin all the way. It was empty. "How is this possible?"

Jill shook her head. Her bottom lip trembled. "I don't know. We need to check the other coffin."

We followed the truck to Lloyd's coffin, repeated the same process, and found the same thing. Nothing. Neither Gabriel nor Lloyd were in their coffins. How was that even possible?

"So, they buried empty coffins?"

"What about the rest of them?" asked Tony. "If Lloyd and Gabriel aren't in their coffins, then what about their families?"

Jill shrugged. "We'll have to get permission before we can do that, but I think it's worth a look." Jill took out her phone. While she called who she needed to, I glanced at the building.

"We should talk to them and ask them how this happened."

Tony looked back at the building. "That is an excellent idea." We walked toward the building. Inside, it smelled like fresh flowers, which surprised me. It wasn't like I expected it to smell like dead bodies or anything, but the floral scent was nice. Jasmine, maybe. In the lobby, there were coral-colored chairs and a beige-colored coffee table littered with magazines.

Across from the sitting area was a receptionist's desk, cherry wood and shiny. An empty one.

Heels clicked on the tile floor. I heard the noise before I saw the woman in a light pink pencil skirt and white blouse. Her long hair was pulled into a tight ponytail, showcasing her sharp cheekbones.

"Can I help you?"

"Yes." I held up my badge. "We need to take a look at your records."

"Why? Did something go wrong with the exhumation?"

"I'm sorry, what is your name?" asked Tony.

"Call me Peaches." Peaches, curious to know if that was her real name or not, was an inch or two taller than me, with honey-blonde hair and dark brown roots. When she smiled, there was a deep dimple on her right cheek. It was adorable.

"Was there something wrong with the body?"

"Kind of." I glanced at Tony. "It wasn't there."

Her long eyelashes fluttered behind her pink-rimmed glasses. "I'm sorry, what? How could it be gone? Where did it go?"

"That is why we need to see your records," said Tony. His lips quirked into a smirk.

She nodded slowly. "I'll have to clear it with my boss. I've only been working here for three months."

She glided to the back of the building. A man, red-faced and huffing, returned with her in tow a moment later. Obviously flustered and confused.

"What is this about missing bodies?" His eyes darted from me to Tony, waiting for one of us to explain.

I explained how we had a court order to dig up two bodies, and both were missing. "How does that happen? If someone came here and dug them up—"

"We would know. There are cameras on the property. And security guards walk the grounds at night. If anything were disturbed, we would know. Someone would notice."

"Did you prepare the bodies yourself?" I asked.

"I'm not sure. Come back to my office, and I will look over my records."

We followed him down a long hallway to a small room with a desk, file cabinet, two chairs, and a bookcase. I sat in one of the chairs. "What is your name?"

"Oh, I'm Andy Marsh." He stopped at a file cabinet and opened one of the drawers. "What was the first name?"

"Gabriel Ortega," I answered.

He closed the top drawer and opened another. "Yes, here." He pulled out a light green folder and opened it. "I see. No, I didn't do this one. I didn't do any of the Ortega family." His forefinger tapped against the folder. "Ortega... I remember now. They were done at another mortuary and then brought here. We didn't handle the bodies. The memorial was somewhere else. I don't think it was an open casket either."

"What about Lloyd Dale?"

"That was another one not done here. The bodies are buried in our cemetery, but we didn't work on them."

"Would you have checked the caskets beforehand?" asked Tony as he leaned against the door frame.

"Not if we didn't have a reason to. And we didn't, or at least I didn't. What about the other members of the family? Are they empty, too?" There was real concern in his voice.

"We don't know. We are in the process of getting a court order to exhume the rest," I answered.

"Well, whatever you need."

I stood up. "Well, one thing. Who handled the bodies?"

CHAPTER THIRTEEN

"**A**RE YOU KIDDING ME!**"**
It wasn't really a question. We both knew that, so without being told or having to exchange a knowing look, we both kept our mouths shut. She wasn't expecting an answer, and we wouldn't give her one. It was best to let Davies get out all of her anger and frustration by asking rhetorical questions instead of trying to engage her by answering her questions, just for her to point out they were rhetorical to begin with. I learned that early on, and it was a lesson that stayed with me.

"So, where are the bodies?"

This was a question that should be answered. "No one knows. Dr. Pittman is still at the cemetery waiting for the court order to exhume the other bodies. She wasn't hopeful when we left."

Davies' hands gripped her hips. A vein pulsed near her temple. "Do you think the bodies are in the coffins? The rest of the family."

I shrugged. I had a lot of time to think about it on our way to the field office. On one hand, I thought it was possible the other Ortega and Dale family members were missing from their coffins as well. I thought of a scenario where when the coffins were delivered, there was nothing in any of them. Nothing but sandbags for the weight. That would mean the bodies were disposed of before the coffins were taken to the cemetery.

Andy said he believed the memorial service was a closed casket service. That made sense to me, especially for the Ortega family. Their bodies were mangled, and while a mortician could fix them, having looked at the crime scene photos, it would never be enough.

Their teeth were removed. Their tongues cut out. Eyes gouged. They were a mess, which was why it was a closed casket. The mortician probably couldn't do enough to make them look how they did before.

The other scenario roaming around in my head consisted of only Gabriel and Lloyd being taken. Whatever this was, it was about them. If it was about the husbands, there wouldn't have been a reason to take the other members of the family too. Their bodies might still be in their coffins.

"I'm not sure. If it was about both families, then yeah, they could have taken all of their bodies. But if it was just about Lloyd and Gabriel, then no, their bodies might still be in the coffins."

"So, you think this is about the husbands alone? Then why kill the entire family? Both of them." She threw her hands up in the air, her frustration palpable. "Did he know this? Bruce? I can't help feeling he orchestrated this whole thing to lure Christopher Balor out of hiding and have him killed."

I blinked. She had a point, and the thought had crossed my mind a few times after Christopher was killed. The thought irked me. Almost drove me crazy thinking we might have given him exactly what he wanted. Making him happy was not something I wanted to do.

"I thought about it, and honestly, I'm not sure. He might have orchestrated it, or he might not have. I don't think we will ever know the truth about that. Not until we figure out who killed the Dale and Ortega families. Which is our focus, not Bruce."

Davies opened her mouth to say something but stopped. She slunk into her chair. "You know what, you might have a point. We need to focus on finding out who killed these two families and why. To hell with Bruce."

"My sentiments exactly."

"That being said, you need to go back and speak to him." She closed a folder on her desk. "Go to him and see what information you can draw out of him without committing to a deal. Something to go on."

"I'm sorry, what now? I thought we were doing this without him." I looked at Tony, who leaned against the closed door. His eyes closed as he drew in a deep breath. His shoulders sank as he exhaled.

"I know. But you need to know where to look next, and right now, you don't. I've sent agents to find the mortician who took care of both families, so don't worry about that. Focus on Bruce and see what you can get from him. I know you don't like talking to him."

"It's fine. I'll go if it will help."

"Thank you."

I followed behind Tony and exited her office. I didn't want to go to Bruce. He either didn't know anything and was just using us for attention, or he orchestrated the whole thing to kill Christopher. Either way, I wanted nothing to do with him. Talking to him made my skin crawl.

"You gonna be okay to go alone?"

I nodded. I could do it by myself. I didn't want to, but I could if I had to. "I'll be fine. You focus on your appointment."

He sighed. "Okay."

"Good thoughts. Everything will be fine. You will be fine and come back with a good bill of health."

His lips quirked up into a smile. "Okay. Call me when you get done. If all goes well, I'll meet you back here."

"Sounds like a plan."

Tony seemed reluctant to leave at first. He stayed by his desk for a long moment, shuffling papers and moving things around. He was less worried about me and more worried about going to the doctor. It was a check-up to make sure his ribs and everything else were healing correctly. The doctor also wanted to check his brain to make sure everything was still okay.

It didn't sound serious, but the question of *what if* hung over his head. What if they found something? Eventually, he left when there was nothing left for him to do. I said a short prayer for him and then headed to the prison.

"He's becoming popular," said the guard as he walked me to the visitor's station.

"Once this is all over, things should go back to normal."

He chuckled. "Hopefully."

We rounded the corner and stopped short. The door in front of us opened. A guard led prisoners into the hallway. The guard, a young, muscular man with black hair, opened his mouth to say something. Before he could utter a word, all hell broke loose. My pulse rushed in my ears as a prisoner, a big white man with more tattoos than visible skin, punched another inmate. The Asian man hit him back, and then everyone started fighting. Arms flailing through the air. Fist smacking into bone. Feet slamming into shins. The guard tried to break it up, but he was one man against seven. The guard who had been escorting me rushed toward the fighting crowd.

He was punched in the nose for his trouble. Blood spurted in the air. My eyes were so fixed on the scene before me that I didn't see him at first. His loud breathing caught my attention. My eyes darted to my left, and there he was, chest heaving, a sinister grin on his face. I backed up, and my right hand immediately reached for my gun, but it wasn't there.

"Damn!" I had to turn it into the security guards.

"You look pretty."

"Thanks." I took a step back.

"Pretty skin. I could add it to my collection."

"I'd rather you didn't. Still using it after all."

His grin faltered for a brief moment before it returned. "You'd have to be alive to use your skin."

I glanced down, and in his hand was something sharp.

"Listen, you can't kill an FBI agent. That's the death penalty."

He smirked. "No death penalty in Hawaii."

The guards backs were to me. My chest tightened like a rope was wrapped around me and pulled until I couldn't breathe. In the next second, there was a sharp crack. I blinked. Bruce stood next to the man, whose wrist was twisted at an odd angle. He howled, and Bruce grinned. His eyes met mine, and his smile widened. The man snatched his hand from Bruce and cradled it against his chest like it was a hurt child.

"Get down now! Or get tear-gassed. The choice is yours!" yelled a voice.

"You came to see me. Mia, I'm touched. Always happy to see you."

More guards stormed the hallway, screaming commands. Bruce and the other inmates fell to their knees and then lay on their stomachs with their hands up. The guard with the broken nose grabbed me by the elbow and led me out of the hallway. I would have felt better if I had been allowed to go back and get my gun. He ushered me into a room reserved for prisoners meeting with their lawyers.

"Stay here. The prison is going into lockdown. I'll bring him to you when I can."

"I think you should be more concerned about your nose. Go get that looked at."

Blood dribbled down the hand that held his nose. His face was a bloody mess. Around his nose, it was already turning purple.

"I will. Just got to get things cleared up first." He closed the door behind him. I sat at the table in complete silence for what seemed like forever. A million thoughts ran through my mind. Had Bruce orchestrated that, too? Had he convinced his fellow prisoners to start a riot? Had he convinced them to fight? I wouldn't have put it past him. He was capable of anything bad. There was no question about that. But would they follow him? I wasn't sure about that.

An hour ticked by. I took out my phone and sent a text to Tony, asking him how it went. I would wait to tell him about the fight until I saw him face to face. It was better that way. So he could see my face and see how relaxed I was. I didn't think it would translate over the phone. Especially not text. While I waited for his reply, the door opened.

My heart hammered in my chest before I saw it was a guard. Not the same one who brought me into the room but another one. An older, more mature-looking man with a well-kept beard and bright green eyes.

"Here he is. Sorry for the wait. I had to clear up the lockdown and get the inmates where they were supposed to be." He chained Bruce to the table, asked if everything was okay, and then left the room. The door clicked behind him.

Bruce grinned. "I thought you'd be back. Well, let me stop lying. I never thought I'd see you again. I figured you'd try to solve the case on your own and then come back when you were finished to rub it in my face." He leaned forward.

"That was the plan, and it was working."

"What happened?"

"Now it's not."

He laughed. "Huh, that's interesting. So, your way isn't working, and now you want to try mine? How interesting indeed."

"Can we cut the shit now, and you tell me what you know."

His smile faltered for a split second. If I hadn't been staring at him, I wouldn't have noticed. His happiness wavered. Bruce's smile was a mask to hide the monster underneath, and when he wasn't getting what he wanted, the mask slipped. But only for a moment. He regained his composure quickly, and the grin was there again.

"Okay. I know why the men were killed and where they were taken after. I'll tell you the basics, but if you want more, then you are going to have to come back here with a deal. Here are the basics: the men worked for a child trafficking ring. This organization has different chapters all over the world. They were part of different chapters, but they betrayed the people they worked for."

"Did they do it together?"

He shrugged. "Not known. But they did it, and the higher-ups thought it was suspicious. So even if they didn't work together, they would be punished together as if they had. A hit was put out, and the two men disappeared only to show up here. Lloyd was flashy, while Gabriel understood the need to lay low. This is what got them killed."

"Where are the bodies?"

"Cremated."

"Okay. Give me a name."

His head tilted slightly. "Bring me back a deal. No deal, no information."

"I should have known that. You don't do anything unless you get something out of it. So what do you want?"

I knew that was where the conversation was going. Of course, he had to get a deal. It wasn't like he'd be doing this out of the goodness of his heart. He didn't have one.

"I want time shaved off my sentence. That's it."

"It's amazing how you say that like it isn't a lot." I stood up and walked over to the door.

"It's not. I am a changed man. Prison has reformed me. I'm not a danger to anyone anymore. I promise. I'll be good. I can be good."

The last sentence sounded more like he was trying to convince himself, not just me. He couldn't be good. There was no good left in him. He was a horrible human being and could never be released from prison. I sighed as I banged on the door.

The prosecutor was not going to go along with this. She made it clear she would not offer him anything. She would not make any deals with him, so what was I supposed to say? I walked out of the prison angry. Angry at Bruce and myself for even going to the prison. I did get one bit of useful information, though. Hopefully, I could make it work for me.

When I got back to the field office and dropped into my chair, Tony pulled a box out of his desk and slid it over. I opened the bright pink box. The smell of butter and vanilla consumed me. I sighed. "Thank you for the bear claw." I took a bite. "Mmm."

"Figured you might have gotten some bad news."

I looked up. "Did you?"

His lips quirked into a smile. "Everything is good. No brain damage, and everything is healing as it should."

"Oh! That's great! I'm so relieved." I leaned back in my chair, tension eased in my back, and my shoulders dropped. "That's so good. I was a little more worried about that than I originally thought."

"Thank you for caring about me. But I'm okay. What did you learn?"

I rolled my eyes and shoved half the bear claw into my mouth.

"I'm going to give you a moment to eat that and calm down."

I nodded. as I bit into the bear claw again. I finished it in four bites. The buttery pastry was still warm and perfect. And I wanted another one, but that was out of the question right now.

I shook my head. "Where do I begin? Well, I was almost attacked by a prisoner." I explained the fight, and the prisoner about to attack me and Bruce stepping in.

"A guy is coming at you with a shank, and you are still a smart ass."

I knew I should have left my comments out of the recap. "I am who I am, Tony."

"Even in death's sight, you have to make a smart-ass remark." He shook his head and chuckled.

"I think it threw him off. My smart-ass mouth might have saved my life."

He shook his head. "Well, at least that's something."

"Anyway..." I recounted what Bruce said as he leaned back in his chair.

"She won't give him the deal he wants, and I can't blame her. He doesn't deserve it. But I learned that Lloyd and Gabriel did know each other. And they were connected to the child trafficking ring.

CHAPTER FOURTEEN

After breaking down everything Bruce said about Lloyd and Gabriel, I bit into the other bear claw while Tony stared at me.

"I guess this has come full circle." His brows furrowed, and his smile slowly dissipated.

"I wasn't expecting this. I wasn't expecting everything to be connected, but I'm not surprised it is. Bruce had to get his other victims from somewhere. Why not use a trafficking ring?"

It made sense. And at one point, we thought he might have used the trafficking ring. His father-in-law definitely did.

"Did he say what they did for the organization or how they betrayed them?"

I finished chewing the last of the pastry before I answered. "He's not saying anything else until I bring him a deal. And he wants time shaved off his sentence. We can't do that. Aisha is not going for that. She made it clear she would not offer him a deal."

"You sound annoyed."

I shook my head and sighed. "I shouldn't be. I knew better. I knew he was going to want something, and I hoped we could solve this without him. Now I'm not sure."

He nodded slowly, his eyes drifting toward his computer screen. "Okay, so let's keep working the case. We can go see Aisha on our way to the crematorium."

"He never told me which one," I said, closing the bright pink box in front of me. I wanted another bear claw.

"Right, but Andy told us where the bodies came from. Davies sent agents to talk to them, but there's no reason we can't go and see them for ourselves. And now we know what questions to ask."

"Fair point."

Aisha was busy and annoyed at our presence. More so at Tony's than mine. She inhaled sharply the moment she saw us.

"What now? Came to tell me what you're hiding?"

"She's not hiding anything," answered Tony. This was the second time I had met with Aisha, and the second time she accused me of hiding something from her about the case. She believed that I had done something wrong, and that was why Mrs. Blackstone had turned down her deal. I had nothing to do with it. And I knew she didn't know what she was talking about.

But it still bothered me. If she thought that way, then who else did? Were the other agents talking behind my back about my connection to her? Did they believe her? I knew I didn't do anything wrong, but I didn't like the idea of someone believing that I had.

Blackstone believed she could get away with it. She believed she could sway the jury in her favor, but that wasn't my fault. But it was something that gave me pause. She was persuasive.

"Right. What do you want? I have back-to-back meetings." Aisha stood behind her desk in a magenta pantsuit and a white blouse.

"We need to talk to you about Bruce," said Tony. He took a step toward her desk, and she recoiled visibly. He stopped moving. "We need to discuss a deal."

"No. I told you I am not making any deals with that man."

"He has information that can help us solve two cold cases. He won't tell us what he knows until he has a deal in place."

Her hands gripped her hips. "And what does he want for his trouble? Oh, let me guess, time shaved off his sentence?" Sarcasm dripped from every word.

I told Tony this was a bad idea. I didn't think this was about Tony, even though she didn't like him. It was more about Bruce than anything else, and I understood why. He was a deplorable human being. I wouldn't want to give him a deal either if these two cases weren't attached.

"Aisha—"

"No. He is not getting a deal. So, you two need to do what you're supposed to do and solve this case on your own. Bruce can't help you."

She didn't even try to listen to the argument. Or what Bruce had said that made me believe he really knew about the case. She didn't want to hear any of it. I didn't know if it was because it came from us or rather Tony, or if she was just adamant about not giving him a deal.

We left the room. She had dug her heels in and wouldn't be helping us. So, we would have to figure out the case on our own. Tony slammed the car door so hard that the car vibrated. Usually, when he was angry, it was quiet. A quiet anger reserved only for him. But now his anger felt palpable. It was in the car with us, hovering in the air like steam.

I thought about saying something. Something comforting. Something wise. I didn't think I was good at those things. But I said nothing instead. Words would not help him. Tony was wrestling with his thoughts, and I would leave him to it. Something about his relationship with Aisha had soured. Turned rotten, and knowing him, he was blaming himself for her attitude. He was the reason she was incredulous. But I didn't think it was about him.

"You can't blame yourself for the actions of others." The words tumbled out of my mouth before I could catch them. He stilled.

"Her actions are not your fault. She doesn't want this to happen. She wants to be difficult, then that's on her. We can solve this case... cases without her. Just stay focused."

In reminding him, I was also reminding myself. We needed to stay focused on the case and nothing else. The Dale and Ortega families needed answers. Deserved answers. And it was up to us to make sure they got them.

"Noted."

"So, let's get to the crematorium and see what's going on."

"Yes, ma'am."

The ride was relatively silent. Not an uncomfortable silent, just silent. It was clear he didn't feel like talking, and I was too busy replaying my conversation with Bruce over and over in my head. Turning over the words and examining them from different angles. Trying to coax any clues from them. He said they both worked for the trafficking organization. He didn't say what they did for them, but I had a feeling I knew.

For a moment, I wondered if that was why Dale's daughters were raped. The killer was sending Ortega a message. If they worked in the trafficking and rape of children and women, then that would have been a strong message. If the men stole money from that group that would have been the second most dangerous thing to do, the first being turning state's evidence.

Stealing their money would have gotten the men at the top beyond pissed about it. And they would have hunted them down to get it back. My forefinger tapped against my knee. That would have explained why Ortega and his family were tortured. The killer was trying to figure out where the money was.

Lloyd was flashy, at least that was what Bruce said. He liked to draw attention to himself. In the crime scene photos, the Dale home was extravagant. Beautiful but flashy. Expensive furniture. Top-of-the-line appliances. Marble countertops in the bathrooms. Quartz countertops in the kitchen.

I took my notepad out of my pocket and wrote it down to check if the Dale family had remodeled their home. If he paid for all those upgrades, then he probably spent most of the money he stole.

The Ortega family, on the other hand, had a lovely, modest home. It was still big, but it wasn't extravagant. There weren't a lot of upgrades throughout the house. He kept it simple. Granite countertops in the kitchen and the bathrooms. Nice appliances. There was nothing over the top. He must have saved his money. He had even gotten a job. He was smarter with his money, which made me think they didn't do it together, but the organization wouldn't have cared one way or another. They just wanted their money back.

"Figured you two would show up sooner or later." A man in a suit met us at the door. I had seen him around the office, but I couldn't remember his name.

"Hey, Tompkins." Tony smiled and shook his hand. "Why were you expecting us?"

Tompkins was tall. Taller than Tony. It strained my neck, looking up at him. He had soft brown eyes and warm chestnut skin. His smile was dazzling, warm, and inviting, with perfect white teeth.

"I heard you two were working the case, so I figured it was only a matter of time before you showed up and talked to the owner on your own."

"You think we wouldn't trust your reports?" I asked.

He smiled. "You could. But if you're anything like me, you'd want to see things for yourself."

"She is like you," said Tony.

I rolled my eyes. He suggested we come here. "So, did you talk to him? What do you think?"

He glanced behind him. "I don't know. There's something about the guy I don't like, but I can't pinpoint it. And you know the right questions to ask, so you might be able to get more out of him. Something is weird, though. I just can't put my finger on it."

"Thank you." We followed him to the back office, where his partner and the owner were talking. The owner, Emanuel, was surprised to see us.

"More agents? I haven't done anything. What is going on here?"

"Clemmons, come on, let's go. They've got it from here." The young agent nodded and followed his partner out of the room.

"So, where to start," I said as I sat in the chair in front of his desk. "We dug up Gabriel Ortega and Lloyd Dale, and their coffins were empty."

"Well, I didn't have anything to do with it. This is a reputable establishment. We don't mess with the bodies. Anything that happened did so at the gravesite."

"The memorial for the Ortega family was closed casket?"

"Of course." He slunk into his chair. "Did you see the crime scene photos? I can work wonders, but I can only do so much. I got them ready as best I could, but I still insisted to Marisol's sister that it would be best if the family had a closed casket ceremony. She insisted on seeing the bodies. I warned her against it, but she kept insisting, so I showed her, and *then* she agreed with me."

"How were they transported?" asked Tony.

The angle of my chair allowed me to keep my eye on Emanuel but also watch the door. A woman walked past the door with two garbage bags in her hand. She disappeared for a moment and then walked by the door again, this time her hands empty. I knew that gesture.

My mother did it all the time when she was trying to listen to your conversation but didn't want you to know she was listening. So, she walked by the door pretending she was busy cleaning or something so you wouldn't ask questions. And you wouldn't think she was listening. But she was always listening.

"Excuse me." I left the room. The cleaning woman rounded the corner, and I followed. I heard a heavy metal door slam ahead of me. It was the door to the outside. I pushed it open. The woman tossed one trash bag into a large green trash can.

"Excuse me?"

She jumped, banging her elbow into the trash can. "Oh, um... can I help you?"

"Yes. I'm with the FBI." I held out my badge. "I need to ask you a couple of questions about your work here."

"Oh, I just clean. That's it. Mr. Emanuel would be able to handle your questions better." She crossed her arms across her chest and then dropped them to her sides. Before I could utter another word, she folded her arms back across her chest.

"I think you know something. Would explain why you look so nervous. And why you keep glancing at the door."

She stepped back, moving closer to the trash. "I—"

"You won't get into trouble, I promise. I just need to know if anything weird or suspicious has been happening here?" She glanced at the door again.

"I can't get in trouble. I need this job."

"I understand. Whatever you say is between you and me. That's it."

She chewed on her bottom lip. "Sometimes the owner stays really late. I always thought that was strange, because why would we need to be open after midnight? You could just pick the body up in the morning. Not like someone was going to have a funeral at midnight."

"That's a good point. Anything else?"

"On more than one occasion, just when I'm about to leave for the day, a van pulls up. It's a white van with no markings or anything. It pulls up, and a body is unloaded. But when I get in at my usual time, which is around seven in the morning, there is no sign of the body. Where did it go?"

I stepped toward her. "Could someone have worked on it overnight?" The words felt strange in my mouth. Who would someone work overnight in a mortuary?

"I don't think so. During that time, Mr. Emanuel would be the only person here. He sometimes works on a body by himself, but usually, he leaves before me. Usually, he leaves during lunch and doesn't come back. Mr. Riet has to stay late and finish up. But on these days, when the white van pulls up, it's just Mr. Emanuel. He sends Mr. Riet home."

"That is strange. And when that mysterious van pulls up, is that the only time that happens? When he sends Mr. Riet home early?"

She nodded.

"Okay. Thank you for your time." I left her to her work and went back inside, curious about how Tony's conversation was coming along. I entered the back office. Tony and Emanuel were still talking.

"Mr. Emanuel, what can you tell me about the late-night white vans that drop off bodies?"

His eyes went wide. "What do you know about that?"

"I know that you stay late and accept bodies from an unmarked white van. And you work on those bodies by yourself."

He jumped up from his seat. Emanuel was a short, stocky man with thick, black-rimmed glasses and a severely receding hairline. Red-faced and out of breath, he threw his hands up in the air.

"I don't need the FBI in here telling me about my business. I haven't done anything wrong. My business is legit, and we don't screw around with dead bodies. I don't know what happened to Gabriel Ortega. And it is no longer my problem." His voice had gone up a couple of octaves. He was frustrated and annoyed with us being there.

"So, here's the deal." I stepped further into the room until the desk touched my thigh. "We got information about your crematorium from a serial killer currently in prison looking to shave some years off his sentence. So, unless you want to be linked to his crimes, you need to start talking."

His eyes fluttered as he slumped to his chair.

"You need to speak up. You might still go to prison, depending on what you give us. But you won't be there as long as him."

His mouth opened and closed. "Where do I start?" Beads of sweat glided across his face and neck. Emanuel started sweating immediately. He took a handkerchief out of his desk and patted his forehead.

"That's a lot of sweat for someone with nothing to worry about," said Tony.

Emanuel looked up. "It's hot in here."

"I feel fine." He looked at me.

"Yeah, it's not hot at all," I added.

Emanuel rolled his eyes. "What do you want me to say?"

"What did you do to the bodies?" I sat back in the chair and waited. We weren't going anywhere until he told us everything we needed to know. Even if we had to call more agents and search every file, nook and cranny, to get the information we needed, we were going to learn something.

"Okay. I'm not hurting anyone. I just want to preface this by saying that. I don't actually hurt anyone. I just... get rid of the bodies."

My spine straightened. "You do what?"

"Explain everything," said Tony. He closed the office door.

Emanuel's eyes were wide and watery. "I get rid of the bodies. Or better still, I allow them to get rid of the bodies they need to."

"So, someone comes in with a body, and then they pay you to what? Toss them in the incinerator?"

He shrugged. "Pretty much."

"Where do the bodies come from?" I asked. This was fascinating. I tried to remove some of the fascination and intrigue from my voice, but I still heard it a little.

He threw his hands up. "I don't know. I don't ask. This only works if I don't ask questions."

"Who drops the bodies off?" asked Tony.

"Again, I don't ask questions. Here's how it works. I get a call from someone telling me to stay late. The body is dropped off, and then I burn it and whatever came with it."

"Whatever came with it?"

"Purse, clothes, shoes, and whatever else. Once, there was a dead dog in the coffin. But I burn everything, and then the person leaves with the ashes."

"They take the ashes with them?"

"Most of the time. Sometimes, I'm told to dispose of them myself. I throw them in the trash."

How many times? How many times had he done this? How many murder victims and accidental deaths had he covered up? The hairs on the back of my neck stood up. It was difficult to fathom. This was not where I saw the case going, an actual cleaner.

"How many times have you done this?"

He shrugged. "I haven't been doing it since we first opened. But it has been a while." He sighed. "Actually, it feels good to get this off my chest. It started a few years ago. Only one time, and then I guess word got around. And it became what it is. I've thought about getting out of it more than once, but some of the guys look pretty scary. Getting out didn't seem like an option. Or at least not one that didn't have dire consequences."

"We need names, Emanuel. We need to know who brings the bodies in or who calls you." I rested my elbows on the desk. "You need to tell me more."

"I understand that. But I can't tell you what I don't know. I don't know names. I make it a point not to know names. It all works better that way."

I sighed. If he couldn't tell us more… I didn't know what was going to happen to him. We couldn't arrest him for murder because, technically, he wasn't killing anyone. He was, however, illegally disposing of bodies and covering up crimes. I wasn't sure if it was something Aisha would want to prosecute. Worth a shot, though.

"I did get a call this morning telling me to stay late."

My spine straightened, and my arms fell from the desk. "You did?"

"Way to bury the lede, Emanuel." Tony took out his phone. "We might get to do a stakeout."

"Around what time will they be here?"

"It varies. Sometimes ten, sometimes not until two in the morning. I'm just supposed to sit and wait."

I glanced back at Tony, who I assumed was talking to Davies. "Well, I guess we'll just sit and wait with you."

CHAPTER FIFTEEN

E MANUEL'S FACE WAS SLICK WITH SWEAT. I DIDN'T KNOW someone could sweat so much for such a long period of time. He had to change his shirt twice, but still, the sweat bled through. His nervousness was going to give the operation away.

Tony cleared everything with Davies. He was able to mute his excitement, but I was not. Excitement pulsed beneath my skin. Not only were we doing a sting operation, but we were trying to catch someone who disposed of bodies for a living. A real-life cleaner.

Well, we had the cleaner. Emanuel wasn't the criminal mastermind I was looking for, though. We were about to meet the person who arranged for the bodies to be dropped off and picked up. And that was exciting. I didn't care what Tony said.

He rolled his eyes at my glee, but that didn't make me any less gleeful. He rolled his eyes at that, too. Tony and I stayed out of sight. When the body was dropped off, Emanuel was supposed to be the only one in the building. He said that was the routine. The caller told him to stay late and to make sure he was alone.

There was something about staying in a crematorium at night that was a little unnerving. I wasn't superstitious, and it wasn't like I believed in ghosts and thought the place was haunted or anything. I didn't. But the room gave me pause. If there was a place on this island that was haunted, I was in it. The ghosts of victims who were dropped off and incinerated, their ashes dumped somewhere. Never able to find peace, much like the murder house.

The hardest part was the waiting. Emanuel didn't know when the men were coming. He just knew it was after nine. Sometimes before midnight, sometimes after. It wasn't like I had anywhere to go. Excitement settled into my bones. No, not excitement. Anxiousness. Curiosity might have been a better word to describe how I felt.

I was curious about what the men looked like who would be dropping the body off and who it was. That was the real question, mine anyway. Who was killed, and how and why didn't they just go to the police?

I paced the back room, far from the front door so no one could see me, and even further from the dead bodies that currently resided in the freezer, waiting. My insistence on being nowhere near the freezer made Tony laugh.

"You see dead bodies every day, Storm."

"It's not the same. We see them covered in blood, and... it's not the same." I had a point. I just didn't think I was explaining it right. I rolled my eyes as he walked through the entire building. Neither of us able to keep still. In an unmarked black van down the street were agents watching the cameras that were hastily set up along with recording devices stuck in places no one would ever look. Backup was also close by in unmarked cars scattered along the two nearest streets. Just in case we needed them.

A little after midnight, Emanuel started sweating again. He rushed into the back room, flushed and glistening.

"They are on their way. Told me to make sure that everyone was gone for the night." He dabbed his upper lip with his handkerchief. "What do I do?" His eyes darted to the door.

"Well, first, you calm down. It's business as usual, that's all. If you look nasty, they will get suspicious."

"If I don't, they will get suspicious. This is my business as usual."

I nodded slowly. I understood that about Emanuel. He seemed like the jumpy sort. Anxious and jittery. The kind of guy who never needed a second cup of coffee; the type of man you would never imagine running a get rid of dead bodies business. He didn't seem level-headed enough or calm enough to do it. But I guess all he was really doing was turning on the incinerator. Didn't take guts or calmness to do it. He did it every day. It was a practiced action. He could probably do it with his eyes closed.

Thirty minutes later, I heard a door slam outside the back door. I hurried into the next room. Tony stood, and he nodded at me. I returned the gesture. We knew what we were supposed to do. Wait for the men to bring in the body and for Emanuel to get paid and start his job. He told us how everything happened every time someone called him. They dropped the body on the table, he started the process, and once he was done and gave them the ashes, he was paid. The same thing would happen tonight, but we were skipping a step.

Emanuel opened the door, and two men entered with a large black bag. There was a loud thud when they placed it on the table. Emanuel looked back at the door as he wiped the sweat from his brow.

"Jumpy as always," said one of the men. "You really need to relax, man. You are an old pro at this. Why are you still so stressed?"

"What if we get caught?" whispered Emanuel.

The man laughed. "By who? No one is looking for us. No one even knows who you are. Stop worrying. I say this to you every time I see you."

"Maybe one day it will sink in." After a few glances at the front door, Emanuel wheeled the body to the back. The men stayed near the back door. He said it usually took him thirty minutes to an hour, depending on the condition of the body. Since he didn't have to embalm it, it wouldn't take as long. He wasn't actually incinerating a body, though.

He was supposed to wait the allotted time and then return with someone's ashes in exchange for the money. I watched them from my hiding spot. One man was tall and lanky with graying black hair and a mole under his left eye. He rocked back on his heels with his hands in his pockets. The other man was short and stocky with strawberry blonde hair and a Celtic knot tattoo on his neck. He sat on a metal stool by the back door. The two men looked like they belonged. Like they had done this so many times before, it was just another day.

Forty minutes later, Emanuel emerged from the room with a bag of ashes. This was the critical part. Money had to exchange hands. The men weren't just dropping off a body. They were paying him to get rid of it. He walked over to the ginger-haired man and handed him the ashes.

"Here you are. Just what you wanted. I also incinerated the bag. It was full of blood, and that was never going to come out. I threw everything in the incinerator. I'll have to rerun it to get rid of the purse and shoes, but it will all be gone by morning. As usual."

The man stood up, reached into his coat pocket, and held up a brown bag. "Pleasure doing business with you, as always." He handed the bag to Emanuel. "We might need you again in a few days. We'll get back to you."

"I'll be here." The men exchanged bags.

He stuffed the bags of ashes into his coat pocket. "Until then."

"Freeze!" I drew my gun and rushed into the room with Tony. Emanuel ran back into the other room just as the ginger-haired man reached for the collar of his shirt. That was smart. Probably the most intelligent thing he had done up until now. If he had gotten his hands on Emanuel's collar, he probably would have strangled him. One last act. If he were dead, he wouldn't be able to tell us everything he knew. Which wasn't much, but it was more than most.

"Hands up!"

Both men slowly raised their hands in the air. A smirk eased across the red-haired man's lips. He was relaxed. The taller man's lips were pressed in a thin, hard line. His face was vacant. No traces of emotion, just a blank stare. It was eerie how calm they were as we arrested them. How little they cared.

I kept my gun steady as Tony used the cuffs and cuffed both men. For a moment, it reminded me of Mrs. Blackstone. Fatima didn't care that she was being arrested for murder. It made no difference to her. She was relaxed, too. Nonchalant about everything we talked about except when it came to facing the death penalty. When it was her own life on the line, she tensed.

I stared at the men as other agents descended on the mortuary. I watched how they paid them no mind as they talked and laughed on their way out the back door. For a moment, the briefest moment, I wondered if they knew something I didn't. If they already had a plan to get out of our custody, a good lawyer, or a name tucked into their back pockets to use in this situation. They were too smug. Too comfortable. They knew something. They had a way out.

"Where did Emanuel go?"

I blinked at Tony's voice, shaking me from my thoughts. I spun around and headed to the back workroom, where he ran as soon as guns were drawn. I heard Tony's footsteps fall in line behind me. I burst through the door to find Emanuel cowering in the corner.

"They're gone," I told him.

"Are you sure?"

"Yes. They've been arrested and aren't even in the building anymore."

He sighed as he stood up, dabbing his slick forehead with his handkerchief. "That was scarier than I thought it was going to be. He was going to kill me… if I hadn't run."

"Probably," I said. The ginger looked like he was ready to attack Emanuel as soon as he saw me. His hands lurched from his body, searching for his throat. At that moment, his face showed true emotion. Anger. Red-faced, scowling.

And then, just as quickly as the look appeared, it vanished. A mask of nonchalance and indifference settled in its place. These were men used to hiding their emotions. Used to keeping themselves in check. What would rattle them? What would make them talk?

Jill appeared a moment later, hands already gloved, ready to get to work. The black bag with the body the men brought in was still on the metal worktable. I walked over as I slipped on my gloves, and then unzipped the bag. The rotting smell of flesh smacked me in the face. I coughed and stumbled back.

"Yeah, that's ripe." Jill waved her hand in front of her face, trying to swat the smell away.

I couldn't even look inside the bag. I backed away until my back pressed into the far wall. Bile bubbled up my throat. I swallowed hard, trying to push it down. My stomach soured. I'd leave checking out the body to Jill. That was her job, after all. Now, we just needed to get Emanuel down to the field office and then interrogate the two men. Maybe we could get them to tell us who the person in the bag was.

We left Jill in the mortuary. She seemed pleased enough to work there but decided to have the body taken to the morgue. The bag was leaking, so she had it placed in a body bag. I was glad not to have that job or have to sit and watch the process.

At the field office, Emanuel was jittery and jumpy as usual. We parked him in an interrogation room. We still had a few questions left to ask him and still needed to write out a statement.

The ginger-haired man was named Killian McDowell, and his partner was Ed Goren. We decided to start with Ed. Killian was too calm, too uncaring. Going to prison meant nothing to him. After researching both men, we found Ed had a family. Granted, they didn't live on the island or anywhere near it, but it was still an angle we could use.

Killian either had no one or was good at hiding them.

Ed sat at the metal table, relaxed. He leaned back in his chair, hands clasped on the table, his body language open. I sat across from him while Tony stood next to the door. He leaned against the wall. The sudden movement drew Ed's eyes.

"Okay, so what can you tell us about the body in the bag?" I asked. I leaned back, mimicking his body language. "Who is she?" I assumed it was a she because Emmanuel mentioned having to burn the purse again.

His lip twitched, but he didn't utter a sound. The silence was defeating. Unrelenting. There was a stillness to Ed... it was unnerving. And frustrating.

"If you didn't kill her, we can make you a deal. Limited jail time," said Tony.

Ed rolled his eyes. He wasn't persuaded.

"Who killed her? Who is paying you to get rid of her?" I asked. I heard the edge in my voice. Judging by his expression, so did he. The corner of his mouth curved slightly. I glanced over at Tony, who shook his head. We left the room and tried our luck with Killian. It ended the same. Neither man would speak about the body or where she came from.

After filling Davies in, we both went home. It was almost two in the morning, and we were both tired, beyond tired. My bones were weary, and my back ached. I wanted to crawl into bed. I should probably eat something first, but I didn't feel like stopping anywhere to pick something up. And neither did Tony. We said goodbye at the elevator, and then he went his way, and I went mine.

The only thing I wanted to do was crawl into bed. No, not crawl, jump. I wanted to leap into bed, yank the covers over my head, and sleep for hours. Days. I could have slept for days if someone would let me. I had never been so tired.

This case was exhausting, and it wasn't just dealing with Bruce or the US Attorney, who seemed to have it out for me. It was a combination of things. It was Tony getting hurt after a yet to be identified assailant beat him. It was finding out that Yumi was a human trafficker and not being able to talk to her so I could understand how she fooled me.

It was my entire life revolving around my job, and there was nothing else.

As I inched closer to my front door, I heard rustling behind me. My blood went cold. My hand found my gun just as I spun around. Harrison held up two glasses and a bottle of champagne.

"Oh! I'm sorry." I dropped my hand.

"No, my bad. I should know better than to sneak up on an FBI agent. Stupid now that I'm thinking about it."

I smiled, glancing at the bottles of champagne. I pointed. "What's that about?"

He grinned, wiggling his eyebrows. "I got some good news a few minutes ago, and you were the only person I knew that would be up."

I sighed. "Yeah. Lots of late nights lately." I glanced back at my door. "Okay. Well, come in and tell me your good news." It'd be nice to hear something good. That was in short supply these days. Harrison grinned. He was practically beaming.

I opened the door, kicked off my shoes while he entered, and then closed the door behind him. I led him into the kitchen, where he popped the cork off the bottle.

Even though I knew it was coming, the pop still startled me. My heart stalled in my chest for a brief moment.

"So what are we celebrating?" I walked over to the sofa and sat down. He handed me a glass and sat next to me.

"I've been working on a paper for a medical journal, and it got accepted. My first one out of twenty, I think, I've submitted. I've lost count over the years. It's a hard journal to get into, and I don't want to bore you. Still, the paper was about behavioral therapy and its uses and how careful mental health professionals need to be when employing this type of therapy."

"What made you write the paper?"

His exhale was loud. His grip tightened around the glass. "I… recently, I lost a patient. I was using CBT, and I thought it was going well. I think I misjudged how difficult it was for her to dig into her painful memories and feelings. She killed herself after one of our sessions."

My chest tightened at the way his voice faltered. He shook his head. "I thought we were making progress. She seemed to be doing well, and then… the therapy triggered something. A memory she might have repressed. I'm not sure. I keep replaying our last conversation… our last session, looking for the warning signs. I wrote it to warn other doctors so they don't make the same mistake I did."

"I admire that. Taking something painful and using it to warn others. I think most doctors would have wanted to pretend it never happened."

"The truth is the truth. It changes for no one."

"Very true." I raised my glass. "Here's to you and your medical journal."

He chuckled as the glass clinked together. We spent the rest of the night talking about his job and mine. And how they both consist of us trying to get to the truth. And how difficult that is.

I wanted to know more about his patients, but I knew better than to ask. There was only so much he could tell me. After finishing the bottle, Harrison looked at his watch.

"I need to let you get some sleep."

I looked down at my watch. It was well after three. I smiled. "Yeah. It is time to go to bed, I guess."

"We should do this again." His voice was low and light. Playful even. There was an invitation on his lips, and I wasn't sure if I wanted to accept it.

I didn't have the time for dating. My mother's voice rang in my head. You'll never have time. You have to make time.

"Are you asking me out on a date?"

"Only if you're accepting." His green eyes twinkled in the light. His smile warm and inviting. Heat pooled at the base of my spine, getting hotter and hotter the longer I stared at him. I looked away as I felt the heat wash over my cheeks.

"I would love to."

CHAPTER SIXTEEN

I WOKE UP TIRED, THE DULL ACHE BEHIND MY EYES PULSING with every moment. I sat up, my feet resting on the cold hardwood floor. I wanted to crawl back into bed. Throw the covers over my head and sleep for a few more hours. Or all day if possible. Excitement pulsed beneath my skin, causing the exhaustion to recede. I wondered if Jill had figured out who the woman was yet.

In some ways, Jill reminded me of myself. When she wanted to know something or when she was faced with a puzzle, she couldn't rest or think about anything else until she solved it. Until she figured it out. She probably worked until the sunrise.

I wanted to know where the woman came from and who killed her. Who had the means to pay someone to get rid of her body, and had they done it before? Were Ed and Killian just delivery drivers, or did they work for the person who killed her?

A million questions whirled around in my head while I got ready. I hoped Jill had the answer to at least one of them. If we could figure out who the victim was, it would make it easier to figure out who killed her. People, more often than not, were killed by people they knew. Especially women. Women were killed by a boyfriend, husband, or sometimes a friend.

I didn't want to assume it was her husband or boyfriend, but if I had to make a guess... I made our breakfast sandwiches and was on my way out just when the elevator doors opened.

"Right on time," said Tony.

I smiled and handed him his sandwich. "You're up early this morning."

He shrugged. "Yeah. I couldn't really sleep last night."

"Were you in pain?" I stepped onto the elevator.

He shook his head. "No, not really. I just couldn't stop thinking about the case. Kept wondering who the body was, and then I started thinking—"

"How many bodies they had done this to?" That was what I had been thinking last night. Images of dead bodies had been swirling in my head all night. How many times did they do this? How many bodies had they gotten rid of? That was my main question. And it was one I didn't think I would ever get the answer to. They probably couldn't answer that question. None of them. Not Emanuel, Killian, or Ed. They probably lost count at some point.

"Yeah. All of that. I can't believe this has been going on for so long. I just kept thinking of all the bodies, all the murders we will never solve because the bodies are gone. All evidence is gone. All the families wondering, and they will never know."

I pressed my shoulder into him. I understood what he was saying. The emotions that realization stirred in me were hard to press down. The frustration of never being able to solve these cases was palpable.

"I know. But what we need to focus on is what we can do instead of what we can't. And what we can do is figure out who the most recent victim is and who killed her."

He nodded slowly. His shoulders fell. "I know. I know."

"But for now, eat your sandwich."

He chuckled as the doors dinged open.

We stopped by the morgue just in case Jill figured something out while we were sleeping. Jill stood in the middle of the exam room, writing in her notepad.

"You're here. I hadn't called you yet."

I smiled. "I know. We were on our way in and figured we'd stop by just in case you had something for us."

Jill snatched off her gloves and tossed them in the trash can. "Come with me to my office." Jill's office was just like her, bright and girly and out of place, surrounded by all these dead bodies.

She had done some redecorating since the last time we had been there. There was a black and gold rug on the floor. Very art deco in design. Her desk was gold with a glass top. In front of her desk were two emerald-green chairs with thick gold legs. The gold framing matched the bookcases on the wall behind the chairs. Her chair was also green.

Pops of green, gold, and black from the paintings on the walls and the curiosities in the bookcase completed the look. It was beautiful but strange when I remembered where the room was... in a morgue.

"You've made some changes," said Tony as he sat down in one of the chairs. I sat in the other. "Looks all fancy, and it smells amazing."

"Take some of the surprise out of your tone, please." Jill pretended to be offended, but it was something he had said before. And it did smell amazing in her office. Hints of jasmine and vanilla surrounded us.

"It is weird to be in a morgue and think, wow, it smells amazing in here," I said.

She laughed. "You're in my office, which just happens to be in a morgue. I don't like the sterile smell in here. Out there, it is fine because of the bodies, but not here. Too much makes my head hurt, and I had to spruce it up a little bit after the mishap."

My body stilled as I waited for her to continue.

"But back to what—"

"What was the mishap?" I asked.

"Explain," said Tony.

The corners of her mouth curved upward. "Right. It's been a while since you had a dead body and stopped by."

There was a slight edge to her voice, not sharp enough to break the skin. Just enough to leave a dent. "Don't act like we don't see you outside of the morgue or a crime scene."

"I mean, usually I'm knuckle deep in a dead body—"

"Why knuckle deep?" asked Tony.

"But there have been a few instances when we saw each other outside of this place—"

"Cut it out," I said. There were more than a few instances when we had seen her away from work. We had our weekly game nights. However, those days had dwindled as of late. Everyone was so busy, and with Tony being hurt, it had been a while since we had all gotten together and just hung out. It had crossed my mind the past few weeks. I missed our game nights, where we ate and played cards or video games.

But I wanted to have more friends outside of the FBI, outside of work. I wanted more friends who were normal, not saying Hattie and Jill weren't regular. But I wanted people in my life who didn't just deal with dead bodies and fighting crime. I wanted to become more well-rounded. I had been in Hawaii for almost a year, and I wanted to immerse myself in the culture more. Meet more of the locals. I wanted to get out more and meet new people, which was something I had done since I moved into my new condo.

Jill laughed. "Anyway. We had a … floater, I guess you could say. A body was discovered in the ocean. Someone was fishing out there, and the body floated by. It was brought back here, but there was some time before I could examine it. It had been cut up pretty well. Anyway. I went to check it out and unzip the body bag, but it's already open. Whoever put it on the table had opened it up already. And then I saw it... a trail of blood."

My jaw dropped. My body leaned forward.

"I followed it, and it ended in my office. I hadn't been in here all day, but there was a small octopus covered in blood and guts on the floor. It was dead by the time I saw it. But the smell in here… smelled like blood and rotting fish. It was disgusting. I had to clean everything. Even though it was only in here for a few hours, the smell was overwhelming. And they cleaned. There was so much disinfectant in there that I coughed every time I walked through the hall. But as soon as I sat in here, the smell was everywhere. So, I just got rid of all the furniture and put a fresh coat of paint on the walls."

I glanced at the wall behind her. It was a light gray now. "I hadn't noticed that before. Paint and everything is new."

"Yeah. I haven't smelled that fishy rotting smell yet, so I guess that was what was needed. But anyway, back to the reason you are here. The body in the bag." She shuffled through a stack of folders on her desk until she found the right one. She placed the folder in front of her and pushed the rest off to the side.

"We have been able to identify the body. Moya Pollard. She worked at a flower shop downtown. There is no record of her being reported missing. I've already checked. And she is married."

"So, either he doesn't know she's missing, or he killed her," I said.

"You know which one I think it is," said Tony.

Jill's lips curved into a smile. "I'm with him."

We were all thinking the same thing. Chances were it was the husband. We all knew that, but we still had to work the case. Jill gave me the folder she had on Moya. Instead of going to the field office, we headed straight for the flower shop. Before we talked to the husband, I wanted to learn more about Moya.

In the folder, there was a picture of her. Moya had bright blue eyes, sandy brown hair, and delicate features. She was pretty. Moya was twenty-eight and had no children. She and her husband Rin had been married for five years. She had lived in Olympia, Washington when they first met. He was from Maui but moved to Honolulu after they got married.

That was all we knew, but I still had a few questions that I hoped her coworkers could answer. We sent an agent to her house, not to speak to the husband but to watch him. He was still at the home and, so far, hadn't left all morning. Tony and I wanted to know more information before we spoke to him. The agent was just there in case someone told him we were asking questions, and he decided to run.

"Hello." I walked up to the counter and took out my badge.

The black-haired Hawaiian woman blinked. "Umm... is this about Moya?"

I nodded. "When was the last time you saw her?"

The woman shrugged. "It's been a few days. I tried calling her husband, but he said she was fine. She is supposed to be with her mother in Washington, but I'm not sure."

"Why?" asked Tony.

The woman chewed the corner of her lip. "Well, I hate to say this, but she hates her mother with a passion. She can't stand her. There is no way she would run off and visit her unless she was dying, and even then, she probably still wouldn't go."

I glanced at Tony. "I see. What can you tell me about her husband?"

The woman sighed. "I…" She glanced around the shop. It was empty. The shop smelled of roses, jasmine, and lavender. The birds of paradise were in the front, vibrant and inviting. It made me want to buy one, but it would probably die within a month. And it was a lot of money for something that wouldn't last.

"I don't know what to say." Her voice was low, like she thought someone was eavesdropping.

"Just tell us the truth," I said. "That's all you can do. Whatever you tell us can only help Moya."

Her eyes softened. "Right. I want to help her. I mean, I don't know what's going on, but I want to help. I know something's wrong. I've known for a while. She wouldn't just leave, you know. But Rin… they had been fighting a lot lately. She said things were fine at first. They were really in love and all that, but it was like once they got married, and he got her away from her family, he changed. He was like a completely different person. She felt like she didn't know him anymore."

"Abusive?" I asked. I leaned on the counter. I felt Tony move closer to me, closer to the counter. The amber and cedar notes of his cologne overpowered the floral scent in the room. "Did he hurt her? Could he hurt her?" I needed to coax as much information from her as possible.

Her sigh was deep, weighted. The silence that followed was so heavy I thought it would crush me. Crush her. But I let it stretch. I didn't say anything to fill it, and neither did Tony. We waited for her to find the words she searched for. And when she opened her mouth, I leaned in.

"I think so. She's never outright said he was abusive. Not to me, anyway. But there are signs. My sister was in an abusive marriage, so I knew what to look for. He was nice when I met him, but the way he watched her. His eyes never left her. He's possessive of her. He doesn't want her to have any friends outside of his or to go places without him unless it was here.

"And he stops by a lot. He doesn't come in. He just passes by the window and waits until he sees her, and then he walks away. We all think it's weird even though she tries to blow it off." She glanced out the front window. "She keeps cutting back on her hours. She was full-time, but now she's only part-time. There doesn't seem to be a genuine reason for it. She seems annoyed by it."

"What about the last day you saw her? How was she acting?"

Her fingers drummed against the counter as she stared out the window. "She seemed… I don't know if paranoid is the right word, but it's the first one that comes to mind. As soon as she walked in, she asked if he had been by. She sounded a little panicked. He hadn't, and when I told her no, she looked relieved. And then she left earlier that day. Around ten, she said she had an appointment, but she didn't say where."

"Is there anyone that would know where she went?"

"You should talk to Hannah Teng. They are really close. Hannah worked here for a while, right after she divorced her husband. They were always talking and still had lunch together even after Hannah left."

"Where can we find her?" asked Tony.

"She works at the boutique across the street."

CHAPTER SEVENTEEN

BEAUTY WAS A HIGH-END BOUTIQUE THAT CATERED TO modern women who didn't want to spend a lot of money. The store smelled like new clothes and incense. As I walked toward the front counter, I stopped to feel a blood-red maxi dress. The red fabric flowed through my fingers like water, soft and buttery.

"You should get that," whispered Tony as he walked by.

"We are not here for this." I didn't have anywhere to wear it. However, I had said yes to a date with Harrison. I didn't know where we were going, but the dress would make a statement. Although it had been so long, I didn't know what the statement was anymore. I took in the dress one last time before following him to the counter.

"You should treat yourself," he whispered.

I didn't even bother looking at the price, but I knew it was too much. I already treated myself to a new apartment. I wouldn't be treating myself to anything that wasn't free for a while.

"How can I help you?" A woman with dark brown hair and hazel eyes emerged from the back room. Her lips curved into a wide smile when she saw us.

"We are looking for a Hannah—"

"I'm Hannah." For a brief moment, her smile faltered, stuttered for a moment before falling from her face completely. "What is this about?" Her voice was soft and lacked warmth this time.

I held up my badge. "Can we talk to you about Moya Pollard?"

She took a step back. "He killed her, didn't he?"

"Why would you say that?" I pressed my palms into the counter.

She sighed. "He was abusing her, and she was trying to get out. She told me. She had had enough. She just wanted to be free. And he refused to let her go."

"Had he threatened her?" asked Tony.

It is well known among officers, agents, social workers, and groups that deal with domestic abuse victims a woman is most at risk when she finally decides to leave. When the abuser feels like he or she is losing control over their victim, they become even more dangerous. Even more vicious. Even more possessive. Even more likely to kill their victim.

"He told her once that if she ever tried to leave him, he'd kill her. She believed he was serious, but she couldn't take it anymore. He pushed her down the stairs and just stepped over her like she was nothing. She thought if he could do that this time, next time it might be more serious. If she was going to get out, it had to be now."

I glanced around the store. It was still early in the morning, so anyone who would shop here was working. We were alone. "Were you going to help her get out?"

She sighed. "I was willing to try, but she didn't want me to get involved. She was afraid he would hurt me to get to her. It happens. But I know how hard it is. It took me ten years to leave my husband, and I was terrified. It's not easy to just walk away.

But I wanted to help her, so I set her up with my lawyer, Neal Hui. He's excellent, and he helped me immensely when I went through my divorce. I honestly don't think I would have made it without him."

"Can you give us his address?" I asked.

She nodded, ripped a sheet of paper out of a small notepad by the register, and wrote down the address of his office. "Is she okay?" she asked as she handed the slip of paper to Tony. "Can you tell me?"

"Not at the moment," said Tony. "That being said, we need you not to speak with anyone about this conversation."

Her eyes went wide for a moment. She blinked several times and then nodded. She understood what we were saying. Or rather, what we weren't saying. Her shoulders fell. "I won't."

I thanked her for her time and followed Tony out of the store. I was almost sure she wasn't going to call or contact anyone. She knew how serious this was, having been in the same situation before… virtually the same problem.

Neal Hui worked a few blocks from the store. It was a short drive as traffic was almost non-existent… well, it wasn't as dense as it would have been later in the day. We parked in an empty spot across the street. The building was modest, tan stucco outside and a black door. 'Hui and Associates' was written in bright gold letters on the door and the large window at the front of the building.

I walked in ahead of Tony. He stopped to called the agent we had sitting on Rin's place, making sure he was still home. We could have gone ahead and picked him up or gone to interview him, but I wanted to have the facts first. I wanted to know more about their relationship and who she was.

Calling her mother wouldn't have been any help as her coworker said they weren't very close. Inside, the decor was simple. Black chairs in the seating area with tan tables and tall palms that might have been fake. I could never tell.

"Hello?"

"Hi." I held up my badge. "Is Neal Hui in?"

The secretary, who was male this time, blinked. His lips pressed into a firm line as his brows pinched together. He glanced down a short hallway at a closed door. "Give me a moment." Instead of using the black phone at his desk, he disappeared down the hall and knocked on the door. Hushed voices, one extremely tense, whispered back and forth for a moment.

A second later, Tony walked in. "The husband hasn't left. He's looked out the window a few times this morning, but no one is in or out so far."

I nodded. Before I could say something, the secretary appeared. "He will see you."

I walked down the short hallway, and Tony followed close behind me. I stepped into the room. Neal sat behind a black and gray desk that was too big for the small room. He stood when he saw me.

"I just want to preface this conversation with the fact that I can't tell you about any of my clients. So, if you are looking for me to turn on them—"

I waved my hand dismissively. The words dried up in his mouth. "We are here to talk about Moya Pollard. What can you tell us about her relationship with her husband?"

He stilled for a long moment. Silence stretched between us, and we let it breathe. I didn't say anything as he stared at me, brows furrowing.

"Moya. Why are you asking about her? She hasn't done anything wrong?"

I sighed. While we didn't tell the last two women about Moya, we had to tell him. I explained how her body was found. Neal collapsed into his chair. His right hand trembled as he brought it up to cover his mouth. "Are you sure?" his voice was quiet with a slight tremble. A hint of disbelief. "Are you sure?" he repeated.

"Yes. The coroner confirmed it this morning. Hannah Teng told us that she referred Moya to you. How close was she to leaving her husband?"

"Her bags were packed. She was more than ready to go. I don't think she'd told him yet. I advised against it. I work with a lot of domestic abuse victims, and once they verbally state their intent to leave, it gets dangerous. I told her to make sure she had all her ducks in a row first. A place to stay for starters. And I told her she should not be in the house when he finds out, and if she has to, make sure to call the police beforehand."

"Do you think she followed your advice?" asked Tony.

"I want to say she did. I really do. But she did tell me that when they fought, he had a way of pushing her buttons. If they argued, she might have let it slip." He sighed. "I can't believe this. She was so close to getting out."

"Do you think he could have hurt her?" Judging by what everyone had said up to this point, I already knew the answer, and yet I still wanted to hear it. He knew her. He had spoken with her. She might have told her attorney things she kept from her friends and coworkers.

He inhaled sharply. "I do. I think she believed it, too. She was afraid of him. Afraid of what he would do if he were angry enough."

"I see. For right now, it would be best that you don't tell anyone about this." I glanced at Tony, who was staring out the window. Hard to tell if he was listening to us or not.

"I understand. Of course. You're still investigating. I can keep my mouth shut."

I smiled. "Thank you."

Our next stop, finally, was the husband. We passed by the unmarked car down the street from his house. The agent gave a curt nod as we strolled by. My chest tightened. I was a little nervous. Not because I was afraid of Rin but because we didn't know what was going on in that house. We didn't know what Rin was thinking. Was he relieved? Did he think he had gotten away with it? Was he nervous? Sure that he wasn't going to get caught? Or was he wondering if the police would come knocking any minute now? It was more the uncertainty that made my heart race.

Not knowing how to approach the situation. Tony knocked on the front door.

There was a rustling sound on the other side of the door and then heavy footsteps. A long moment later, the door opened.

A man with reddish-brown hair stood in the doorway in dark blue sweatpants and a white tank. He frowned when he saw us.

"Whatever you're selling, I'm not buying." He started to close the door, but I wedged my foot between the door frame and the door.

"We aren't selling anything."

He froze. "Then what do you want?" The door obscured most of his face.

I held up my badge. The door eased back.

"We want to speak with you about your wife. Her coworkers say they haven't seen her in a while. They are worried and filed a missing persons report."

Wide-eyed, he stumbled back. "I told them she went to stay with her mother for a few weeks." There was an edge to his voice, sharp and icy.

"Can we come in?"

He glanced back into the house and waited a long moment before he moved out of the way and allowed us to enter. Lemon-scented bleach wafted into the foyer. Someone had been cleaning. Rin didn't offer us a seat in the living room or anything to drink. He closed the door, turned around, and leaned against it, his arms folded across his chest.

"What else do we have to talk about?" His jaw was set, and his eyes narrowed.

"Do you have a number where we can reach her? Just to make sure she's okay. Her friend said she tried to call her but never got an answer. Have you heard from her?"

"Of course I have." He pushed himself off the door and stood up straight. He was just as tall as Tony. "I talk to her every day. I'm telling you she's fine. She and her mother are trying to work on their relationship. Finally. That's all it is."

"And you're probably right," said Tony. "I'm sure you are. But we need to do our jobs once a complaint has been made. I'm sure you understand. Just to be on the safe side and put everyone's minds at ease." Tony smiled.

Rin's eyes narrowed at him, and the corners of his mouth turned down. "Sure. I guess I can find a number for her. Give me a moment." He walked away from the door.

I followed him down the hallway, slowly with quiet steps, my hands in my pockets. I felt Tony's movement behind me. I didn't look back, but I knew he was there. He was always there. "That's an interesting choice of words," I said.

"What words?"

I rounded the corner. "You said you can find a number. If you've talked to her every day since she's been gone, why wouldn't you just look it up on your phone?"

His hands stilled over a stack of papers on his desk. I leaned against the door frame. At that moment, I felt like Tony. It was very much a him thing to do. Leaning against the door frame, hands in pockets, asking questions nonchalantly. The thought curved the corners of my mouth upward slightly.

His eyes, dark and hooded, stared up at me. Searching me. Looking for what I knew or what I thought I knew. Looking for a way out. Tony moved behind me, right into his line of sight.

"I don't know what you mean."

"You said you talk to your wife every day. Isn't her number in your phone?"

He blinked. "Oh, I hadn't thought of that." He chuckled.

I smiled. "I understand. How was she the last time you talked to her? How did she sound?"

He straightened. "Good. Annoyed. A little, anyway. She and her mother don't see eye to eye on a lot of things. They are trying to work it out, but she still knows how to press her buttons."

"I see." Silence curled around us like smoke. I let it for a long moment. "The phone."

"Right…"

"Maybe you could go ahead and call her so we can speak with her and fix all this up. That's doable, right?"

He smiled tightly. Beads of sweat cascaded down the side of his face. "I don't see why not."

"I mean unless you are worried that she won't answer. Like she might not want to talk to you, or maybe she's too busy hanging out in a crematorium to answer your call."

"I—What?"

"Maybe you don't want to call her because you know she's dead. You killed her. And you know she won't answer."

Rin blinked. His lips quivered for the briefest moment. "I don't know what you're talking about. Like I said, she is with her mother. Why don't you go look up her number and give her a call instead of bothering me?"

I smiled. He was tense. Glances to the door kept falling on Tony. He was looking for a way out.

"Well, this was fun, but I'm done playing this game now. We know you killed your wife. We know you paid to have her body disposed of. And we know these things because her body is in our morgue. And we have the men you paid to get rid of her in custody. What we don't know is why you killed her?"

"I—I didn't."

"Well, the coroner has her body, so you can tell us what we don't know. Or you can let us find out for ourselves. Keep in mind if we find out for ourselves, it will be worse for you in the long run."

His bottom lip trembled before he pulled it into his mouth. He staggered back until he fell into his desk chair.

"You might as well come clean," said Tony. "Start talking before someone else does."

CHAPTER EIGHTEEN

U NDER THE THREAT OF PRISON AND A LIFE SENTENCE with no chance of parole, Rin spoke. Short burst of sentences tumbled out of his mouth, the words knocking into each other on their way out. It amazed me how little people knew about the law in Honolulu. Especially those that weren't locals. He begged and begged us to not give him the death penalty. That was a deal I felt fine making. The State of Hawaii hadn't had the death penalty for decades.

"The death penalty is no longer an option, but you could either spend the rest of your life in prison or get out before you're seventy. It's up to you," I said. Those words seemed to relax him. His shoulders, once bunched around his ears, dropped as he sighed.

"It was an accident, I swear."

There was something about his tone that rang unbelievable to me. Maybe if he hadn't been abusing her, if he hadn't threatened her, I would have thought it possible that he killed her by accident. But he had said he was going to do it. He had warned her.

"Explain," I said. I kept my voice flat and matter-of-fact.

"We—we were arguing on the stairs. I tried to grab her arm, but she snatched it out of my grasp, and when she did, she fell back. Look, I know I wasn't the best husband. I know I might have threatened her before, but it was just words. I knew what people would think… that I did it. But I swear to you, she fell down the stairs. There was this sickening crack. Wet. I ran to her." He dragged a hand through his hair. "Her eyes were open…blood oozed from her ears. She was gone."

I sat with his words for a moment. A long stretch of silence. Weighing them. Weighing their believability. Weighing the source. And truth be told, I just didn't trust him.

I couldn't trust him. If it had been an accident like he said, why hadn't he just called the police? He could have explained everything. There would have been evidence. Whether she had been pushed or fallen, there would have been evidence to prove this story.

But no, he hired someone to get rid of her body. He made an effort to get rid of her body and to hide what truly happened.

There was something about that that didn't sit right with me. None of this sat right with me. Not what he said. Not the way he said it. Or the way he knew who to call.

That stuck out to me. His wife lay dead at his feet, and he knew there was someone he could call to get rid of the body. How did he know that?

"We still have to take you in, accident or not," I said. "I am curious, though… how did you know there was someone you could call to help you get rid of the body?"

He stilled. Even the subtle rise and fall of his chest stopped. The firm line of his lips told me he was done talking for the day. Tony handcuffed him, and I called ahead to let Hattie know that we needed some crime scene techs at the Pollard home.

The smell of bleach still lingered in the air. He had cleaned up, which brought another question to the surface of my mind. If she just fell, what was there to clean?

He said blood oozed from her ears, but it couldn't have been that much. I glanced at the stairs on my way out the door. The marble flooring went throughout the house, including the stairs. The white marble and the black iron spindles on the railing were eye-catching. There was no blood. No markings. No hint that something had happened, that a body had rested on the floor a few inches from my feet.

As I stared at the steps, his story seemed more and more plausible. The marble stairs looked slick and dangerous. In the heat of an argument, when one wasn't paying attention, slipping could happen. Suppose one was angry enough, distracted enough, and not wearing the right shoes. It could have happened the way he said. But since he tampered with evidence, we might never know.

And I still wanted to know how he knew who to call. Had he done this before? The more I thought about it, the more questions bubbled to the surface. I followed Tony and Rin out of the house. We put him in the car and then waited. I leaned against the driver's side door while Tony leaned against the trunk.

Five minutes later, the forensics team arrived and rushed into the house along with two other agents. With them on the scene, we got in our car and headed to the field office. Once there, we placed him in an interrogation room. He hadn't said anything the whole way to the office. Completely silent. It was eerie.

He had nothing to say. Or maybe he was trying to figure out what to say next. What we knew, what we could prove, and what he could spin to work out in his favor. Killian was waiting in one of the other interview rooms. I burst into the room. Killian's eyes were as wide as saucers. It was the first time he showed an ounce of emotion.

"We found Rin Pollard," I said, breathless. My pulse rushed in my ears.

There was a hint of surprise in his eyes that quickly dissipated. "What does that have to do with me?"

"I'm just letting you know. We found him, and he already told us how his wife died and that he called you two to get rid of the body. You might not have killed her, but there are still some charges we can drum up for you. Just to get us started. I'm sure once we really start looking into you two, we will find so many new charges."

Before he could utter another word, I spun around and walked out of the room, closing the door behind me. I didn't care what he had to say. It no longer mattered. He wasn't going to tell me anything anyway, and that was no longer my problem. I still had a million questions, one of them being who he worked for and who else he had done this kind of work for. How long had he been in business? Maybe it was more than one question. But they might never get answered, and I had to be okay with that.

I wasn't, but I at least needed to act like it. And I felt like we were getting off track. We should have been working on the Ortega and Dale murders. We were trying to figure out where their bodies went. Now that we knew the bodies were cremated, we needed to figure out who killed them. Were they killed because they had taken money from the child trafficking ring?

Just because Bruce said it, it didn't make it accurate. I found it challenging to believe half the shit that came out of his mouth. But it could have been true, and that was my issue. Unless we spoke to him again, we wouldn't know the full story. We wouldn't know what he knew or how he knew it. I wanted to know how. Had he used the cleaner company before?

Every time I spoke to him, it just raised more questions, but how could we get answers if the US Attorney would not make a deal with Bruce? I understood her vehement resistance to the idea. I didn't like it either. What he had done… he deserved to be in prison. If there was ever a criminal who deserved the death penalty to be brought back for one day, it was him. But if he had information on another crime… was it worth making a deal?

I wasn't sure. But we needed to do something. Anything. There had to be another way to get the information we needed. Emanuel didn't know anything. To work with this organization for as long as he had, he didn't ask any questions. Ever. He knew nothing. They brought him bodies, he got rid of them, and they paid him. That was the extent of their relationship.

We needed to speak to Bruce.

I chewed on the thought as I walked back to my desk. Rolling it over and over in my mind. Examining it from all angles. It was true from every angle. We needed to speak with him again, but how would I broach the topic not just with Aisha but with Tony as well? I glanced over at him. He sat at his desk, shuffling through papers.

"Is there something you want to say?" he asked without looking up. He felt my gaze and knew I had something to say. He always knew when I had something I was thinking about. It was both annoying and comforting.

"We need to speak to Bruce again," I said, trying to keep my voice as flat as possible. His fingers kept moving over the pages. He didn't look up.

"He won't say anything without a deal. A deal we can't offer him, and she won't agree to."

I sighed. "I know. I know. Maybe we can persuade her to at least hear him out." I looked up at him, hopeful. His eyes stayed on the papers in his hand.

He sighed. A long, slow, calculated exhale. "We can try again. But I'm telling you, don't get your hopes up. When she says no, she means it." There was a slight edge to his voice, but it wasn't sharp, just pointed. It wasn't an invitation to talk about how or why he knew that.

I swallowed my words, my questions. Their personal relationship should not be a problem, and it wouldn't be as long as she didn't make it one. We left the office and headed over to her office. We didn't have an appointment, but there was no reason she shouldn't have been there. And if she was in court, we could wait. We weren't doing anything more important than this.

She was in her office, and she wasn't happy to see us. She was on the phone when we walked in, a slight smile on her lips. As soon as her eyes fell on me and Tony, the corners of her mouth turned down and then turned into a grimace when I closed the door behind us. Her brows furrowed.

"Judge Henderson, I will get back to you on this matter."

"Be sure that you do." His tone was flirtatious. The smile on his lips heard through the phone. She hung up.

"Why are you here? What have you two done now?" Her arms folded across her chest.

"Why must you assume that we did something? We haven't done anything wrong."

She rolled her eyes at me. "Every time I see you, you are pleading the case of why a serial killer needs less time."

It was my turn to roll my eyes and cross my arms across my chest. How dare she? She had no idea what I went through to close those cases. The sleepless nights, the bodies I saw. The victims I interviewed. I had to talk to him to get his confession. It was hell, a form of one, anyway. He belonged in prison, but if he could help us close other cases, that angle needed to be explored. Why couldn't she see that?

"I'm not pleading his case. I'm pleading the case of the Dale family, the Ortega family, and their loved ones. They deserve to know what happened to the members of their family. It is our job to find the people responsible."

"Then do your job! Making deals with serial killers is not your job. Putting your nose to the pavement and finding suspects or witnesses is your job! Have you tried that, or do you only want to take the easy way out? Is that what this is? You don't want to do the work? Like with Fatima Blackstone."

My jaw twitched as my fist clenched at my sides. Why was she always going on about Blackstone? Why did she think I did something with her? "Again, I didn't do anything with Fatima. I did my job."

She sucked her teeth at me. "Right. That's why she won't take a deal. Because you did your job and not because she thinks she has an FBI agent on her payroll. You wouldn't be the first agent to take bribes. I heard about that agent who hung himself because you all were closing in. I don't put anything past you."

"You don't even know me!"

"I know enough."

My blood pulsed in my veins, hot and bright. I could hit something. I could punch her right in the nose. That might be frowned upon... an agent hitting the US Attorney because she had a slick mouth and no evidence. I drew in a deep breath and slowly exhaled, counting the seconds.

"I don't know what your problem is, but you need to get over it," I spat. "This is about the victims. Real, true victims who have lost multiple members of their families and still don't know why. They deserve answers."

Her eyes narrowed. "Then I suggest you help them find those answers without Bruce Weisman."

I bit my tongue. A metallic tang bloomed on my tongue. I threw my hands up in the air.

"You're not even trying to hear us out on this," said Tony, but his voice was calm, measured. He stepped forward, and instinctively, she took a step back. "We are right about this. We need information, and he seems to be the only one who knows anything."

She shook her head. "Stop cutting corners."

"We are not cutting corners. We are using all of the resources at our disposal, and that includes prisoners," said Tony, his voice an octave higher than before.

"I will say this one last time. I will not make deals with Bruce Weisman, the serial killer. He deserves every bit of the life sentence he is serving, and I will not do anything to shorten it. This concludes our business, and from now on, when you want to stop by, make an appointment."

"Why are you making this so difficult?" asked Tony. If there was a wrong thing to say, that was it. Her lips curled into a snarl. Her hands curled into fists, ready to punch something. "You're not being reasonable. You won't even hear us out on a plan."

"There is no plan, and how dare you call me unreasonable. That's rich coming from you."

Their voices became so high, so filled with anger and resentment, that it was difficult to make out all of the words. The room vibrated with rage from both of them. Aisha's hand pulsed at her side, her fingers itching to slap him. He seemed aware of it and kept his distance. They yelled at each other for what seemed like minutes instead of seconds. Both accused each other of not listening. Both screamed about betrayal.

"Shut up!" The words scrapped against my throat like knives. "Both of you shut the hell up. What is wrong with you two?"

Tony dropped his head. Aisha stared at me wide-eyed. They were acting like children.

"I don't know anything about your personal relationship, and I don't care. If you can't put it aside and do your job, then you need to request a transfer."

Aisha's jaw twitched. She opened her mouth to say something, but I spoke first, cutting her off. I didn't care what she had to say. I didn't care what either of them had to say. They both needed to shut up and listen.

"It is not my business, nor is it my problem. The focus here is the families. Dale and Ortega. Their families. The people they left behind, and it is our job to help them find closure in any way we can. That is our job. Our *only* job."

She rolled her eyes. The second they landed on Tony, she looked away.

"He does deserve life in prison. Every bit of it. But we don't need to make a deal with Bruce. We just need to make him *think* we are making a deal with him based on the information he gives."

Her shoulders dropped a little. "Explain that."

I explained my plan to make Bruce think we were willing to give him a deal as long as he told us everything. We would only give him a deal once we checked the validity of his information and made sure he could not be tied to the crime in any way.

Tony looked back at me and smiled. It was a good plan. I hoped he fell for it. Bruce wasn't stupid. Insane and a sociopath, yes, but not stupid. He might see through the plan, but he might also fall for it. I wouldn't know until we talked to him.

"I guess that could work." She sat down at her desk. "If he falls for it, and that is a big if."

She just had to say something negative. She had to say something that made me think it wouldn't work. But still, it was a plan. A plan to extract information from a ruthless killer. It was more than she offered up. All she gave us were negative comments and condemning looks. At least I was trying to get the families justice.

I swallowed the words perched on the tip of my tongue. Waiting to be unleashed. Tossed at her like shuriken. Even if I had said them, they wouldn't have hurt her. They wouldn't have stuck. Aisha had a pointed tongue. Practice in throwing insults that sliced through you. Her words knew how to cut deep and burrow in bones. I could tell based on my limited interaction with her. Everything told me, do not piss her off. She will hurt your feelings.

"Thank you for your enthusiasm. It might work. It might not. But we have to try something. We need this information, and right now, he is the only one we know that has it."

Tony sighed. "She has a point. Bruce is all we have, and he isn't giving anything up without getting something in return."

Aisha didn't look at him. She kept her eyes trained on me like she was actively avoiding his gaze. What happened between them? A million scenarios bubbled in my mind. I wasn't sure which one felt right. At first, I thought they dated, and maybe Tony cheated on her. He didn't seem like the type to cheat. I just couldn't picture it. But she seemed to hate him. Her anger towards him was superlative. It wasn't an emotion. It was a living, breathing thing. It was in the room, filling up the space between them. She didn't even try to hide it.

Tony… didn't seem to hate her. He seemed more hurt than anything else. And whatever it was, he didn't want to make it worse by talking too much. Maybe she cheated… but then he would have been the angry one. There was something there, but I kept my thoughts and questions to myself. They might have been written all over my face, but they wouldn't come out of my mouth. I wouldn't pry or push. It wasn't any of my business.

"In order to sell it, you will need to join us," I said.

She frowned, her brows pinching together. I watched as she tried to think of a way to get out of it. A way to send someone else in her stead. But we all knew that Bruce would only believe the deal if it came from the US Attorney. Not a proxy. Not someone who didn't have the authority to make phone calls let alone sentencing deals. It had to be someone with authority. Although it was clear she didn't want to go.

"Fine. I'll go. You better hope this works because I will not be pressured into making a deal with that man." She glanced at Tony then. A long, narrowed look daring him to say something. He looked at me and then started toward the door.

"We will meet you there." He opened the door, and I followed behind him. The walk to the car and the ride to the prison was long and quiet. It was a silence filled with unsaid words. Questions not asked. His hands tensed on the wheel.

He never said anything, but I felt his anger. Tony's anger wasn't loud or screaming or curses thrown around. Tony didn't fight with words. He didn't sling them, hoping something would stick to you or cut you open.

His anger was quiet. Reserved for himself only. Reserved for his thoughts. He worked through his anger in his own mind until he felt calmed. And when he did, the space between us, the space in the car, would change. It would feel lighter, and safe, and normal. We weren't there yet. And with Aisha following us, it was bound to get worse. A lot worse. One of us might need a stiff drink after this.

And it would most likely be me.

CHAPTER NINETEEN

WE WAITED NEAR THE FRONT DOOR FOR AISHA TO arrive. It took her thirty minutes. It's likely she procrastinated, stayed in her office to finish her call or to make a new calls. Whatever the reason, she strolled calmly to the front door of the prison thirty minutes after us.

"Let's get this over with." She walked past us and headed inside without another word.

I glanced at Tony, who only shook his head as he held the door open for me. Inside, there was something different about the prison. The place was practically vibrating. My heart stuttered in my chest for a moment before resuming its regular beating.

There was something wrong. The air was thick with something. It hung around us like a cloud. My chest tightened as we walked over to the security station and went through the process of being checked for weapons. Once we turned our guns in, we were led down the hallway. The same hallway where a prison brawl had taken place. A guard ran by and turned down another hallway. My heart sank into the pit of my stomach when another guard and then another one followed.

The guard who accompanied us ushered us into a room and closed the door without another word. The door was locked from the outside.

"What the hell is going on?" Aisha's voice trembled slightly.

Out of the corner of my eye, I saw her inch closer to Tony. She didn't like him but wanted his warmth and comfort when she was scared. *That's interesting.* I sat at the table while Tony and Aisha moved to different corners of the room, far away from each other.

The seconds ticked by, slow, agonizingly slow. No one said a word. I sat at the table. Fear pulsing beneath my skin. A shiver ran down my spine in the hot room, and I knew. Something was wrong, and that something had to do with Bruce. Bruce had done something, or something had been done to him.

Maybe he escaped or beat up a prisoner. I couldn't picture him beating up a prisoner, though. Bruce wasn't the kind of man who used his fist to make a point. He was calculating like a scalpel. He would rather carve chunks out of you than beat you bloody. No, it wasn't a fight. It had to be something else. My ears pricked up as I heard footsteps near the door and then hurry away.

Maybe he escaped.

I shook the thought from my head. If he had escaped, things would have been a lot louder. Sirens would have gone off. The place would have been on lockdown. No, it was more than that. It had to be more than that. Something else was going on. I couldn't put my finger on what it was, but I felt it. The feeling hummed beneath my skin. Vibrated. My leg shook beneath the table, unable to keep still. I wanted out of the room. I wanted to know what was going on.

I glanced down at my watch. Fifteen minutes had gone by. It felt more like an hour. Keys jangled on the other side of the door. My back straightened. Aisha and Tony both pushed themselves off the wall just as the door opened. Half expecting to see another guard with Bruce following close behind, my breath caught in my throat when the warden stepped into the room.

"What did he do?" The words were out of my mouth before I realized it. I stood up. He must have done something. The warden's eyes narrowed at me for a brief moment before softening. His eyes softened, and his shoulders relaxed.

"He, I suppose you're talking about Bruce Weisman. And if you are, I hate to break it to you, but he's dead."

"That's not bad news," said Aisha. "Not at all."

"Are you sure?" I inched closer to the warden. He stepped back.

"Easy, Mia." Tony's voice was calm as usual. A beacon in a turbulent sea of confusion. I stilled.

"Are you sure it's him? He didn't escape and kill someone that looked like him?"

The warden smiled. His dark brown mustache rippled as the corners of his mouth curled upward. "Pretty sure that only happens in the movies."

"I wouldn't put it past him," I said. I heard it. The frantic octaves of my voice. The panic. He took another step back.

He couldn't be dead. How were we going to solve this case without him? How could he be dead? I blinked. My chest tightened. Tony's firm hand gripped my shoulder.

"Breathe, Storm. He's gone. He's dead. It's over."

I shook my head. "I need to see him. I need to be sure."

Fear crept up my spine. What if he wasn't dead? What if he escaped and was on his way out of the country? It could happen. If anyone could do it, Bruce could make it happen. He could run away without a trace.

"Umm…" The warden looked over me at Tony. I didn't know what Tony did or mouthed, but when the warden's eyes settled back on me, he nodded slowly. "Sure. I'll take you."

I followed him out of the room, almost tripping over myself. My feet finding it challenging to find a sure path.

Bruce? How could he be dead? It's impossible.

I tried to keep it together as I followed behind the warden. We rounded several corners and ended up in the prison showers. Guards crowded around the last stall. The warden pushed past the group. I followed, trying to mimic the amount of space he took up.

"Here he is." The warden stepped out of the way. Guards followed. A haze of faces moved out of the way. And then there he was. Eyes wide open and glazed over. A smirk tugged at his frozen lips. Blood soaked through his prison uniform. His hands balled into fists.

My mouth twitched. My pulse roared in my ears, blocking out all the other noise. He was dead. Frozen. Stabbed to death. Part of a shiv stuck out of his chest. He had been stabbed multiple times. I tried to count the slits in his shirt but lost count after seven.

Seven times. He had been stabbed at least seven times before anyone could get to him. How was that possible? Where were the guards? My mouth was dry. I wanted to say something. I had something to say. Words sat on my tongue, ready to jump. But they wouldn't come.

The words felt like sandpaper, harsh and raw. I swallowed them. Now was not the time to ask my questions. My eyes lingered over the body. Slowly taking in every inch of him. Every blood stain, every curve.

"That's him, Mia." Tony's voice was quiet behind me. His words just for me. I nodded slowly as I backed away. Tears stung my eyes, wet and hot. I hurried out of the room. I followed the warden back toward the front and then rushed outside. I practically ran. As soon as the slight breeze swept over my face, I wanted to scream. Tears streamed down my face. I gulped in the fresh air. My legs felt like jelly as I walked over to the car. I leaned against it.

He was dead. How were we going to solve the case without his knowledge? Without whatever information he knew or was hiding? How were we going to do this without his input? My head was swimming. I felt like I was drowning. Pulled underwater, unable to get to the surface. Unable to claw my way to the top. To get any air. A question cut through my panic. Who killed him and why?

I rested my chin on my hands. From where I was, I could see Tony and Aisha walking out of the prison. Aisha glanced over at the car and then quickly looked away. She and Tony exchanged a few words, and then she promptly walked away.

"You okay?" He stopped next to the driver's side door. "You need anything?"

"What are we going to do now? How are we going to figure this case out?"

I hated how small my voice sounded. How childlike. I hated sounding weak, but I was tired. Exhausted. And I didn't feel like making myself sound strong. I needed answers, and he was my way of getting them. I could not live the rest of my life with this case roaming around in my head. The victim's bodies taking up space. Haunting me. We had to figure this out.

"What are we going to do?"

"We are going to lunch." Tony opened the car door and got in.

We went to Aunt Mai's diner and had lunch. I ordered potato soup and a grilled cheese sandwich. I didn't feel like eating, but Tony wouldn't talk until I put something on my stomach.

"We will figure it out," he said when the waitress came and took our plates. Aunt Mai wasn't there. It was her one day off a week. Tony was surprised that she actually stayed away today.

"Usually, she says she is going to stay away, but she never does. She always finds a reason to come in and micromanage things. I'm kinda proud of her."

A smile tugged at my lips. "It's good that she can take a break now and then."

"Yeah, it is. Maybe we need a break."

I pressed my lips together. We didn't need a break. We needed to figure out who killed the Ortega and Dale families. We needed to find justice for them. That's what needed to happen, and it wouldn't until we figured out who killed them and why. His brows furrowed as he stared at me.

"I know. I know, Storm. We will figure out what happened to them, but for right now, we need to regroup. That's all this is."

"He was stabbed several times," I said.

Tony sighed. "Was he? Warden said he probably killed himself. There was a razor by the body. On our way out, the warden said he didn't know where it came from. Or how he got it. They are strict about contraband there."

I nodded slowly. He was right. Bruce was dead. We have no other leads right now. We needed to regroup. We needed to come at it from another angle. "Why would he kill himself?" My voice was quiet, but I knew he heard me by the expression on his face. How his eyes pinched together, and the corners of his mouth turned down. He had been thinking it, too.

"I don't know."

"He was trying to get a deal. Actively trying. Why would he kill himself knowing we might come through? That doesn't make any sense. Not to me... and are you sure it was a suicide? He stabbed himself more than seven times? Who would do that?" How would he have done that? Who had the strength to stab themselves more than once? That doesn't make any sense.

Tony's right eyebrow raised slightly. I knew we were thinking the same thing, but neither of us said it out loud. He didn't kill himself. He didn't. He couldn't have, and saying he did didn't make any sense. None of this made any sense.

"I don't know. I know what I think, but I don't know how true any of it is. And I don't want to say anything until I know for sure."

"But it's weird, right? How he could just kill himself while trying to get a deal to shorten his sentence."

He nodded. "It is. I want Dr. Pittman to take a look at the body, but I know the prison has its own doctors and what not for all of that. I sent a text to Jill and asked her to see what she could do. Hopefully, she can pull a few strings."

"Hopefully," I said. I hoped she could look at the body. The angle of his body didn't make sense if he killed himself. His balled-up fist. If he stabbed himself to death, why were his hands balled up when he died? It wasn't possible for him to kill himself that way.

I saw something on a true crime show where a prisoner killed himself by slicing the veins in his legs and arms and slicing his throat. He was dedicated to his suicide attempt. I couldn't picture Bruce being that dedicated to anything. Something didn't sit right. "What about the shiv?"

Tony blinked. "Where was it?"

"Stuck in his chest." Was that what I saw? I replayed the image in my head over and over. I saw it. I had seen something sticking out of his chest. I didn't see a razor. When I recounted what I saw to Tony, he frowned.

"I didn't actually see the body. Once you looked and you rushed out, I followed you. I'm just going by what the warden said, and I don't know why he would have lied about it."

My fingers drummed against the table. Why would he lie about it? I had more questions than answers. By the end of lunch, I still had no answers. Instead, I had even more questions than when I got there. Nothing was answered. We knew nothing. We were nowhere. It was frustrating. And that wasn't going to change today.

We went back to the field office. Davies stood outside her office and waved us over before we could sit down. I sighed.

"He killed himself?" Davies sat at her desk. "Why did he kill himself?"

"That's a good question," said Tony.

"He was trying to get a deal, so I don't know why he would kill himself until he knew for sure that he wasn't getting it."

Davies looked at me and nodded. "That makes sense. I mean, why kill yourself if you are trying to get time shaved off your sentence? You think about it, maybe, but you don't go through with it until you know for sure it won't happen. Maybe something happened to him. Or someone said something that made him think it wouldn't happen."

I blinked. The first thing that popped into my mind was Aisha and how long it took her to join us at the prison. It took her thirty minutes to arrive, and when she did, there was no explanation as to why she was so late. Had she called the prison? Had she spoken with Bruce and warned him we were trying to trick him into thinking he was getting a deal but that she wasn't agreeing to anything?

That could have been the reason. The real reason. One of them at least. My finger tapped against my knee. Why did he do it? That was everyone's main question. Why? But that wasn't mine. I wondered about something else entirely.

Did he do it? That was a much more important question.

CHAPTER TWENTY

With the way my date ended, I had a lot of time left to think last night. I wasn't sure if that was a good thing or not. Being left to my own devices for so long, but I was, and all I did was think. It would have been nice if I could have thought about Harrison. If I spent the rest of my night grinning from ear to ear and thinking about our date and our conversations and the way he looked last night.

How his green eyes sparkled every time he spoke about his work. Or every time he asked me a question.

How the tattoo on his forearm played peekaboo all night. I caught myself staring at it multiple times before dinner ended abruptly, trying to figure out what it was. It looked new. The drawing had scabbed over slightly. I could only make out the edge, which sent my imagination into overdrive.

What kind of tattoo would he get? Images of a sofa with a client lying across it. He was a psychiatrist. Maybe a pen and a white coat.

But no, thoughts of Harrison were not what occupied my mind. I wish they had been. But no, I had to spend the night thinking about dead serial killers and who killed them. All night, Bruce Weisman roamed in and out of my subconscious. Making himself at home in my dreams. I dreamt of a beach. Tony and his brother were trying to teach me how to surf and failing miserably. We were laughing as King attempted to catch a wave.

And then there was Bruce on the sand next to me. Neck bent, a line of crimson from ear to ear. Perfectly still. Frozen in time. Red bloomed on his shirt, starting with the space right above his heart. And then again and again. I stopped counting after seven. The spots harder to see. They all blended together.

I woke with a start several times in the night. No matter where my dream took me, no matter what I was doing, Bruce always showed up. Dead, neck bent, blood pooling on his shirt. It was a sign of something, but I wasn't sure what it meant. Well, I had a feeling, but it meant nothing until I could back it up. No one would take my word for it because I had a dream. I wouldn't even be able to explain it to Tony, although he might believe me.

I watched him when we were having lunch. I watched how he tried to make it all make sense, and it wasn't. It wasn't adding up, and brows pinched closer and closer together. He looked confused. I wasn't the only one who didn't believe Bruce killed himself.

Around six, I pulled myself out of bed and started to get ready. I wasn't in the mood for a run outside. Although I could have used the treadmill in the gym in the building, I didn't feel like going all the way down to the gym, coming back up to get ready, and then going back down to leave. I could have done it, but I didn't feel like it.

I got dressed, made breakfast sandwiches, and decided to meet Tony by the elevator before he showed up at my front door. I wanted to surprise him. The elevator doors dinged open just as he closed his door behind him.

He blinked. A smile eased across his face like it had always been there. "You're early."

"Figured I'd surprise you." I handed him his sandwich as he stepped into the elevator.

"Color me surprised. Did you sleep?"

I watched as he took me in, his eyes raking over my body and stopping at my eyes. I slathered on a bit of concealer under my eyes to hide the bags. They were deep and a shade darker than the rest of my face. I shrugged at the question, hoping he would drop it. His eyes lingered. I stared at the elevator buttons, all dim except for one.

His eyes burrowed into the side of my face. My skin burned under his gaze. He sighed, a heavy, weighted sigh. It filled the space between us.

"Did *you* sleep?"

It was his turn to shrug and my turn to search his face and look for the truth. The thing he wouldn't say. The skin around his eyes was dark. A shade darker than the rest of his face. He hadn't slept either. I leaned into his shoulder.

"I see you couldn't sleep either."

He smiled. "What were your dreams about?"

As we sat in the car eating our breakfast, I told him all about my dreams and how Bruce showed up no matter what I was doing. He nodded in between bites.

"There's something weird about the body," he said around a mouthful of bread, cheese, sausage, and eggs. "I think that's what your subconscious is telling you. There is something off about the body."

"I thought that while I was looking at it. I made sure to take in everything from head to toe. And I thought there was something weird about this. I hope Jill can get the body."

"Yeah, me too. If there is something off, she will find it."

At the field office, Pollard, Killian, and Ed were in interview rooms. Now that we didn't have Bruce, we had to speak with someone who actually dealt with the bodies. They knew something. We just needed to get them to tell us.

"Okay, I can offer you a deal," I said as soon as I walked into the room. "Whoever talks first gets the best deal."

Ed and Killian sat next to each other, stoic and perfectly still.

"The first person to talk gets the lesser charges and, therefore, gets the lesser sentence. The second person to talk gets the second lesser sentence, and the last person to talk gets everything we can throw at them. Which is a *lot* of shit."

"What do you want to know?" Both men opened their mouths, but words came out of Killian's first.

"There we are."

Ed let out an exasperated exhale. It was good they both wanted the deal. That meant we could get more information out of them. I wanted everything they could tell me.

"Right. I want to know who you work for, and I want to know why Mr. Pollard knew to call you to help get rid of his wife."

The last question drew out a laugh from Killian. It was the second time his face showed any emotion, and it looked wrong and out of place. He should never laugh or smile again.

"He's a frequent flier. At least, that's what I call him. This is the second time he's used us."

"Third," corrected Ed. "The third time."

Killian stared at him for a long moment, his right eyebrow raising slowly. "Remember the girlfriend with the fiery red hair."

Killian's head cocked for a moment, and then he nodded slowly. "Right. How could I forget about her? She was gorgeous, but it was such a waste. I think he shot her. There was blood everywhere. Someone had to clean that up."

"You?"

Killian shook his head. "I don't clean up blood and guts and all the shit. Not in my job description. We pick up the bodies, and we drop them off. That's it. Someone else does the cleaning."

"So, he killed his girlfriend. You got a name?"

He shook his head, stopped and glanced at Ed to confirm, and then shook his head again. "Nope. I think she was trying to leave him. That always seems to set him off."

"It appears that way. When was the first time?" I leaned back in the chair. Giving them room and space to talk. Space to figure out what they wanted to tell me.

"Three years ago," said Killian. "That was the first time that I had ever seen him or done a job for him. Not saying that was the first time he used the service, though. I just started working for him three years ago." He looked at Ed.

Ed shrugged. "I've been with them for a few years, but the last three years were the first time I saw him. I had heard things though from others. He hates it when people walk away from him. He can never let go."

"He loves deeply," said Killian with a chuckle.

Ed shook his head. "Crazy how often we mix up love and ownership. Pollard feels like he owns these women. That's why he gets upset when they try to leave. That's all it is. It isn't love. Never was."

I blinked. *Look at him being all philosophical.* I smiled. Killian nodded his head and smirked like he was proud of the answer.

"They said he used the service often. I don't know how often," said Ed. "But it was a lot. More than three times."

"Huh..." My fingers drummed against the table. "How does this all work?"

The two men exchanged a long look like they were weighing who should go first. Killian was the first to speak. He explained what he knew, and Ed filled in the rest.

The two men worked for a cleaning crew. Instead of cleaning filthy homes, they got rid of dead bodies and cleaned up murder scenes. There were tiers to the organization. They got rid of the bodies. Another tier was responsible for cleaning the actual murder scene, and another tier was responsible for dispatch.

Dispatch was called when a body needed to be gotten rid of. They took the information and dispatched who they needed to the location. As Killian and Ed described what happened, it sounded like a real business. Like a well-oiled machine. You had to admire the tenacity.

They saw a need and decided to fill it. Although I wonder how they discovered there was a need for body disposal. Who were they talking to that made them think, "You know, I wonder if there is a market for that?" Or maybe they killed someone and saw that getting rid of a body was a lot of work and wished they could have hired someone to do it for them.

Wasn't that how it worked? Wasn't that how all businesses came into being? There was a need, and someone tried to fill it. It was infuriating that there was a market for that kind of thing. There were so many murderers on the island there needed to be a cleaning business. And we were just finding out about it. Neither man knew how long the organization had been in business. But they both believed it was for a long time. More than five years, less than twenty.

Longer than I had thought. "What's the name of your boss?"

Both men quieted at that question. They became so still it was almost as if they had disappeared. That I was alone in the room, talking to myself. But they were still there, weighing their answer. Killian sighed. Ed leaned back in his chair. The answer on the tip of their tongues. Neither wanted to be the first to say it. They waited each other out. And then, finally, after the minutes ticked by in complete silence, Killian opened his mouth.

"Violet Wise. That's her name."

I blinked several times. My back straightened immediately. It wasn't what I was expecting. Women had been known to murder, but to be cleaners? I wasn't sure why I pictured it as something exclusively done by a man. I could have kicked myself, some feminist I was. If women could kill, they could be cleaners as well. After all, some men believed cleaning came naturally to women. However, getting rid of dead bodies probably wasn't what they had in mind.

"A woman?" My head tilted slightly. "A woman." The name hung at the tip of my tongue. Violet Wise. Interesting name. "How do you get in contact with her?"

Killian shrugged while Ed chuckled. "Never had cause to meet her. I've never even seen her or spoken to her. Never heard a voice. There are hushed whispers about who she is and what she looks like, but I can't say whether they are true or not."

"I heard her family was in the mafia or something. Some crime family. That's why she started the business," added Ed.

I wanted to roll my eyes, but I caught myself. I swallowed the retort that bubbled up to my lips. The number of people who liked to claim they were part of a crime family was laughable. And most of it was bullshit. Now, there were still some crime families out there, but not in Honolulu. At least, I didn't think there were. That part didn't make any sense. It was possible, but I doubted it.

That being said, I believed the rest of what they were saying. It was wise not to let too many people in the organization see you. If few people knew what you looked like, it would make it more challenging to get caught. She should have kept her name under wraps, though. However, who's to say that Violet was her real name? It could have just been a name she made up. I slid two notepads across the table and told them they had to write everything down in order to get the deal.

They picked up their pens and started to write. I got up and walked out of the room. Tony sat at his desk. He went first, telling me everything Mr. Pollard had said. And then I told him everything Killian and Ed told me about Pollard and the organization. When I said her name, his face perked up. His eyebrows lifted. He was surprised, too, by it being a woman… if it really was.

It could have been. We both agreed on that. But it also could have been a front. A name told to those who needed a name. It could have just as well been a man trying to throw people off his scent. That was something I could believe.

I searched the name, and it did belong to a person. We were both shocked. I half expected the name to come back to nothing. Not a real person. That would have been smart. But no, Violet Wise was a real person who lived on the island in a nice neighborhood. She didn't live in a mansion, which also surprised us. She had two kids and a husband named Miles. I pulled up a picture of them I found on the internet. They looked like the perfect family. All that was missing was a white picket fence and a dog.

"If I were making so much money from disposing of bodies, I would live in a mansion," I said.

Tony chuckled. "And that is how you would get caught."

"She doesn't live in a mansion now, and she still got caught."

Tony's eyes rolled instantly. "Well… we should go pick her up."

CHAPTER TWENTY-ONE

VIOLET WISE LIVED IN A QUAINT LITTLE HOUSE ON A quiet little street surrounded by lush trees and vibrant flowers. It wasn't the kind of house I pictured a cleaner would live in. I wasn't sure what I had envisioned. It was something I never really thought about. But now that I was, I couldn't stop thinking about it. Granted, when she started the business, she probably didn't have a slew of people helping her. She probably cleaned the blood herself and got rid of the bodies herself.

The house didn't look like it would belong to someone who, as Jill would have put it, was often knuckle-deep in blood. Bright pink blooms framed the front window.

Backup descended onto the street by the time we walked up to the door. I didn't think there was going to be a problem. I doubted she wanted to go down in a blaze of glory, but it was better to be safe than sorry.

It was not lost on me that I would not have been thinking this way if the cleaner was a man. My thoughts would have been harsher. I wouldn't have been so at ease with the idea of walking up to his house. I would have waited for backup first or, better yet, sent units ahead of us. But there was something about the cleaner being a woman that set my mind at ease. Relaxed me. Subdued me.

She had a family. She had two kids and a quiet life. She didn't kill the victims. She just got rid of them. It doesn't make her any better. The more I thought about it, the angrier I got. She erased dozens of murders. How many victims would never get justice because of her?

And yet, even though anger pulsed in my veins, there was still no fear of her. I knocked on the door as Tony slowly drew his gun. We didn't know anything about her, so I wasn't sure if she was armed or dangerous. I doubted with the children home. But it was better to be safe than sorry. I knocked again. There was a light rattle on the other side of the door. The door jerked open.

"Oh! You are not my nanny." She glanced from me to Tony and then the space behind us. "How can I help you?" She smiled tightly.

"Are you Violet Wise?" I asked as I took out my badge and held it up.

Her eyes narrowed and then softened. "I won't say anything without my lawyer present. Give me a moment to get my purse and keys." She backed away from the door for a brief second and returned with her purse and keys in hand. "Your car or mine?"

I glanced at Tony, who shrugged. I had never arrested someone who was so… it was like she was waiting for us. She expected us to visit. If not us someone. Maybe she had been expecting this knock for years. I took her purse while Tony arrested her. I checked it for any weapons. There was nothing. We led her to the car.

It was one of the most uneventful arrests of my career. No need for backup or guns. While we went to the car, techs and backup descended on the house with our warrant. I wasn't sure what we were looking for. Part of me hoped for records. If I were a cleaner, I would have kept meticulous records on everybody I worked for. Everybody I disposed of. I would have written down names, dates, murder causes... everything. It would have been my get-out-of-jail-free card.

We took her to one of the empty interview rooms and left her there until her lawyer showed up. She didn't look the way I pictured her. She resembled a typical housewife. Caramel-colored hair, light brown eyes, and perfectly manicured nails. She wore white capri pants and a peach-colored top with tan sandals. She looked like she was ready to run errands, not dispose of a body.

It was strange to see her and think about the company she ran. I could have passed her on the street and never have put it together. I wondered as I walked to my desk if her family knew. If her husband had any idea of the kind of business his wife ran. How could he not? I pushed that thought away. Women have been married to serial killers for years and never put it together. Maybe that was what happened to them. Sleeping next to someone day in and day out didn't mean you knew them.

We waited for her lawyer, who seemed to take her sweet time. Violet sat in our interview room for over an hour. And then, when the lawyer did arrive, calmly strolling onto the floor, she talked to Violet for thirty minutes before we were permitted into the room.

Violet sat next to her lawyer, poised, hands clasped onto the table, back straight. Her lawyer, Yana Robinette, sat next to her in an expensive teal suit with gold buttons and a white blouse underneath. Her thick black hair was pulled back in a loose ponytail. She smiled at me as I sat at the table. There was an ease to the women. They were practiced at this. Old pros who knew we couldn't prove anything. Who knew that what we had was hearsay? Words from two men caught trying to dispose of a body.

Yana smiled. Less of a smile, more of a smirk. "We both know what this is. You have no evidence, no bodies. You have nothing. So why are we here?"

I returned her smile. "Well, she seemed to be expecting us. She didn't even ask what this was about, and I find that interesting." My fingers drummed against the table as I waited for one of them to say something.

"We have two men that work for her and were discovered trying to get rid of a body at a crematorium. They gave us her name as the boss and told us how her organization works. A deal can be made for information."

Violet whispered something into her lawyer's ear. "Have you corroborated this information? How do you know it is true? Maybe the two men just lied and gave you a name so they could get a deal."

"And they both just happened to give us her name? A woman who had her lawyer on speed dial and wasn't the least bit surprised to see two FBI agents at her door," said Tony. "Does that make sense to you?"

"Doesn't matter what makes sense to me. What matters is what makes sense to a judge. And seeing you have no proof of anything to link her to these crimes…" She shrugged.

My stomach soured. She was right. All we had were the words of two men caught trying to get rid of a body.

"You're right. But now that we know about you, we know what to look for. And now we know who to talk to." I jumped up and left the room.

When I got to my desk, Hattie stood near my chair. I shook my head as I sat down. Tony followed suit.

"She's not wrong. And I already asked Killian and Ed to explain further how it all works. Killian said they don't do names, and they don't talk on the phone. They get a text that disappears after a few minutes, telling them where they need to go. He said that's it. They've met other guys when there is a big job, and they chat during those times, but they don't tell their names. Some of the guys wear masks to keep their identities a secret."

"She does not have a foolproof organization," I said, mostly trying to convince myself. She couldn't. How was that even possible? "We need to check her financials. Perhaps there is something there."

"I'll get on that," said Hattie. "Jill wants you two down at the morgue. She found something." Hattie's voice wavered at the end, unsure. Jill had told her she found something but hadn't told her what it was.

I glanced at Tony, who shrugged. We jumped up and walked out before she could say anything else. I wondered what Jill had found the whole ride there. It was either about Moya or Bruce, or both.

When we walked into the morgue, she was in her usual spot. In the middle of the room, between two bodies.

"You two just keep dropping bodies on me. You keep me busy and intrigued."

"You're welcome," I said as I stepped into the room.

The corners of her mouth turned up slightly. "Anyway, I was able to get Bruce's body, and I… something isn't right. His wounds don't match up to what they are saying happened. First, I was looking at the amount of blood." Jill spun around, walked to the back table, and picked up a folder.

"I was looking at the blood around the body, and something was not adding up. First, his wrist was slit, and he was stabbed ten times. If he were alive when this happened, blood would have been everywhere. But this small puddle…" She walked over and handed me the picture. I looked at it. Tony leaned over my shoulder to get a better look.

There was blood on the floor around Bruce, but it wasn't a lot. If he had stabbed himself, slit his wrist, and then his throat, his blood would have still been pumping as he inflicted each wound. He should have been covered in blood. Blood should have snaked around his body and into the other stalls. We should have been wading in it on our way to see the body.

"I thought something looked off. I just couldn't put my finger on what it was," I said.

"I understand that. At first glance, it looked off, and then once I examined him, I figured out what it was."

"So, what do you think happened?" asked Tony. He straightened, the warmth of him gone.

"Well, from what I can tell, he was dead before he was stabbed. Smothered, I think, judging by the petechiae in his eyes and the white fibers I found underneath his nails. I think those were from a pillow. And that brings me to his wounds. Bruce was right-handed. The cuts on his wrists are from the wrong angle, and the slit across his throat is also from the wrong angle."

"So, he didn't kill himself," I said. I didn't think he had, but it was nice to hear that I was right.

"Right. Those are my findings. Definitely not a suicide. I will say whoever killed him he didn't see it coming. Other than the pillow fibers underneath his nails, there are no other signs that he fought back."

"So, he wasn't expecting it," said Tony.

Who would want to kill Bruce? I thought about it for a moment. The list was long. I was reasonably confident he hadn't made many friends in prison—he was a serial killer and a rapist. Serial killers were popular in some prisons, depending on how scary and gruesome their crimes were. Other prisoners also looked at who they targeted.

Rapists, especially child rapists, were not well-liked in prison. Often being attacked by the other prisoners, while the guards looked the other way. Bruce was both a serial killer and a rapist, and he was arrogant. I doubted anyone liked him.

The list of people who would want to kill him was probably long, both inside the prison and outside. Hell, I could have been a suspect. I hated him, but not enough to kill him. I didn't hate anyone enough to kill them. But he definitely got under my skin.

He was the kind of person who burrowed deep into people. Down into their bones and made himself a home there. He was the kind of person that, even though you didn't want to, you took him everywhere with you. He was hard to shake. Invaded your dreams, your nightmares, your every thought.

I tried to put him out of my mind, but he kept creeping back in. Sneaking through a hole or something. I sighed.

"Is that not what you wanted to hear?"

I glanced up and found her staring at me intently. Her brows furrowed. I wasn't sure if that was the answer I wanted. I wasn't sure what I was looking for. I didn't think he would kill himself, so I was relieved to know that I was right.

But relief gave way to annoyance. Now, we had to investigate Bruce Weisman's murder. Of all the things I thought were going to happen before the new year, this was not on my bingo card.

"Now we have to investigate the murder of a known serial killer and rapist. A man that every bit deserved to die," I said.

"I mean, I can throw my findings away. I haven't put anything into the system yet." Jill threw her hands up. "Entirely up to you."

I glanced at Tony. I didn't care who killed Bruce… well, I did care, but not because he was murdered. I cared because whoever did it stopped us from finding out what happened to the Ortega and Dale families. That's what pissed me off. The murderer took that lead from me and their families.

"I am curious, though," I said. "Why kill him now? And how? I doubt a prisoner could have done this without help."

Tony shrugged. "Good point. As long as he has been there, why wait to kill him now?"

I sighed. "I guess we will solve it. Not to bring him justice but to satiate my curiosity."

CHAPTER TWENTY-TWO

I DIDN'T CARE THAT BRUCE WAS DEAD. I DIDN'T. I WOULDN'T go as far as to say that I was happy about it, either. It made no difference to me. Bruce had blood on his hands. He was soaking in it. It wasn't just on his hands but in his hair, on his clothes, soaked into his skin. It was a part of him. He could have scrubbed himself clean for the rest of his life, done a million plus good deeds, and it still wouldn't erase what he had done. He was not a person to mourn. His death made no one sad.

And while I did not care, I still had to investigate his death. Not because I wanted to or because I felt a duty to see justice served. It was more due to my curiosity. I wanted to know why someone had waited until now to have him killed. I wanted to see if it had anything to do with the Dale and Ortega murders. I wanted to know if any of his victims or their families thought spending the rest of his life in prison was too good for him.

If I thought about it, some of them must have been thinking about it, too. We went to Davies and Ayanna to fill them in. It was a good thing the door was closed. Judging by Davies's face, she was about to blow her top. When I had finished talking, her face twisted as a variety of emotions rose to the surface. Anger was up first, shifting her features into a scowl. She pressed her lips into a hard line. Probably to stop herself from saying something she shouldn't.

The room was quiet for a long moment. Davies stared at her desk for a beat. "It's wrong, but that is the best news I've heard all week."

My mouth hung open. I hadn't expected her to say that. I expected more yelling and questions. Why hadn't we placed him in protective custody? Why was no one watching him? Why wasn't a deal struck sooner?

She didn't ask any of the usual questions. Her shoulders dropped a little as she leaned back. "I mean the *best* news. I know we aren't supposed to wish death on people, but it couldn't have happened to a worse person. Now all of his victims' families can move on with their lives."

Her voice wavered for a second. I figured she thought about the Dale and Ortega families at that moment. I had. I was relieved Bruce was gone, one less serial killer in the world. But then I thought about the Ortegas and the Dale family and everything we didn't know or couldn't prove without Bruce. And that made me angry. But more than anything, it made me sad.

"So, what are you going to do now?" Davies' gaze flipped from me to Tony to Ayanna.

"Well, Dr. Pittman said it was murder, not suicide, and I am curious as to why someone would wait until now to kill him. I wonder if it has something to do with the murders."

Davies' nodded. "Good point. That is curious. Where do we stand on the murders?"

I glanced at Tony, and he sighed. "Right now, we don't know anything. All of our leads have been exhausted. Bruce was our last resort, and now that he is gone, I don't know where we go from here. I wonder if the person who killed him knew he was going to tell us and was trying to stop him. We are hoping that by solving his case, we will learn more about the other cases and hopefully solve them eventually."

"Okay. I wonder why the warden said it was a suicide?" Davies said the words primarily to herself as she tapped the arm of her chair. "I'll have to get to the bottom of that. Until then, keep digging into Bruce's murder."

I nodded and jumped up to my feet. I wondered the same thing. The way Bruce was killed, the way Jill described it, it was difficult to picture it as a suicide. So why would he say that? It was clear he was stabbed several times. Why would they immediately assume he stabbed himself? That didn't make any sense to me. Didn't make sense to Jill or Tony either, and now not to Davies, either.

"Well, I guess that leaves me to work on other things," said Ayanna as she closed the door to the office behind her.

"We will keep you in the loop if this circles back around to your cases," I said.

The corners of her mouth lifted slightly. "I appreciate that. And good luck. I know what it's like to solve a case of someone you hate. It's hard and infuriating because you don't really care about the person, or you are happy they are dead. That being said, if you ever need the extra motivation, remember that solving his case may lead to solving mine."

I nodded slowly. Who had she hated that she had to solve their murder? I didn't know a lot about Ayanna. She had an excellent closing record and was a hard worker. She had also worked alone since the death of her partner. But that was all I knew. She didn't seem like the kind of person who liked to share a lot about herself, so I didn't ask.

Tony and I walked over to our desks. I slumped into my chair.

"What do we do now?" I mainly asked to myself. Bruce was probably hated in prison. He was hated outside of it, too. He had an annoying arrogance. He thought he knew everything, and it was something I didn't think he could turn off. His arrogance was infuriating, and the other prisoners and the guards probably hated him for it.

That left the suspect pool too deep to wade in. Not to mention there were suspects outside the prison, too. Bruce's ex-wife had reason to want him dead. So did his sister and his victims that he didn't kill. Maybe they were tired of thinking about him, knowing he was still on the island. Still alive. And then there were the families of his deceased victims. The ones Bruce had killed and buried. All those women had families. Had people who loved. People who were angry that Bruce was still alive. Still allowed to draw breath. It didn't matter that he was behind bars. He was living while their daughters and sisters were not.

I shuddered to think about Charles Tanaka's victims and their families. We would never know the extent of his crimes or all the people he hurt. Not with him dead. Even if he was still alive, I doubted he would have told us anything. He would have taken his secrets to the grave. Bruce knew more than he told us. He had to have. He participated in many of those killings. I doubted his death had anything to do with Tanaka or someone seeking revenge.

I needed to stay focused. This was about Bruce Weisman and his crimes. Or something he was going to tell us. We just needed to figure out which.

"So, you worked that serial killer case? That's exciting." Harrison's smile wavered for a second as he poured our drinks. "Working the case, not the murder parts."

A smile tugged at my lips. I understood what he meant. My father had said almost the same thing before correcting himself and bringing up the dangers of my work.

"I know what you meant. I guess it was at first. But then... it got really dark and difficult. Especially when you look at the scope of the things he's done." I shook my head.

He set the glasses on the coffee table. Harrison's condo was a little like mine, only with a better layout, and it was more expensive. I respected his minimalist approach to decor even though it wouldn't have worked for me in my condo. He believed in only keeping what he needed. He didn't need much, apparently. We sat in his living room on a bright white sofa. There was a glass coffee table in front of me. And two white chairs on the other side of the table. There was a plant in the corner of the room next to a bookcase that housed some books and family photos. He and his sister were close. He kept pictures of her and his nephews in several places throughout the condo. There was one picture of his parents and his brother.

"I just mean, being able to catch a serial killer has to be exhilarating. You bringing all those families justice and solving all of those open cases. It has to make you feel like you are truly making a difference."

I sipped my bourbon. I guess he was right. In a way, it did make me feel like I was making a difference while still making me feel like I wasn't doing enough. I always felt like I wasn't doing enough. If we had found him sooner. If we had figured it out sooner. If someone had noticed the correlation between the missing children in the area and the rise of child trafficking and child sex workers. Then Dane Wesley wouldn't have become a serial killer.

I always felt like I should have been doing more. Worked harder. Tony had told me early on that thinking this way would only drive me crazy. He wasn't wrong. It would eventually. It was such a hard thing to shake.

"I guess it does. But it also makes me feel like I should have done more. I could have done more if I had been smarter or had seen the clues sooner. If I had been more on my game, then maybe it wouldn't have happened." I took a long sip of bourbon. Heat bloomed in my chest. The warmth filled me as my body relaxed.

"I get that. I've had plenty of patients that I wished I had met sooner. As a psychiatrist, you only see people when they are at their lowest. Sometimes, I wonder if they had come to me sooner if I could have prevented a lot of what happened to them."

"In what way?"

Harrison glanced at me and then looked down at his drink. His shoulders raised slightly in a half-shrug. "I can't get into specifics, but there was a patient who had gone through a horrendous childhood. The things her father did to her… that her mother allowed… shaped her entire life. And when she came to see me, she was still... dealing with it. During our sessions, I've always wondered if I could have started with her sooner, maybe she wouldn't have made bad decision after bad decision."

"It sounds like a difficult job. Trying to change the course of someone's life. Trying to undo how they view themselves and the world. It sounds exhausting."

"It can be. But it is also exciting and satisfying. When you see someone you've helped for years finally making strides in becoming the person they have always wanted to be... there's nothing like it. But it can also be heartbreaking when you watch patients throw away all the hard work they have done and slide back into old habits."

"Tony is always telling me you can't get too emotionally involved. I have a hard time with that sometimes. Most of the time. With Bruce, I was a little too invested. I hated him. I hated everything about him. Everything he did... all the people he hurt." I shook my head. "And now to have to solve his murder case. I wish I could just walk away. I wish we could just walk away and leave it unsolved. No one cares. I'm sure his ex-wife doesn't even give a shit."

"I understand the impulse."

I finished the last of my drink and set the glass on the table. "Yeah. But if we want to solve this other case, solving Bruce's murder might be our only hope. So, we have to, I guess. No matter how dirty it makes us feel. Or how much we don't care. Does that make me sound like a horrible person?"

He laughed. "I don't think you could be a horrible person if you tried. It just makes you... human. You're human. And most humans loathe serial killers."

I sighed. The tension in my shoulders eased. I didn't think I was a bad person for feeling the way I did about Bruce, but hearing it from a psychiatrist made me feel better.

CHAPTER TWENTY-THREE

Investigating Bruce's murder was mildly infuriating. Annoying. More than annoying. But now that we knew Bruce was murdered, we had to investigate. I still had hope that solving his case would lead to catching the Ortega and Dale family murders. Tony wasn't so sure.

"You don't think so?" I asked as I placed a hashbrowns on his plate. He poured creamer into my coffee cup before placing it next to my plate.

"Of all the reasons someone could have killed Bruce for, knowing something about those murders isn't really high on the list. I think it might have been one of the victim's family or someone in his family. They all seemed pretty upset when they learned what he had been doing."

"I bet. Although I doubt they were surprised. I don't think it was the family, but we should still ask. And I'll ask Love to check the names of his victims and see if any members of their families have been on the island lately."

"Good idea."

Our breakfast together was filled with our usual comfortable silence with short bursts of conversation.

"How did your date go?" His tone was light. He focused on his plate of food.

I watched out of the corner of my eye. He ate slowly as he waited for an answer. I had told him Harrison and I were going out on a date and that I was excited about it. My first actual date in a long while. I had had that brief thing with Eli, but I wasn't really feeling it, and we never properly 'went out.'

It was just never the right time. I was focused on my work. I had goals that I wanted to accomplish and I always felt like a man would distract from that. And I couldn't afford to be distracted. Not now. But Harrison understood that. He understood my ambitions and my work and how important it was. He was understanding of my schedule and never pushed or sounded annoyed when I had to cancel.

A smile tugged at my lips. "It was nice. At least, I think it was nice. I had fun, at least."

"Are you guys going to do it again?"

"I hope so." We had drinks last night, but that wasn't a date, nor was it planned. We just happened to get home around the same time, and we both looked and felt exhausted. It had been a long day for both of us.

"Look at you." He chuckled.

"Shut up." I pressed my shoulder into his. I wanted to ask him about his dating life, but I refrained. His mother asked him enough questions for both of us and frequently. So much so that it annoyed him, and I didn't want to add to it. I was curious, though, but I swallowed my curiosity and chased it down with a bite of hashbrowns and a sip of coffee.

"That's good. You getting out more." He sipped his coffee.

"Have you been getting out more?" I lifted my eyebrow slightly just as he glanced in my direction. I couldn't resist asking. I hoped he was getting out now that he was feeling better. His bruises had healed, and he was feeling stronger every day.

He sighed, deep and heavy. "You sound like my mother."

"I know, and I'm sorry. It was just a question. I won't push, so you don't have to answer if you don't want to."

He nodded. "I'm not doing anything. Not really, anyway. I think I want to spend some time by myself for a little while. I haven't done that in a while. Just been single."

"I get that."

"My mother doesn't."

I nodded slowly. His mother was like mine. "She sees herself getting older and feels her chances of playing with her grandchildren are running out. And if you don't have any before she dies, she won't get to meet them."

His eyebrow ticked up. "Is that supposed to make me feel better?"

I sipped my coffee. "No, it wasn't. Just telling you why she pushes so hard. And she wants to see you happy."

He sighed. "I know. Doesn't make it any less annoying, though."

We finished our breakfast and coffee. I placed the dishes in the dishwasher while Tony cleaned off the counter and tied up the trash. He dumped the trash bag down the chute while I closed and locked the door behind me. We got on the elevator and rode down in silence.

I wanted to ask him about Aisha and the nature of that relationship, but I swallowed my questions. Her name, her presence felt like a sensitive topic with Tony. A button too sensitive to touch. He didn't mind working with her, but... they changed around each other. She was angrier while he was more quiet. She made her presence known, while he made himself smaller so as not to upset her. It was strange seeing him like that, and it made me dislike her. It made me not want to work with her, but we had no choice.

We left the building and drove to the prison. I wanted to speak with the warden and ask him why he thought Bruce's death was a suicide. At first glance, the body on the scene looked like murder. Where did he get suicide from?

As soon as we entered the prison, the atmosphere changed. It never felt like a good place to be. The air felt hostile, which made sense, it being a prison and all. But it wasn't just the prisoners. It was the guards, too. There was something about the people who worked there. The guards at the front watched us carefully as we locked away our guns.

"How is your day going?" I asked the guard watching the front door, trying to make conversation.

He blinked. His warm brown eyes vacant and narrowing at me. He shrugged, but he didn't open his mouth to answer me. None of them said anything. It was odd. They didn't even ask us who we were there to see. It was like they knew we had come to see the warden. They expected us to show up. I wasn't sure how I felt about that.

We followed a red-haired guard down a series of hallways. The warden's office door was wide open as if he were expecting us to. The guard stopped by the door and knocked firmly.

"They're here." He nodded at the warden before walking away without another word.

"Come on in."

I stepped into the room. Tony followed close behind. The warden smiled at us as he gestured to the two chairs in front of his desk. His smile was wide and fake, not reaching his eyes. There wasn't an ounce of warmth anywhere on his face or in his office. It was cold and sterile. The walls were bright white, almost fluorescent, with nothing on them. His steel desk was close to the back wall facing out. There were two file cabinets and a fake plant in the corner, but that was it. The two chairs in front of his desk were uncomfortable. Not made for long conversations.

The metal pressed against my back, forcing me to sit up straighter. Impossible to relax. Whoever came to visit him, he did not want them to get comfortable or linger. He sat down at his desk, a smile still painted on his face.

Looking at it made me wince. It looked painful for his face to stretch that way.

"So, is this about Weisman's suicide? Do you need me to sign something?"

"The coroner says it wasn't suicide. It was murder."

His smile faltered for a brief second. "Was it?" He leaned forward, resting his elbows on the desk. "Or can we all agree that it was a suicide and be done with it? Weisman doesn't deserve any more of our attention." His smile returned, smug and proud.

"We can't do that, and you even saying those words makes me wonder how many murders have been treated as suicides in this prison. Curious." I glanced at Tony. The smirk on his lips made me chuckle.

The smile dropped from the warden's face. His eyes narrowed. "I see."

"His wrists were slit, but he was also strangled and stabbed quite a few times. If he had been alive when those things happened, there would have been a lot more blood," I said. I kept my tone flat, removing every ounce of the emotion I felt. It irked me how he could just pass it off as a suicide like we wouldn't know a murder when we saw one.

It irked me that he thought we would go along with it. And it irked me that part of me wanted to. If we could all agree that it was a suicide, it would have been easier on everyone. It also would have been wrong. Deep down, I knew that. We didn't get to pick our victims, and like it or not, he was a victim.

The warden took a deep breath and exhaled slowly. "What do you need from me?" He asked finally. His tone was light. It was clear that he didn't care about Bruce or what happened to him.

For a moment, I wondered if that was why the guards stared at us the way they did. Were they worried we wouldn't go along with the agreed upon story? Did everyone know it was murder but agreed to call it suicide because of who he was?

He was a serial killer, after all. All the people he killed, all the people he hurt… did it matter that he was dead? Was the world not a better place without him in it? Did they all feel that way?

I understood the feeling, but I couldn't lean into it. "We need to know who hated him?"

He laughed. "Everyone. Everyone hated him. He was an arrogant prick who killed a shit load of people. Who would like him?"

He had me there. I swallowed my agreement. "He didn't have any friends? There must have been someone in this prison he talked to."

He rolled his eyes. "The guards would know more than me. I doubt it, though. He thought he was so high and mighty, like he was too good for us. Like he didn't get caught murdering a bunch of women. It was the oddest and most infuriating thing. To everyone."

He was arrogant. He seemed to enjoy getting under people's skin. Making a home there. He lived for it.

"He had a knack for that. But we still need to investigate his murder, and you need to make every guard he came in contact with available to us. And any prisoner he was friendly with or that hated him. Especially the ones that hated him," I said.

The corners of his mouth turned up. "I guess the F… B… I… will be taking over the case now. I guess I have no choice but to do what you say." He stood up and gave a curt bow.

"Good. See that you do." I intentionally added an edge to my voice, sharp and pointed. I wanted him to know that if he did not comply with us, there would be trouble. There was something about the warden that I didn't like.

The way he ran the prison… I wondered for a moment what really went on in the prison and if we would ever know. Part of me wanted to do a deep dive into the prison and examine the records and the staff. Do background checks on all of them.

"The two guards that had the most contact with Bruce Weisman are William O'Brien and Rich Anela. As far as inmates, they would know more than anyone." He stood up and gestured to the door. "I'll show you where you can find them."

CHAPTER TWENTY-FOUR

My chest tightened as we followed him. To say I didn't trust the warden without my gun was an understatement. He could have us killed and labeled it a suicide without a second thought.

He wouldn't get away with it, but he would definitely try. We followed him through a maze of hallways until we came to a gate where a group of guards stood talking. There were no prisoners around. I figured they were on break. The group of men grew quiet as we neared them.

"O'Brien. Anela." Two men stepped away from the group and walked toward us. One was tall and muscular, while the other was tall and thin. They towered over me but were the same height as Tony. He stared them in the eyes, and they didn't look away. Not until the warden cleared his throat, getting everyone's attention.

"These special agents want to speak with you about Weisman. They've decided it was a murder, so tell them everything you know about him and who he hung with." There was a slight edge to his voice. He didn't want them to say anything. He didn't want us to be here at all.

"We didn't decide, the evidence did," I corrected. "The evidence proved that it couldn't have been a suicide, so here we are."

Anela rolled his eyes. "Yeah, the evidence. Someone murdered a serial killer. How sad for his family. Oh, wait, no one cares. They don't care. They never came to see him. No one did except for his lawyer and you."

I glanced at Tony. I figured he didn't have many visitors. His wife wanted nothing to do with him. Ayame was done with him, filing for divorce before he was sent to prison. She moved fast. She had moved out of their home before he even confessed. It wasn't surprising that she never went to visit him. I wondered for a moment if she had visited Chika.

Chika had killed their father, Charles Tanaka. Knowing what he had done to his children, the murder was understandable. He tortured them, and not just when they were children.

He loved controlling their lives long into adulthood. He approved of Ayame's marriage to Bruce, and he knew what he was. He knew he was a serial killer. He had taught him everything he knew. Why… How could he hand his daughter over to a monster?

I hope she didn't hold it against her sister. Chika did kill someone, but in the end, she saved both of them. Her actions released them from their father and Bruce. I'm not saying it was right but I understood it.

"I'll leave you to it." Without another word, the warden turned around and headed back toward his office.

"What do you need to know?" O'Brien's voice was soft but firm. There wasn't an ounce of the hostility that laced Anela's. Anela just seemed annoyed for having to talk about Bruce.

"Who did he hang out with? Was he allowed around other inmates?" I asked.

O'Brien nodded. "He was. There wasn't a reason to keep him out of gen pop. We have female guards, and that was a concern, so we treated him like our other rapists and tried to keep them away from the female guards. We did the best we could, but sometimes, if someone called in sick or something, it couldn't be helped."

"Did he get along with anyone?" asked Tony.

O'Brien shrugged. "There were two. Of course, they are convicted rapists. No one else wanted to be around them. But that was it, really. He kept to himself outside of those two. He thought he was too good to hang out with the other inmates, but Sully and Kingston worshipped him. I figured he was the kind of rapist or whatever they wanted to be. Seemed to be they would do whatever he asked them. I doubt they had anything to do with his murder."

"Was there anyone that hated him?" asked Tony.

I noted that O'Brien answered our questions. He was the only one that opened his mouth. Anela stayed silent. His eyes narrowed at Tony every time he asked a question.

"I mean, there might have been a few people. Who wouldn't hate him… seriously. Who?"

He had a point. "Who hated him the most here?" I asked.

O'Brien sighed. He named two prisoners that were on his list. They hated him for a variety of reasons. The main ones being they didn't like rapists and they loathed Bruce's arrogance.

"I think he thought that when he was released into gen pop he would be a star. The guys would love him because he went so many years without getting caught like it was a marvel or something.

Do you know how many guys here went years without getting caught? A lot," he said, not waiting for an answer. "He wasn't the first, and he won't be the last. But he acted like he was, and that irked a lot of the guys. I guess they didn't act like he wanted. He tried to throw his weight around, and the guys let him know that wasn't going to work."

"He got into some fights?" I asked. I could see him walking around like he owned the place and quickly getting put in his place. The prisoners here weren't unsuspecting young women with no one they could depend on. They were men. Real, big, depraved, violent men. Just like him.

Anela chuckled. "Yeah, he got into some fights. Quite a few." He rocked back on his heels. "To say the least. He thought he was big and bold, but he wasn't. He really wasn't."

I wished I could have seen it. When I came to see Bruce, he looked like he was having a rough time. It looked like it hurt him to sit down. He was definitely bruised underneath his prison jumpsuit. I wish I could have seen him getting beat up. That would have made my day. Him walking into a fight where he thought he was about to take someone down, only to get the shit beat out of him. Part of me couldn't picture him fighting.

I couldn't picture him walking up to a man and striking him. That wasn't Bruce's style. He was the type to sneak up on someone. Lure them into a false sense of safety and pounce. Or warp someone's mind to get them to do whatever he wanted. Nothing that involved brute strength. Although I guess moving a dead body required strength.

"Okay, so we need a list of his friends and a list of inmates that he fought with," said Tony.

Anela smiled. "We'll get right on that."

"Well, we aren't leaving until you do, so yeah, get right on that," I said.

Anela winced. The smirk dropped from his face and was replaced by a frown. I meant what I said. We were not leaving the prison until we got what we came for. O'Brien smiled and agreed to give us what we needed. He was the more sensible guard between the two. Anela's disdain for us was palpable.

If O'Brien didn't like us, he was adept at hiding it. Anela didn't even try. We followed the guards to the security room near the front of the building. I called it the security room, but it was really a security post. Two security guards sat in a small room and kept track of who went in and out of the building.

O'Brien stepped into the room and grabbed a clipboard and a pen. "I'll write down the names. You know, in order to speak to them, you need to clear it with their lawyers. I think some of them still have cases pending."

I nodded. "Understood."

When he was finished, he snatched the paper from the clipboard and handed it to me. On it, he had written their names and their prison numbers. It surprised me he remembered their numbers. But if they had to call them out every day, it would make sense why he could rattle the numbers off.

"Thanks." Tony and I left the building as soon as the paper was in my hand. The guards we passed seemed happy to see us go. We'd be back soon, though.

"That was weird," said Tony when we finally got back in the car. Outside, the sky was blue but graying around the edges. A storm was brewing. I hoped it didn't go into effect until later when I was home and ready to go to bed.

"Next stop, the field office." As we drove back to the office, I had a feeling I would be spending the rest of the day on the phone.

My first call was to Aisha. Tony and I both agreed that I should be the one to make the call.

"I don't really feel like hearing her voice at the movement. Not while I'm in a good mood."

I felt my eyebrow raise slightly. "You are in a good mood. Better than usual."

My head tilted slightly. Maybe he was in a good mood or better than usual. He just seemed like himself. But I took his word for it and called her anyway. Her tone was sharp and pointed as soon as I said who I was.

Actually, I think her tone shifted at the sound of my voice. My voice annoyed her. She didn't even have to see me.

"Yes?"

I wanted to say something smart. A smartass remark to further sour her mood. To shock her into silence. I wanted to, but I swallowed the words. I couldn't think of anything particularly witty anyway.

"We need to interview some of the inmates at the prison. I was told that I would have to contact their lawyers because some of their cases are still pending—"

"Right. If their cases are pending, then anything you have to say to them has to be said in front of a lawyer. That just ensures that you don't ask them questions about their current case. What are the names?"

I ran through the names on the list. She sighed on the other end of the phone, deep and heavy.

"Some of those are mine. Sully and Kingston are two cases that have had charges added to their pending cases. You can't speak to them without their lawyers. You can set it up yourself. Bye."

The other line clicked before I could say another word. I guess she wasn't in the mood to talk. "Pleasant as always," I said, half to myself. He shrugged.

"Yeah. What did she say?"

"Not much. She said that I can't talk to Sully and Kingston without their lawyers. And that I can set it up myself. And then she hung up."

He nodded slowly. "Yeah, that sounds about right. So now we need to find their lawyers and set up a meeting."

"Yup."

It didn't take us long to figure out who their lawyers were and find their numbers. Tony took one, and I took the other.

"You need to speak to my client about what? Another inmate?"

"Yes, that's right. Bruce Weisman—"

"The serial killer?"

"That's the one."

There was a sharp intake of breath on the other end of the line. I waited a moment because it felt like he had something he wanted to say. He didn't say anything, so I resumed talking.

"Like I was saying, he was killed, and we heard that he and Kingston were friends. Close friends. Kingston practically worshipped him."

"I told him that wouldn't look good when he went to court. I told him that every time I saw him. But he just goes on and on about Bruce and how great he is. Dude is a serial rapist and a serial killer. He should not be your hero if you want the court to believe you can be reformed. I mean, come on."

I blinked. This conversation took a completely different turn. I didn't have to say or ask anything. His lawyer, Mr. Redwood, just talked. Words spilled from him like water from a faucet. I just had to stay on the other end and catch them.

"He went on and on about the man and his methods. Like I cared. I tried to prepare him for court, but he was more interested in Bruce and how his case was going. He thought the

FBI was bringing more charges against him. I told him I didn't know, nor did I care."

Was he even allowed to tell me all of this? Wasn't it against attorney-client privilege? I didn't ask. I just listened until he asked a question.

"So, you need to speak with him about Bruce. You think he knows something?"

"We aren't sure. We know he and Bruce were friends, and we think he might know the inmates that he had a problem with."

"Oh, I see." Silenced stretched a beat, and then he sighed. "I can meet you there tomorrow morning. Around ten?"

"That's perfect, thank you." I hung up the phone and smiled.

Tony grimaced. "No luck. He's apprehensive about us talking to his client and wants to make sure we don't talk about any of his current charges. I told him this was just about Bruce. He said he would have to clear it with his client."

"Seems like he's afraid his client knows something important about the case, or he's afraid his client can't hold water and will say something incriminating," I said.

He shrugged. "Might be both."

"Well, I got in touch with Kingston's lawyer. We're on for tomorrow."

"I guess that's better than nothing.

CHAPTER TWENTY-FIVE

Before I went home for the day, I called Jill. It had been expressed to me several times that I was not allowed to speak with Yumi. Even though I believed that I was one of if not the only person that could get her to talk. We had a relationship after all.

Granted, she was just my neighbor, but still, we knew each other. And I still had so many questions. I wanted to know how much of this was planned. If she became my neighbor because she knew I was an agent.

While I spoke to Sully's lawyer, an idea popped into my head. I had to pinch my lips together to stop the words from slipping out of my mouth. I called Jill and asked her to run Yumi's DNA.

"And what am I looking for exactly? Are you trying to catch her for other open cases?" Jill had that light and playful tone to her voice she got when she was excited or really interested in what she was asking about.

"I want you to look for relatives. Maybe if we can find someone she cares about, they can get her to talk. Or we can learn more about her. We need to get her to talk and threatening her with prison time is not getting it done. We need to come at her from a different angle. Maybe there was someone she cared about. Someone that she'll listen to."

Jill sighed. "Maybe. Or maybe she's too far gone, and no one can reach her. But I'll do it anyway. I'll let you know if and when I get a match."

I hung up the phone. Jill might have had a point. Maybe Yumi was too far gone. I didn't know who she was… who she really was, or what happened to her to make her do what she did. Mrs. Blackstone said Yumi was a liaison between her and a trafficking outfit that supplied her murder victims. What could make someone get into that line of work?

Something bad had to have happened to her when she was younger. I didn't want to believe she just woke up one day and decided to sell people. Maybe she didn't have a choice. Maybe they were hanging something over her. Coercing her in some way.

"Or maybe she's just a bad person," said Tony when I brought it up. "Maybe she is just rotten to the core and found some people who shared in her depravity."

He had a point. In this line of work, I had learned that some people were just born bad. Some were curated based on their surroundings. I just wanted to know which it was for Yumi. I needed her to talk to me. To *someone*.

I checked my watch before following Tony out of the building. Harrison and I were supposed to go to dinner and a movie. Judging by the time, the movie might have been pushing it. But we could still do dinner.

"I'm so sorry I'm late." Harrison burst through my door in a frenzy. "I'm so sorry. I had to stay later with a patient than I intended. They were really upset, and I wasn't sure about leaving them, and then the police came…"

I blinked. "Did you have to call the police on your patient?" I closed the door behind him. When I turned around to face Harrison, his bottom lip quivered.

"What happened?"

"I shouldn't tell you. I can't…"

But he clearly needed to say it.

"You can tell me. Your confidentiality is safe with me, Harrison."

He let out a heavy breath of air.

"My patient killed his parents." A tear streamed down his cheek. He threw his hands up in the air. "I don't know what happened. I thought we were making strides with his feelings toward his parents. I really thought… he seemed better. His parents even said so. He seemed like a different person. A better person. I don't know what happened last night. And the police wouldn't let me talk to him once they arrested him."

"His lawyer will. You just have to wait until he gets one."

His shoulders dropped. He looked on edge. Full of anxious energy with nowhere to put it. I knew it would be a few days before he could speak to his patient, if not longer. His lawyer might allow him to speak with him, hoping he would say the patient was legally insane.

"Do you still want to go to dinner?" I thought it might cheer him up, but it could also make things worse. I stared at him as an array of emotions flickered in his eyes. Sadness and anger and then nothing. A completely vacant stare. "We could just stay in. Order something."

His eyes turned bright in an instant, and he smiled. "No, let's go out. I could use something to take my mind off of everything. It would be nice." He glanced down at his watch. "A little too late for a movie, though, but we can still go to dinner."

"That works." He said exactly what I wanted him to say.

I didn't really feel like going to the movies now anyway, but I was hungry, as usual. He went to his condo and got dressed while I finished getting ready in mine. I kept it simple: tight dark blue jeans and a white off-the-shoulder top. Then, I added dark lipstick, eye shadow, and mascara. I hadn't worn this much makeup in a while. Being an FBI agent doesn't really allow me to get dressed up. Not like I used to.

It was nice. I stared at myself in the mirror for a long moment. I almost didn't recognize myself. *I should dye my hair,* I thought. My hair has always been black, but it might be time for a change.

I met him in the hallway next to the elevator.

"You look beautiful as always." Harrison had changed into a pair of dark blue jeans and a long-sleeved black shirt. He smelled of cloves and vanilla and warm spices.

"You look nice too."

He smiled and smoothed down his shirt. "Thank you. Just something I threw together."

The night air had a hint of coolness to it. The sun was gone, but the scent of rain was still in the air. It hadn't rained yet, but it was on the horizon.

Harrison took me to Olay's Thai Lao Cuisine downtown. I had never been before, but he had. Two of the waitresses recognized him as a repeat customer for lunch.

We sat at a table in the back next to a beautiful plant that was probably fake. I didn't touch it to see, but I was tempted.

"You come here a lot?" I asked once the waitress, a young Asian girl with dark eyes and black hair with bright pink tips, handed us our menus and walked away.

"Few times a week. It's good and close to my office."

I glanced at my menu. "I thought you worked at a psychiatric hospital or the psychiatric ward or something."

He nodded. "I do with a few other psychiatrists. We rotate. But I have my own practice, clients, and office."

"Oh, that sounds exciting." I glanced over the menu and settled on a few things that I wanted. I couldn't say exactly what made his job seem so exciting, but it did. Excitement buzzed underneath my skin every time he talked about it. Maybe it was understanding the human condition.

I always wondered what made people do what they do. The *why* behind the decisions people make or their choice to kill. I would have loved to have a better understanding of these things, and he did. His job allowed him not only to understand people but help them understand themselves and modify their behaviors accordingly.

I wondered how many people I had arrested would have chosen another path if they had met someone like Harrison. Someone who could have helped them.

"It is interesting. I feel like I learn something new every day. And that is something that I love. I love learning new things and learning about people. One of the reasons I love this job so much."

I smiled. He really did love his job. He enjoyed it. I heard it in his voice. There were some complex cases, but overall, it brought him joy. My job might have had the same effect when a case was resolved with the desired outcome. But some of them were hard to let go.

The waitress appeared next to the table, ready to take our orders. I ordered Thai iced tea, spring rolls, pad ki mao, and fried fish. The pictures looked good. I had tried drunken noodles before, and it left a lot to be desired.

Harrison ordered the basa fish fillet and pad woon sen or fried long rice. We handed over our menus, and she disappeared again.

"How was your day?"

I shrugged at the question. How was my day? It wasn't a question I was used to answering. My mother asked me how my day was, but that was over the phone and not face to face. I could hide over the phone. But here, under the fluorescent light in the restaurant, I couldn't hide my irritation. Or my fear. My chest tightened for a brief moment and eased once I started talking.

The words just spilled out of me. Once the tap was turned on, it was hard to turn it off. I told him a lot more than I intended to, only stopping when the waitress came back with our drinks and then our food. Once I had finished telling him about my day, I was so thirsty I gulped down my iced tea.

"That sounds rough. To have to investigate when you… your feelings for the person are so negative. And everyone else's feelings as well. How do you investigate the murder of a person who elicited such hatred from every person they came in contact with?"

"That is the problem. He had so many enemies we need to narrow them down. That's going to be difficult. I wouldn't say I hated him." *Not out loud, anyway.* "But I did dislike him. And I get why someone would want him dead."

"That's something I can understand. You just have to find someone with the right motive. Someone who would have gained more pleasure or happiness in his death than him wasting away in prison."

"Everyone." I stuffed a forkful of noodles into my mouth. It was pure heaven. Salty and tangy goodness. The fish was crunchy and smothered in chilis. It was the right kind of spicy. Not too much or too little. Would have gone perfectly with a drink, but I sucked down my iced tea instead. I had had enough liquor for the week.

We talked about our work and our families and what we liked about both.

"I love my mother, but she can be a little pushy at times."

That made him laugh. "Mine too. She wants me settled and soon. Keeps going on about grandchildren, but I'm not sure if I want any kids. I tried telling her that, but she didn't want to hear it. She continued with the conversation like I never said anything."

"Mine too. I'm not sure if I want children either." I leaned forward and placed my elbows on the table. "I never really thought about it before, but once I started this job… My first case dealt with a serial killer whose sister was kidnapped by a child trafficking ring and never found. I don't think anyone was looking for her except for him."

Harrison's brows slowly knit together. His eyes focused on me.

"After that case, the thought of having children just doesn't sit right with me. Not now, anyway. Maybe one day I will change my mind. I know my mother hopes so, but… children are never safe. No matter how hard their parents try to protect them and shelter them from the world… the world always has a way of creeping in and ruining things. Ruining lives. I don't think I could ever have a child knowing no matter how hard I tried, I could never truly keep them safe. It would drive me crazy. Drives me crazy now, and I don't even have kids."

"I know that feeling. Not just protecting them from the world but also from themselves. That seems impossible. I suppose if you never think about it or you aren't faced with it every day, it might make it easier to bring a child into this world, but right now, I don't see myself doing it.

Before I became a psychiatrist, I did want children. I'm not sure if I really wanted them or saw it as a way to undo the hiccups of my childhood. A way to make things right. But that's not a good reason to have a child."

"I couldn't agree more."

He told me more about his parents and his childhood. He was adopted and didn't remember his birth parents, nor did he have an urge to find them.

"They gave me away, and while they may have had their reasons—and those reasons might have been the right ones—I just don't… I guess I don't care enough to figure out what those reasons were. I've had a good life. It was a little rocky in the beginning, but everything worked out fine. I don't need to know what I don't know."

"That's an interesting way of looking at it. I'd want to know. No—" I waved my hand dismissively. "I'd need to know. It would irk the hell out of me until I figured it out. It would drive me crazy. I like puzzles. I like figuring things out, and I would have to sort through all of that until I knew who they were and where and why."

He shrugged. "I don't need that kind of control. They let me go, and I can let them go, too."

"Must be nice not to have to know everything." I have always seen people and situations as puzzles. When I was young, I was always looking for the right pieces. Always trying to figure out everything. Once I got a whiff of a question or a mystery, I had to know everything. If I didn't, it could drive me crazy. I needed answers, and I couldn't stop until I found them… all of them.

If I was raised in a foster home, I would have to find my biological parents. And then I would have to know why. Why had they given me up? Why couldn't they keep me? The questions would circle round and round in my head until I had the answers. Even as an adult, when I worked on a case, it was hard for me to focus on anything else until it was solved.

It was challenging to think about anything else. To talk about anything else. My mind would always circle back to the case and, the suspects and what I was missing.

Even on the date with Harrison, I was still thinking about Bruce and his dead body. I didn't care about him, but I cared about the mystery surrounding his death. It had to be a guard or an inmate. Who else could have tried to stage it as a suicide? They probably figured we wouldn't care because of who he was. And we didn't, but it still needed to be solved.

And once my brain finished with his death, it circled around to the bigger mystery, the Dale and Ortega families. What did Bruce know about their death, and how did he know it? Was his willingness to talk to me about the murders what got him killed?

That was the only thing I could think of. If it wasn't about the murdered families, then why wait until now? Why kill him now? That was the thing that didn't sit right with me. Why wait to kill him now? If it wasn't about the family murders, they could have killed him weeks ago. Why wait until now? Until he decided he was going to try and shave time off his sentence in exchange for information. It had to be related.

We finished our dinner, paid the check, and then headed out. The night air was cool and the sky ink black. A soft breeze brought with it the smell of the salty waves not far from us.

"You want to go for a walk?" Harrison shoved his hands in his pocket and rocked back on his heels. "Walk on the beach?"

I smiled. "That sounds lovely."

CHAPTER TWENTY-SIX

"SO, YOU'RE THE GREAT SPECIAL AGENT MIA STORM." Sully leaned back in his chair, his cuffs rattling with his every movement. Sully looked like the kind of man that would worship Bruce Weisman.

His small features and curved back, accompanied by his beady eyes, made him look like a rat to me. He smiled, showcasing his beige and brown teeth.

"He talked about you all day long. He was obsessed. I can see why. You're pretty."

A shiver ran down my spine. He was just the type of man Bruce would have hung out with. Before our meeting, I took the time to study his file. Sully had six cases currently pending against him. Five rapes and one rape and murder. At first, his rapes weren't that brutal, but he escalated into murder. Each victim after the first, suffered through unimaginable horrors. To me, it seemed like Sully was trying to find his footing. He was trying to figure out what he liked doing. One of the women was tortured, another had her breast cut off, and another was beaten with a bat so badly he crushed her skull and several bones throughout her body.

She stayed in the hospital for months and still has problems with her motor skills. The woman he killed after he raped her, he slit her from the neck to her belly and, while she was still alive, started digging around in her abdomen.

What kind of person would do something like that? *The sort of person who would be friends with Bruce Weisman,* I told myself.

"Did he really?"

Sully grinned. "Of course he did. He wanted to get to know you better. He was intrigued by you. Wanted to figure out what made you tick. He hoped you would come and visit him more."

"Why would I do that?"

Sully shrugged. "I guess he hoped you wanted to know what made him tick. You know, the detectives who constantly talk to serial killers, trying to figure out if they were linked to any other murders. I think he hoped you would be like that."

"I didn't want anything to do with him. If he hadn't contacted me, I could have gone the rest of my life, never seeing him again. But here we are." I gestured to the room.

His lawyer sat next to him, silent. He wasn't there to ask questions, just to monitor what questions were asked and answered. I had no desire to learn more about his crimes. I didn't want to know his reasons for doing what he did or if he had committed any other crimes. He was not my mystery to solve.

"Did he have any enemies? Did he ever say that someone was after him?"

Sully sighed. "I don't know about all that."

Tony sighed heavily. I jumped at the sound. He was so quiet I had forgotten he was at the back of the room. He leaned against the wall with his hands in his pocket, watching the door.

Judging by the look on Sully's face, he had forgotten Tony was back there too. When we walked in, Sully's face soured at the sight of Tony. We had talked about it before we entered the prison and decided I would handle most of the interview. He probably didn't like talking to men.

"He... some people didn't like him. You know how people get about guys like us..."

"Rapists and child molesters? Yeah, people usually hate them," I said.

"He was no different. Some people couldn't see his genius."

My stomach lurched. Bile coated the back of my throat. Bruce a genius? Only a depraved individual would think that.

"They only see him as a sick person, but he was a genius. He had to be to have gotten away with this for so long. Bruce had to have been a smart man to go so long without being caught. You know how long he had been at this? He was a teenager when he started. It took you this long to catch him."

Instinctively, I chewed my bottom lip. I hated that he was right. I didn't think that made him a genius, though. It just made him a great liar. A great deceiver, but that was it. Not a genius. A master manipulator, maybe. But that was it.

"Yes, I know. It did take us a while to catch him, but we did in the end. Didn't we?"

His eyes narrowed. "Maybe he wanted you to. I doubt you could have done it if he didn't."

"Why would he have wanted to get caught? He was doing what he loved, wasn't he? Then why get caught?"

His head tilted slightly. "Maybe it was about you."

I blinked. My mouth went dry. What did I have to do with Bruce wanting to be caught? This interview was getting off track. I didn't need to know about his crimes or his reasons. I just needed to know who would have wanted to kill him. That was it.

"He liked you the second he saw you. The way he talked, I don't think anything in his life happened that he didn't want to happen. You couldn't have caught him if he hadn't let you."

"You think he wanted to die because that seemed to happen without his consent."

His brows furrowed as he stared at me. He chewed on his bottom lip. "Maybe he did."

I glanced at the back of the room. I was getting nowhere, but I wouldn't give up. He knew something about Bruce. Something he wasn't telling me.

"Whatever you are holding back, you can tell me. He's dead, and I'm just trying to catch his murderer."

He sucked his teeth. "I don't think you care about who killed him. No one does."

"You're right. No one does. No one wants us here, but here we are. Trying to do our jobs and solve his murder. Help us since we seem to be the only ones who care. And maybe you. If you care, tell us what you know. Who hated Bruce?"

"Everyone." He adjusted in his seat. His lawyer glanced at him. He had been silent the entire time. Mostly staring at his hands or on his phone.

"True, but who had the opportunity to kill him?" asked Tony. "Everyone might have wanted him dead, but in prison, only a few could actually get it done."

Sully nodded. "That's a good point. And usually, if an inmate got something like this done, there would be talk."

"Who's talking?"

He leaned forward. "That's just it. Nobody. No one I've heard. Which makes me think it wasn't a prisoner." his dark beady eyes glanced toward the door. "That's the only explanation. Inmates talk. A lot. And for no one to claim what happened to him even though they all hated him doesn't sit right with me."

"You think it was a guard," I whispered. It wasn't a question. The thought had been rolling around in my mind since I saw Bruce's body, but I hadn't let the words pass my lips. It made sense. A guard could move through the prison freely. A guard would have access to Bruce and could move him to where he wanted him.

Sully shrugged. "Maybe. Or a prisoner that was given orders by a guard."

"That happens?"

Sully smiled. "Of course. A guard doesn't like a prisoner and gets a bunch of inmates to jump him."

"How?"

"By opening his cell when everyone has gone to bed. How do you think Bruce got the shit beat out of him so much?" Sully tapped a finger on the table three times. "Always after lights out. He came out of his cell in the morning, bruised and limping, and blood in his underwear, and unable to sit down for a few days. We all knew what was going on. We had all been through it. The night visits."

"Just the rapists have to go through it?" asked Tony. I glanced back at him as he pushed himself off the wall. "Do they do it to everyone?"

He shrugged. "Everyone that pisses them off. Or steps out of line. And yeah, rapists or child molesters."

"Were there any guards that seemed to hate or dislike Bruce more than the rest?" I looked from Sully to his lawyer, who stared at his phone.

Sully laughed. "Yeah, Rashad Weaver. He *hated* Bruce, and it wasn't like the rest. It was like Bruce had done something to him personally, you know what I mean? Like he had hurt him before he came here. He couldn't hide it. He couldn't even pretend to."

My forefinger tapped the table. Had Bruce hurt Rashad before he came to the prison? Bruce had killed a lot of women. Most of them hadn't been identified yet. I was pretty sure we didn't know all the people he killed. He probably killed more than he claimed. Had he hurt someone in Rashad's life? I wouldn't put it past him.

I wouldn't be surprised at all. "Thank you for your time, Sully."

"I hope you find what you are looking for."

CHAPTER TWENTY-SEVEN

After we spoke with Sully, we had to speak with Kingston, who said much of the same thing. He sat next to his lawyer, hunched over the table. Where Sully had rat-like features, Kingston was built like a tank. Tall and muscular. He looked like he could have broken those cuffs if he wanted to. Split them right down the middle.

He was quieter than Sully. Not as smug. He didn't smile or smirk at me. Instead, he just sat quietly until I asked him a question. It was strange and yet nice at the same time.

"What can you tell me about Bruce Weisman? Who hated him? Did anyone want him dead?"

It took a moment for him to answer. His lawyer nudged him with his elbow.

"Nobody liked him. Not really. He was nice, though, to me anyway."

"But there were people that didn't like him?" I leaned forward. The movement seemed to cause him to lean back. While Sully enjoyed talking to women, Kingston did not. He never looked me in the eye or even acknowledged I was the one asking questions.

"We spoke to Sully," said Tony. "He said some people really hated Bruce."

Kingston's neck practically snapped as he looked up at Tony. Him, he would acknowledge. I kept my mouth shut and let him take over the interview.

"Some people. Some more than others. He could be a little arrogant sometimes. Sully liked to say he was an acquired taste. I guess he was."

That was an understatement. The understatement of the year. He was an acquired taste, alright. Rancid and sour and rotten.

"That's a way of looking at him. Who really hated him here?"

Kingston sighed. "No one really liked him, but I can only think of two people that hated him. I mean, really hated him. They couldn't hide it. Every time they saw him, they got angry. It was almost like Bruce had done something to them. I asked him once if he knew them, and he said no. He seemed a little worried about it. One was Rashad Weaver, who is a guard. Don't know if you've met him yet. And the other was Watson. Don't know his first name. I've never heard anyone call him anything other than Watson. He's another inmate. Murder, I think. A few of them."

"Okay, we'll look into that," said Tony.

I noted that Sully never mentioned Watson. If they were both friends of his, then why wouldn't Sully have mentioned him? That seemed weird to me. Before we could speak with Watson, we would have to clear it with his lawyer and Aisha.

But first, we should find Rashad Weaver and ask him about his disdain for Bruce Weisman. We left the room and walked back to the front. The guards watched us as we walked.

"Where's Rashad Weaver?" asked Tony.

A female guard eased over to us, trying to pretend she wasn't listening to what we were saying. The two male guards next to us looked at each other. A silent conversation passed between them.

"What do you need him for?" asked one.

"Is he even working today?" asked another.

A ghost of a smile touched the female guard's lips. "He's here. Don't know where, though."

"Find him," I said.

She rolled her eyes and walked away. These guards were so irritating. I cut my eyes at Tony, who shrugged. "Should we go back to the warden?" I asked.

"We'll find him," said one of the male guards. He was tall and stocky, with tattoos snaking down his arms.

I took note that the guards didn't really seem worried about us. They weren't concerned with the police or the FBI. What scared them? I had suggested to Tony that the prison needed to be investigated.

"I know. I was thinking that, too. Something is going on there, and I can't figure it out. The guards are running this place, not the warden. He's just the figurehead, but once he goes home, the guards run everything."

"You think he knows?"

Tony nibbled on a French fry. "He has to. He probably just doesn't care. As long as no one dies, then everything is fine. Well, until Bruce. Now, it might come out, which is probably why they don't want us there. Once the inmates start talking, it could end badly for everyone involved."

"Something needs to be done. I don't care about Bruce being killed, but whatever is going on in this prison needs to be sorted out. How can we do that? Can we?"

Something needed to be done. *Something*. The guards were so odd that I just knew they were doing something they shouldn't be doing. Now that I knew what they did to Bruce and the others, I wasn't surprised.

Something I learned years ago was that men in prison don't take kindly to rapists and child molesters. I figured Bruce would have a hard time. That was not what surprised me. The guards orchestrating it did. It surprised me a lot. I couldn't say why. It made sense. In order for the prisoners to move around at night and attack other prisoners, the guards had to be in on it.

The part that surprised me was when Sully said it wasn't just them that suffered this kind of abuse. If someone angered the guards or did something wrong or said something wrong, they orchestrated their abuse. How did the guards choose? And what could set them off?

I wondered how big or small the infraction had to be for them to get beat up. To be raped. If an inmate stepped out of line or made an off-handed remark, could that cause something bad to happen to them?

It was a scary thought. I understood the inmates were in prison and needed to pay for their crimes, but that didn't include being raped and beaten on the whim of certain guards. It was hard to say who actively participated and who just sat back and let it happen. Harder to say which was worse.

"He's down in block B," said the female guard. "I'll show you where he is."

I glanced back at the guards and then turned to follow her. Silence filled the air behind us. We rounded a corner, and a shiver floated down my spine. There was something I didn't like about this prison. The air was too heavy. Too thick. Suffocating.

"What can you tell us about Rashad Weaver?" I asked, trying my best to make conversation. There had to be someone in this prison who was easy to talk to and who wasn't a prisoner.

She shrugged. "He's pretty new here. Only been at this prison since earlier this year. He's not bad. Some of the inmates don't like him, but that's to be expected, really. I haven't had any problems with him, though."

"Did he hate Bruce Weisman?" asked Tony.

She chuckled. "Who didn't hate that asshole? I swear the way he used to look at me made my skin crawl. He was a creep. Everyone hated him."

"What about an inmate named Watson?" I asked.

She stilled for a moment, stumbled, and then continued walking like nothing had happened.

"Yeah, he didn't like Bruce. Don't know why, though. Louis Watson is in for murder. Multiple murders. He killed a family a few years ago. He just knocked on their door, the father let him in, and then he killed the father, mother, four daughters, two sons, and a cousin who was spending the night."

"Why?" I asked.

She shrugged as we rounded another corner. "He never said. He didn't steal anything. He stayed in the home for a couple of days, eating and drinking their food, watching TV, and then he left. He started killing another family, and one of the daughters got away and ran to the neighbors. He killed the mother, father, one of the daughters and the son and the grandmother. Poor old lady, he killed her in one of the rooms upstairs. She was in a wheelchair after a stroke and couldn't get away."

"Damn." My blood ran cold. The murders sounded awfully familiar. I glanced at Tony, his brows furrowed as she talked.

"Do you remember the names of the families he killed?" he asked.

She shook her head. "No, it's been a while since it was in the news. I can't remember their names, but it's in his file." We rounded another corner. I saw a group of guards at the end of the hall, laughing. She stopped short and pointed at the guard next to the wall. "There he is." She turned around and headed back in the opposite direction.

I looked back. I guess she wouldn't be any help with the rest of this. Or she didn't care and didn't want to get involved. The four guards, all male, got silent as we neared them.

"Rashad Weaver?" Tony's voice was loud and echoed off the walls.

The man she had pointed to had short black hair and a medium build with skin the color of brown sugar. He stiffened against the wall.

"Who the hell are you?" His voice was rough and deep.

I held up my badge. "We need to speak with you about Bruce Weisman."

CHAPTER TWENTY-EIGHT

THE MAN NEXT TO RASHAD MOVED IN FRONT OF HIM. Tony walked over to him while I stood back. He and the man were face to face. Eye to eye. Chest to chest.

"We heard you hated Bruce," said Tony.

"You don't have to answer their questions, Rash. Get a lawyer. Or better yet, how about you two just leave," The guard folded his arms across his chest.

"We don't need to speak to *you*," said Tony. "We're here to ask him a few questions. So just let us ask our questions, and then we can leave."

"If you don't have anything to hide, then you shouldn't have a problem answering our questions," I said. The man with his arms folded cut his eyes at me. His red hair blended in with his skin.

"You shouldn't be treating us like we are the criminals. What the hell gives you the right to do that?" demanded the red-haired man.

I held up my badge. "We are trying to solve a murder. And I don't care how loathsome Bruce was, or how deplorable his actions were, or how annoying he was. And we all know he could be an annoying son of a bitch. Someone murdered him. Someone took the law into their own hands, and that needs to be dealt with."

"You don't need to ask him anything," said the man who had put himself between Tony and Rashad. He was just as tall as Tony and only a little more muscular. Even with that, I still had money on Tony. He could take him. I reached for my hip. No gun. *Damn it.*

"It's okay." Rashad stepped away from the group with his hands up. "Calm down, Paul. You too, Trevor. They're special agents, and I didn't do anything that's worth all this trouble. It's cool." He inched over to me. "We can talk."

We backed away from the men and followed Rashad down the maze of hallways to the front of the prison. We retrieved our guns from the lock boxes and followed Rashad outside. He told the guards he was going on his break. Eyes glared at us as we followed him out. He wasn't under arrest or anything. We just needed to ask him a few questions.

What was so difficult about that? The cool noon air caressed my skin and mingled with my sweat. It was hot in that prison. Stifling. I gulped down the fresh air.

"Yeah, the air in there can be kind of rancid," said Rashad. He placed a cigarette in his mouth and lit it. A plume of smoke rose up around him, obscuring his face. "What do you need to know?"

"Why did you hate Bruce so much?"

"Didn't everyone?"

Why did everyone say that? I mean, it was true, but still. I shrugged. "Yes. They seemed to."

"I don't like rapists."

I glanced back at the prison. He followed my gaze.

"I know. I know. Bad place to work if that's how I feel. I needed the job. I really needed the job. Just down on my luck, and then this showed up. I figured I could push down my feelings for the paycheck."

"And then Bruce Weisman showed up."

He shook his head and then took a slow drag from the cigarette. "He was a disgusting human being. You know what he did?"

"We are the ones who arrested him, so yeah, we've got an idea," said Tony. "Hard to think about sometimes."

In two more drags, Rashad finished his cigarette. "Yeah, it is. And he wasn't even ashamed or remorseful about what he had done. He was proud of it. How disgusting was that?"

He was right. Bruce was proud of what he had done. If anyone asked him about it, he would proudly proclaim what he had done and who he had hurt. That made me hate him even more.

"Was that why you hated him?" I asked. I wiggled my hands into my pockets just for someplace to put them.

He took another cigarette out of his pocket and had gone through half of it before he answered. "My sister was raped when we were younger. It never… she could never get past it. She could never move on. It was like she was stuck. Eternally stuck. She killed herself a few years ago."

I rocked back on my feet. That explained why he hated him. Why he didn't like looking at him. His sister had been raped, and that was what Bruce did to almost every woman that crossed his path. I would have hated looking at him, too.

"That's why you didn't like him," said Tony.

He nodded. "I couldn't stand him. But I didn't kill him. I didn't have a reason to. I… that's not something I could do. I would never kill someone. Not even him."

I believed him. I couldn't say why. I wouldn't dare give credit to my gut. Not out loud, anyway, because of how annoyed Tony got at that sentiment. But maybe that was it. I just looked at him… looked into his warm brown eyes, and I believed him.

"Did anyone else hate him enough to have killed him?"

He cocked his head to the side. After the last pull from his cigarette, he tossed it on the ground and stamped it out. "The only name that really comes to mind is Desmond Holmes. Desmond couldn't stand Bruce. He seemed to go out of his way to mess with him."

"Is he an inmate?" I asked.

He shook his head. "No, he's a guard."

After we finished with Rashad, I was reluctant to go back into the prison. I didn't want to return to the heavy and hostile atmosphere. It felt hostile because of the guards, not the inmates, and that was something that needed to be addressed.

Instead, I decided to go back to the field office to do some research. I wanted to research Watson and Desmond Holmes. I wanted to know more before we brought them in to interview them. I found it helpful when I knew which questions to ask beforehand.

At the field office, Hattie was pacing by our desks with her tablet. She was reading something, her mouthing silently. I walked over to my desk and plopped into my chair. I was tired. The tension building up in my shoulder blades eased slightly as I reclined back in my chair. I sighed.

"Long day?"

Tony sat in his chair and reclined back. He answered her with a grunt. She smiled.

"I'll take that as a yes. Where were you two?"

I told her about our time in the prison, who we talked to, and who said what. She listened quietly, making notes on her tablet.

"I see, so you need info on Desmond Holmes and Louis Watson. I feel like Watson sounds familiar, but I can't remember specifics. Okay." She tapped her screen twice. "The files have been sent to both of you." She turned to walk away but stopped cold. "There is something off about that prison. I think I might do some investigating of my own." She walked away before I could say anything.

"The next interviews, we do them here," I said. I didn't want to go back into that prison if I didn't have to. And I hoped I didn't have to. I glanced over at Tony, who nodded. I felt exhausted but curious at the same time. I sat up and turned on my computer. I immediately pulled up the files Hattie had sent us and started reading through them.

I opened the Watson files first. His murders sounded very familiar. He killed two families for no reason. A thought circled around my mind. What if he killed the Dale and Ortega families? Bruce could have learned about it from being in prison with him.

Was that why he killed him? Bruce could have learned about what he had done, and then Watson could have figured out Bruce was trying to make a deal in exchange for information. That made sense to me. If Watson was already in prison for those crimes and didn't want any more added to his sentence, he could have killed Bruce to keep him quiet. I could picture that.

I could picture Bruce using his ways to gather information on the other inmates and then turning around and exchanging the information for a better deal. He used people.

Watson's file was disgusting and hard to read, and yet I read through every page. The murders were so much like the Ortega and Dale families. There was no forced entry. Nothing was stolen.

There were some differences. Watson had killed each member of the Crow and Milthrop families quickly. He had moved through the house swiftly and efficiently but then resided in the Crow home for days after the murders. He ate their food and watched their television. He used their bathrooms and took showers. He had made himself comfortable in their home while their bodies were decomposing.

What kind of person could do something like that? I didn't think even Bruce could do that. There was no evidence that any of the female victims had been raped or molested. So, there was no sexual element to the murders. One similarity was that nothing was stolen.

It didn't make any sense. He killed just to kill. There was no rhyme or reason to it. They were senseless crimes. My blood started to boil in my veins.

Watson had been caught murdering the Milthrop family when the daughter, Billie, jumped out of her second-story bedroom window when she heard her mother screaming. She ran across the street to her neighbors, who called the police.

The most interesting part of the case was that Watson didn't stop stabbing Mrs. Milthrop even though he knew the girl had run. He saw her through the front window while he was stabbing her mother.

He knew the police were on their way, and yet he still didn't stop. He didn't try to run away or hide. When the police entered the house, he was still crouched over two of the bodies, alternating his stabs between the two. There were pictures in the file of the bodies and of Watson.

A shiver ran down my spine, and I shuddered. The picture of Watson with his hands cuffed behind his back was startling, unsettling, and yet I couldn't look away. He was steeping in blood. Smeared blood covered his face and arms and his neck. His shirt was so bloody it clung to his chest.

My stomach turned as bile threatened to bubble up my throat. I swallowed hard. The crime scene looked familiar, almost exactly like the Ortega and Dale family crime scene pictures.

Did we find the murderer of the Dale and Ortega families?

CHAPTER TWENTY-NINE

I waited until Tony read through the file. I knew the moment he was finished by the way he looked up and stared at me. His jaw set, his eyes narrowed.

"Yeah, that's what I was thinking."

He shook his head. "The murders are similar. Strikingly similar. I'm not saying he did it, but he could have. Did Bruce know, or did he know that Watson didn't do it?"

I blinked. "I hadn't thought about that." I figured Bruce knew that Watson killed the families. But what if he knew someone else had done the murders, and they killed him before he could say anything?

My mind flipped back and forth between both scenarios. Either could have been possible. I no longer thought he was killed because someone hated him. That was too simple.

There was something else to it. Do we speak with Watson, or do we talk to Holmes?

"I want to talk Bruce's ex-wife." The words were out of me before I fully understood why. "Maybe if we could figure out what he had, we can figure out why he was killed."

"So, you think he had something? To give or show to us?"

I shrugged. "Whatever this was, he had to have proof. If he were trying to prove that someone else killed the Ortega and Dale families, he would need to be able to prove it. It's not like we would just take his word for it. So, he had to have something."

Tony leaned back. "Right. That would make more sense. So, if we can find what he had, we can figure out who he was talking about." He tapped his finger on his chin. "You think she would know?"

"Maybe she kept some of his stuff." Even as I spoke the words, I felt my eyebrows raise as if I were questioning my own statement. Maybe she did. I wouldn't have, though. I would have burned everything as soon as he went to prison. I would have set it on fire and watched it burn, and then I would have moved.

To another island, to another state, somewhere else. Somewhere I would never have to see ore be reminded of him again. She didn't, though. Ayame still lived on the island.

I figured she stayed on the island to be close to her sister, who was still in prison and would be for years to come. Chika wasn't given life for killing her father, but she would have to serve for some time before her possibility of parole.

"I guess we should at least try. Maybe she did keep some of his stuff."

"Okay. It's worth a shot. I would be surprised if she kept anything, though. And we don't know what we are looking for, so that's something."

I shrugged. It was worth a shot. Ayame no longer lived in her old house. She moved out as soon as she could. She lived in a nice house in a gated community with round-the-clock security.

Every woman that survived Bruce found themselves in heavily secure areas. They were probably afraid that he would get out one day and find them. After bypassing security, we entered the neighborhood.

It was quiet. The manicured lawns were well taken care of. Lush green grass and vibrant flowers filled every yard. We stopped in front of Ayame's house. I had called her before we left the field office. I didn't want to surprise her. The last time I saw her, she was on edge.

Every little noise made her jump. She looked like she hadn't slept in days. The bags under her eyes were three shades darker than the rest of her face and big enough to carry luggage. I worried about her then. Really worried about her. I was afraid she might kill herself, but Tony didn't think she would.

"She'll be fine. She'll go home and be by herself for a little while. And when she gets out of the self-pity stage, she'll get angry. And the anger will fuel her for a long, long time. She'll be fine in the end."

He believed the anger would fuel her until she could work through what Bruce had done. I wasn't so sure. I didn't think her rage would be more potent than her grief.

As we walked up to the door, I wondered which one of us was right. I knocked on the beautiful wooden door. After a long moment, the door opened.

Ayame, or at least a woman who looked like Ayame, stood in the doorway. Her skin was flawless, her hair was red, and she wore makeup. I blinked several times. She didn't look like herself. She looked amazing.

She wore a curve-hugging, blood-red dress that stopped just below her knees. "Hello? Is there something wrong?" Her eyes darted from me to Tony and back.

"Um..." I glanced at Tony. "Can we speak with you for a moment?"

She sighed. "Is this about Bruce?"

I nodded. A slight smile dropped from her face. She backed away from the door, allowing us to enter.

"What has he done now?" She closed the door behind us. "Well, I know he's dead."

"Yes, he is dead," I said as I followed her out of the foyer and into the living room. This house looked nothing like her last one. It was a home that she was allowed to decorate all on her own. And that was clear. The decor was more minimal than her last house. There were very few pictures on the walls, and the ones that were there were of her and her sister. They didn't even include her brother or his wife.

I found that interesting. The living room had a sofa, a loveseat and two bookcases in the far corners of the room. I sat on the couch while she sat on the loveseat.

"So, what has he done now?" she asked. She looked so relaxed. Like she didn't have a care in the world, even though she asked about what he had done, it was evident by the look on her face that she didn't really care.

"You look amazing," I said. The words were out of my mouth before I could catch them. But she did look amazing. She looked like she had been taking care of herself. She looked happy. Stress free. It was an amazing thing to see.

I had been worried about her, but Tony was right. She was okay. She was thriving. I wondered for a brief moment how her brother and his wife were doing. He wasn't as innocent as his sister. He was the man his father had molded him to be, and that was not a good thing. I hoped he could be molded into something else. Now that his father was gone, he could be his own person. Or try to be a better one.

Ayame's smile lit up the room. Without the stress her husband and father had caused her, she was quite beautiful. The skin around her eyes crinkled.

"Thank you so much. It's amazing how good divorcing a serial killer is for your skin. I felt a hundred pounds lighter as soon as I signed the papers. It was like this weight that had been weighing me down my entire life was gone, and I could sit up. I can think. I can live my life."

I understood what she was saying. She sat in her chair, her back straight. Her head held high. Before, she looked small, so small. Like she was afraid to take up any space, she was afraid for someone to notice her, which was understandable. Growing up in a house like hers. Being noticed was probably a dangerous thing in both houses, not just when she lived with her father.

"For the first time in my life, I feel like I can breathe. And I can't even describe to you how amazing that feels." Her eyes turned watery. Tears pricked the corners of my eyes. I was so happy for her. She didn't let them ruin her. She didn't let either man break her. I was so proud I wanted to hug her. But I kept my arms to myself.

"But back to Bruce. What has he done? Did you figure out who killed him? Are you looking?"

I chuckled at the last question. And to my surprise, so did Tony. A smile pulled at her lips. She laughed lightly.

"I guess that's a mean thing to say, but honestly, I wasn't expecting anyone to care about his death. I know I don't. As soon as I heard about it, I felt relieved. I had been a little worried about him getting out. I know he was supposed to be in prison for life, but… Bruce could always find a way to get what he wanted. I just knew he would walk through those doors one day."

"We are investigating," I said. "Albeit reluctantly. Did you keep any of his things?"

Her lips slowly curled into a smile. "I'll admit I wasn't sure what I should do with it. I wasn't sure if it was illegal to throw any of it away. I burned most of it. His clothes and whatnot. But the papers… I don't know why I kept them. I really don't. I guess I imagined one day I would be sitting here having this conversation about his stuff. They seemed important, although I can't say why. I didn't know if maybe there were hints to help find the other women he killed. I know he killed more women than he went to prison for. I just know it."

I thought the same thing. Tony and I both discussed it, and we believed he killed more women not just on the island but in other states he lived in as well. Murders that would probably never be linked to him without DNA or without finding the bodies. So many stories without endings. So many stories unknown. It was depressing when you really thought about it.

"Can we look through them?" I asked.

"Oh, of course! What else am I doing with it?" She jumped to her feet. "Just follow me."

We followed her into the kitchen and through the door to the garage. The garage was clean sans the boxes in the corner.

"I just dumped everything in here. I didn't really want it in the house. I wanted nothing of his in the house, so I figured this was good enough."

"Thank you," I said.

Tony walked over and started examining the boxes. Simple boxes used for packing. There were six of them stacked on top of each other.

"Thank you, Ayame. We'll just look through the boxes, and then we'll be out of your hair."

"That's fine." She turned around to walk away.

"How's your sister?"

She spun back around. "Well, you know prison." She shrugged. "That being said, it's the first time she's ever been able to have a good night's sleep. It's the only time in her life she hasn't been scared or worried. I went to see her, and she looked refreshed and happy. It had been a long time since I had seen her smile. So, she's doing fine."

I blinked. It was amazing she had to go to prison to actually get a good night's sleep. But there, she knew her father was dead and that Bruce couldn't get to her. I felt so bad for Chika. I understood she had to go to prison. She killed a man, and her father at that. Though he did deserve to die.

After everything he had done to her and the rest of their family, Charles had deserved to die. That being said, I didn't like the idea of her being in prison for so long. But it was good to hear that she was doing well, finally.

She must have felt so relieved now that both of those men were gone and never coming back. I'd probably sleep well, too, knowing that Bruce and Charles Tanaka were dead. She went back into the house and closed the door behind her.

"So, what are we looking for?" I asked as I walked over to Tony and the boxes. "Anything in particular?"

"A flash drive or something. Something that can hold information."

We divided the boxes and started searching. There were a lot of papers, most of which I didn't feel like reading. His handwriting was also hard to read. I searched my boxes for something that could hold a lot of information. I thought of a flash drive like the one we found in my first case. Where else would he keep the information?

I doubted he would have written it down. The likelihood of someone coming along and reading it was too great, even though Ayame probably didn't go through his things. He would have kept it somewhere that was easy for him to get to and that no one else would think to look.

I searched through the last box and found nothing. I picked up the box to move it out of the way when I heard something slide across the bottom of the box. I stopped and set the box in front of me. Underneath one of the bottom panels, there was a gold key.

"You find anything?" I asked as I examined the key.

"Nope. Not a thing. Maybe he kept it somewhere else."

"Like a bank deposit box?" I turned around and held up the key. "Maybe whatever he was hiding might be here."

CHAPTER THIRTY

THE SMALL BANK ONLY HOUSED DEPOSIT BOXES. WE were both curious about what he decided to keep there. While I was curious, I was a little afraid about what it could have been. Bruce was a horrible man. I could picture him recording what he did to those women and keeping the videos in a lock box. I didn't want to see the videos if there were any.

"Yes, Bruce Weisman has a box here." The banker eyed us suspiciously. "Why?"

I held up my badge.

"That's why," answered Tony. "We need to get into his box."

"I'm sorry. You need a warrant or something, don't you?" He glanced at the front door. He clearly didn't want us to be there. His fingers drummed against the counter.

"He's dead. His next of kin has authorized us to look into it. And we have a key, so we just need to see the box," answered Tony.

The banker, a tall man with short light brown hair and hazel eyes, froze. "What? He's what… are you sure?"

"Very," I said. "Do you want to see his body?"

His face scrunched up as he shook his head. "I'd rather not. I'll take you to his box. I would like to say beforehand that we are not responsible for what is in the box. I know he's gotten in some trouble, but that has nothing to do with us here."

He closed the ledger on the front desk and stood up. He walked around the desk and headed toward a door in the back. We followed.

It seemed like the banker and I had the same idea. Bruce might have kept pictures or videos of his crimes in the box. This told me that he knew about Bruce being a serial killer.

The back room was lined with boxes. Every inch of the wall was covered. In the middle of the room was a large black block. The banker walked over to a box and waited.

"The key, please."

In order to get into any of the boxes, you needed two keys, one supplied by the bank teller and the other by the owner of the box. That was a good way of keeping things secure.

I walked over to the box, fished the key out of my pocket, and stuck it into the free keyhole. We turned the keys, and he pulled the box out of the slot and set it on the black block in the middle of the room, next to Tony.

"There you are. If you need anything else, please let me know." He exited the room without another word. He walked faster out of the room than he did walking in.

It was clear he didn't want to be in the room to see what was in the box. I wished I didn't have to be in the room with it, either. Once he was gone, Tony opened the box. For such a big box, there was a lot of wasted space. It made me think he had planned on putting more stuff in the box, but instead, there was just a flash drive.

A lonely flash drive.

"That's interesting," I said as I picked it up.

"I shudder to think what's on it, though," said Tony as he closed the box. I shuddered, too. But the only way we will ever know is if we open it up.

We went back to the field office and went straight to Love.

"And where did you get this?" She stared at the drive, turning it over in her hands. Eli stuck his head out of his office, saw us, and walked over.

"What are you three doing?"

I explained to both of them about Bruce and his wife and what we found in the box.

"We need to know what's on it, even though we don't want to know what's on it."

"I don't want to know what's on it, either," whined Love. "I can only imagine. You know what? No, I can't even imagine what's on this drive. He was a sick, sick man. He probably recorded his rapes and murders to watch later. So he could watch them, jerk off, and then figure out what he could have done better."

"You've given that some thought," said Tony.

"No, that was just off the top of my head. And you know I'm probably right. He was a sick man who did sick shit, and now we *all* have to watch it because I am not sitting here and watching it by myself."

She eyed the three of us as she pushed the drive into her computer. From the look on her face, she was making sure none of us walked away or closed our eyes. She meant what she said. If she had to see it, so did we. I wouldn't want to watch it by myself, either.

A window popped up on the screen, and she moved it to the bigger screen on the wall across from her. We all adjusted ourselves to see the screen. "Okay, what are we going to see?" I said to myself.

"Wait," I said after a thought popped into my head. "The killer was probably after the key. If Bruce had something on him, then he might have forced him to tell him where it was before he killed him."

"You think Bruce told him about the key?" asked Tony. He rocked back on his heels. "He could have. I don't think Bruce was good at taking pain. It wouldn't have taken him long to tell."

"Yeah, he didn't seem like the type that could take torture. Inflicting torture, yes. Taking it, he would have talked in a matter of seconds." If he was looking for the key and we found it, then he was still looking for it. "How can we catch him?"

"Who do you think it is?" asked Love. She started looking through the files on the flash drive while we talked.

"Not sure. But whoever it is, they will be looking for the drive. Which means they will be looking for the key. So, we need to put the key back and wait for them."

Tony nodded slowly.

"You might as well because we aren't getting anything off of this right now," said Love. "There are three files. And in each file, there is a number or maybe a code. It's just a series of numbers. There's nothing else."

I stared at the screen.

"There was nothing else in the deposit box. Why would he keep this?"

Love shrugged. "I don't know. There is nothing else on this drive. Not that I can tell, but give me a little time to mess with it."

"Until then, we should put the key back. Someone's looking for it."

Tony nodded. "Okay. We should warn Ayame, though. See if she has a friend she can stay with."

"That's a good idea, just in case something happens."

"Sounds like you two are going to have a stakeout," said Eli.

A smile tugged at the corners of my mouth. I tried not to grin or show how happy I was on the inside. I got to do a stakeout. A real stakeout.

"Tamper down your excitement," said Tony as we left the It department.

"I didn't say anything. I'm not even smiling."

He glanced at me. "I *feel* your excitement. You always get excited about stuff like this. It's loud." He shook his head and chuckled. "Loud. Real loud. Makes the room vibrate."

"I'm sorry I'm excited about a stakeout. It's my curiosity."

It took a couple of hours for everything to get approved by Davies and the US Attorney.

Aisha was annoyed, but she approved our request. Davies was curious because she wanted to see who killed Bruce, and she wanted to know why. I was curious about why, too.

I called Ayame on our way to her house and told her she needed to leave for a few days. Once I explained everything, she agreed.

"His mess will forever haunt me," she said.

"Hopefully, this will be the last of it. I think someone wants the key to his deposit box."

"You think that was why someone killed him?"

"I think it is a possibility. And if it is, you shouldn't be at the house if the person finally shows up."

"I don't want to be here if that happens. I have a friend I can stay with for a few days. Just let me know when I can go home."

"Will do."

Tony stopped at the store to grab a few snacks for the stakeout that he was not happy about. He got back in the car with three bags. One with drinks and two with snacks.

Protein snacks, jerky, beef sticks, cheese sticks, chips, and snack cakes. I pulled a beef stick out of the bag and opened it.

"It's for the stakeout."

"That we are actively on our way to, so it counts." I bit into the stick. It was more salty than anything. I took a bottle of water out of the bag.

"Are you going to eat all the snacks before we get there?"

I shrugged. "I might." I wasn't. We hadn't eaten lunch, and I was hungry. We pulled up in front of the house. Tony went inside, placed the key back in the box, and then ran outside. We moved the car across the street and down two houses and parked.

We settled in for what we both assumed would be a long night. I sighed as I leaned back in my seat. I was already tired and ready to go home.

I wasn't even sure if this plan would work. It was my idea, but it was a half-assed idea that I had just thought of on the fly. We didn't know if the killer would try to come to his house. If the killer was an inmate, they wouldn't have been able to.

But if it wasn't, and I didn't think it was, then the killer might be looking for Ayame. She was the only person that would have access to Bruce's things, and Bruce might have told the killer where to find the flash drive.

But why did the killer want it? And what did it have to do with the Ortega and the Dale murders?

CHAPTER THIRTY-ONE

A PIT FORMED IN MY STOMACH. WHAT IF THIS WAS A stupid idea and nothing came from it? I sighed even heavier. What if this was a waste of time?

Tony looked back at the house. "So, how's life?"

I smiled. "Life's pretty good. Will be even better if this works out."

"And how is Harrison?" There was a laugh on the edge of his voice.

"What do you know about Harrison?"

"He asked me where he should take you on your date. I told him food was your favorite pastime and just about the only hobby you have."

"I don't know how I feel about that, and I have other hobbies."

"Name them. I'll give you some time to think about it."

I folded my arms across my chest. I had other hobbies. I couldn't think of any at the moment, but they were there. They had to be. I did other things besides eating and working. Right? I needed to get some hobbies. Before I could say another word, I felt my phone vibrating in my back pocket.

"Uh-oh." I looked at the screen. Jill calling me at night was never a good sign. "What's wrong?"

"I just wanted to tell you about the DNA results you asked for. I was going to wait until the morning, but I didn't think I could hold it that long. I ran Yumi's DNA, and I finally got the results back. Yumi is Dane Wesley's sister."

My blood ran cold. My phone slipped out of my hand. I caught it mid-air and lifted it back to my ear.

"Are you sure?"

"I ran it twice, and both times, it came back positive. She is his sister."

I hung up the phone, blinking back the tears pricking my eyes. Yumi was his sister. All the people he killed were looking for her. All the things he did, trying to find his sister, and here she was in our interrogation room.

Tony's voice echoed in my head, but I couldn't focus on it. I couldn't focus on anything else. Anyone else. Yumi was Dane's sister!

Did she know? Did she even remember her brother? Yumi was kidnapped when they were younger, and no one really looked for her. It was believed that she had just run away from their adoptive family.

But Dane didn't believe it. He believed that his sister was kidnapped by a child trafficking ring, and he did everything he could to try to find her. He figured out who had taken her and then went on a rampage and started killing people who were associated with the trafficking ring.

He did it all, looking for her, and here she was. Selling people. Doing to others what was done to her. How disappointed Dane would have been in her.

"Mia?" Tony's voice was soft in my ear, his hand firmly gripping my shoulder. "What happened?"

I snapped out of my trance and looked at him. Tears streamed down my face.

"What happened?"

I shook my head. "Yumi is Dane Wesley's sister," I said slowly. My voice sounded so foreign to me. Distant and cracking. My chest tightened. I felt like I couldn't breathe. Did she know her brother was dead? Did she even remember him?

"Seriously?"

I nodded slowly. It was all I could do. All I could muster. He squeezed my shoulder. "Well, now we have our in. I wonder if she knows her brother has been killed or if she knew what he was doing before he was killed."

"That's the question. I can't Imagine that she could have known and still worked with those people."

"But if they got her when she was a child, you don't know what they did to her. She's probably brainwashed. If she didn't have a place to go, she would have stayed there as long as possible."

"Who is that?" I looked up into the rearview mirror. A dark figure slinked across Ayame's front yard, inching closer to the door. I hadn't seen any car lights. He probably parked down the street.

I watched him as he hovered near the door. "You think that's him."

"I hope so. I'm ready to get out of this car." Night had fallen. The sky was inky black, and most of the lights on the street were out. I wondered for a moment if the killer had something to do with that.

We watched as he broke into the house. We watched as he closed the door behind him, and then we waited. Just long enough for him to get used to the house and wiggle his way through the house to the garage. Ayame said she sent Bruce a letter. Only one, telling him she had a few of his things in the garage and if he wanted her to send them somewhere to give her the address. He never wrote her back.

He might have liked the fact that she kept a few of his things. He might have liked the idea that he was still with her in a way. And he might have told the killer where he could find the key.

I said a short prayer as I got out of the car. I hoped it work. I wanted to get through this case so I could talk to Yumi. I needed to talk to others about her brother. I rounded the car and shook my head.

Focus. I had to stay focused on this case at this moment. No mistakes. We ran up to the house. Tony pressed his ear against the garage door. He looked back at me and nodded. I fished the garage door opener out of my pocket.

My heart pounded in my chest. Fear and anxiety snaked underneath my skin as I pressed the button. The silent door lifted slowly. Tony and I drew our guns. As the door continued to lift, a black figure ducked behind the boxes.

"Seriously?" Tony glanced back at me.

"FBI! Come out with your hands up!" I shouted. "Come out now, or we start shooting."

The figure darted up with his hands up. Tony looked back at me, and I nodded. He holstered his gun and walked toward the figure who was moving toward us slowly. He cuffed him first and then removed his mask.

"Huh," I said. Desmond Holmes. Now that's interesting."

Tony shoved him in the backseat of the car. We had looked into both Holmes and Watson. Between the two, Holmes was the straight arrow. He didn't have any priors and no complaints during his work as a prison guard. He had never been reprimanded for anything. He hadn't bought anything out of the ordinary. Why would he want Bruce dead? Did he hate him that much?

When Tony had Holmes secured in the car, Tony and I exchanged a look of shock. I couldn't say who I was expecting, but it wasn't him.

We were both eager to get him back to the field office and ask him a shitload of questions.

"Lawyer," Holmes said as soon as we got back in the car.

I looked at Tony, who shook his head. Should have seen that coming.

CHAPTER THIRTY-TWO

After setting him up in the interrogation room and giving him his phone call, we left the room, annoyed. I was ready to talk to him. I was ready to figure out why he killed Bruce and what he knew about the Ortega and Dale murders.

My phone rang, and I fished it out of my pocket. "It's Love."

"Come to the IT department." And then she hung up.

"She wants us to come down. I guess she found something. I hope she found something." I followed Tony to the elevator. I hoped she'd found something, anything, that could tell us how to decipher the codes in Bruce's flash drive.

"Finally. You both need to come look at this." She pulled something up on the big screen. "I think Hummel and Bruce knew each other."

"What makes you say that?" I inched forward until I stood right in front of the screen.

"Well, it's a theory or... let me just show you." She pulled up another screen. "On Bruce's drive, there is a file labeled 'codes.' I wondered what the codes went to because, of course, it doesn't say. So, I ran the codes through the system to see if we had anything that it could unlock. And we did. The codes unlocked the files on Hummel's drive."

"What?" I stared at the screen. On Hummel's drive, we now had access to the cities the organization operated in, the names of the people used to procure the children or people trafficked, among other things. One of the codes unlocked a file on Bruce's drive.

"What is that file on Bruce's drive?" I asked. Love pulled it up.

"On his drive, it looks like these are their clients. They arrange them by their license plate numbers. I put two numbers in the system, and I got two names already. And not just in Honolulu."

"Did Bruce just solve one of our cases?" I asked, my voice barely above a whisper.

"Let's not give him that much credit." Love said. "He probably was using all this information to blackmail those people."

She was right, but still. He had all this information right at his fingertips. He could have brought so many people to justice, and yet he refused to do it until it worked in his favor. My blood boiled in my veins.

He could have helped so many people. Tears stung my eyes. I stepped away from the screen and walked out of the room. While I was already on the verge of tears, I might as well go all out. I grabbed Dane's file out of my desk and stormed into one of the interrogation rooms.

Yumi was brought to a room almost every day, and someone would ask her a bunch of questions that she refused to answer. But not today. She had to answer my questions today. Davies would be mad, but let her be bad. I needed answers.

I uncuffed her hands. Yumi still looked the same. Her long black hair pulled back into a sleek ponytail. Even without makeup, her skin looked flawless. I opened the file and slid it across the table.

"You should read that," I said on my way out the door. As I closed the door behind me, a man with a briefcase started walking toward me.

"I'm looking for my client, Desmond Holmes." His lawyer was younger than Tony but older than me. His sparkling blue eyes were still vibrant, even behind his glasses. I walked over to the other interrogation room and opened the door.

"Here he is."

He walked into the room, and I closed the door behind him. I walked over to my desk and sat down.

"What did you do?" Tony sat at his desk, watching me.

"I gave her her brother's file."

"You don't think that was a little cruel?"

I shrugged. "I think it was what the situation called for. If I told her what happened to her brother, she wouldn't believe me. She has to see it for herself. So now she can."

Desmond's lawyer stuck his head out of the door and waved me over. "I guess he's ready to talk."

Tony looked over at him. "I guess so. This should be interesting."

Desmond Holmes sat at the table, looking like a giant. He was a big man. Not just tall but wide as well. He was taller than Tony. He didn't look that big when he was wearing all black. They do say black is slimming.

"Why did you kill Bruce?" I asked. "Now, before you answer... before you say you don't know or that you didn't do it, let me tell you what we have. We have already decoded Bruce's flash drive. We know where the operations are. We have the client lists. We have everything. So, you can either tell us what you know, or you can go down with the ship."

He opened his mouth to say something, but I cut him off.

"At this point, we can charge you with whatever we want. Breaking and entering to start. But as soon as the organization learns that you are in prison, they are going to send someone to deal with you."

"Talking might save your life," said his lawyer in a loud whisper.

Desmond blinked several times. He stared at the table for a long moment. I didn't say anything else. This was his time to think, and he needed time to make his decision.

"What do you want to know?" The words came out as a sigh. He was hunched over the table, his chin touching his hands.

"Everything. Starting with who hired you to kill Bruce." I sat down in the chair across from him.

He sighed. "The leader of that organization. I don't think it has a name."

"The one that deals in child trafficking?" asked Tony.

"That's not all they do," he said. "It might be all you know about, but they have their hands in everything flesh-related. Not just children."

I blinked. I thought about Yumi and how she supplied Mrs. Blackstone with her murder victims. They had a hand in that, too. What else did they deal in?

"He wanted Bruce dead because he knew everything. A lot more than he should have. Not sure how he got all of the information. Bruce had used their services before and found them through his father-in-law. I think the guy was afraid that Bruce would turn him in, which sounds like something Bruce would do. So, he wanted him dead."

"Where is he?"

CHAPTER THIRTY-THREE

THE LEADER OF THE ORGANIZATION WAS NOT HARD TO find. It both amazed me and pissed me off at the same time. The more I learned about this guy, the more my blood burned.

Gage Wellsworth was born to a Japanese mother and a British father. His parents divorced when he was younger, and he lived with his father.

His early years beyond that were not well known.

I wondered if he stayed out of trouble when he was a kid. I wondered what happened to make him think selling flesh was a lucrative way to make money.

Love pulled up everything she could find about him. He wasn't hiding. That was the part that pissed me off the most. He lived in a lovely home that had three stories on five acres of land. And a lot of security.

The security I expected. I half expected him not to live on the island. Or even more, to not live so out in the open. It was like he believed he was never going to get caught. Like nothing or no one could touch him.

Well, all that was about to change.

Before we made a plan of action, I went back into Yumi's interrogation room.

She sobbed into her hands. Tears pricked the corners of my eyes. My heart dropped into my stomach. Maybe showing her the file was cruel, but she needed to see it. She needed to see what her brother was trying to do for her, how he tried to avenge her, how he held on to her memory.

"I thought he was dead," she said. "I just knew they had killed him. There was never a reason for me to come back if he wasn't here."

"If you tell us what you know, we can and will protect you. Finish what your brother started." I slid a notepad across the table with a pen. "Write down everything." I grabbed an agent and asked him to stay in the room with her.

I wasn't sure about leaving her alone, especially with the pen.

§

"This is going to be an intricate operation," said Davies. "Agents and SWAT will need to go in and get him. It's hard to say who he has there with him. It could be armed security guards, or it could be trafficking victims. Sometimes, they like to break them in by throwing parties and letting men take turns on the girls."

"I don't think we should wait any longer. I mean, we could wait until we know more about the area, but that is just going to give him time to get rid of evidence or escape. We need to get him now while it will still be a surprise."

Davies nodded. "That's true. She's right. If we are going to do it, then we need to do it now."

As an FBI agent, things can happen slowly or so quickly it is all a blur. This was a blur. The time I left the field office with Tony to the time we found the house whizzed by so quickly, I scarcely remember the route we took.

We pulled up to the beautiful house, and then chaos swarmed us. We were through the doors in a matter of seconds. Armed agents and police.

SWAT moved in front of us, ready to fire on anyone that popped up. My eyes fixed on the stairs as bullets buzzed over my head and whizzed by my ears. My feet ran toward the stairs before I could think. My chest tightened as I gasped for air. I ran up the stairs, ducking and dodging the bullets raining down on us.

"Hello," I said as I aimed my gun at a man in a large, minimally decorated room.

A smirk danced across his lips. "Wasn't expecting to see you here, Special Agent Mia Storm."

A chill ran through me. He knew my name. How?

He chuckled. "Yeah, I know all about you, and I find you quite interesting. First case and you stumble upon a serial killer. And you solve it. Rare. And most impressive."

"Well, thank you. I try to impress." I inched further into the room. Only then was I fully aware that I was alone with him. Everyone else was either still downstairs or searching the rest of the house.

Anxiety snaked under my skin. I tried to control my breathing so my hands didn't start shaking. "Put your hands up and get down on your knees."

The right corner of his mouth curved slightly. "So, who gave me away? Let me guess." His forefinger tapped against his chin. "Was it Bruce? No, he's dead. Desmond? Yumi? Zora?"

I blinked. *Who's Zora?*

There was a twinkle in his dark eyes. It was unnerving as he watched me. Out of the corner of my eye, I caught a glimpse of something metal. It was a gun. But he wasn't inching toward it. In fact, he was several feet away from it.

He should reach for his gun. I wanted him to reach for it. I wondered for a moment if he could read my mind. He glanced toward the dresser at the gun.

But instead of moving toward it, he threw his hands up in the air and got on his knees.

"Can't shoot me. I'm surrendering."

I didn't lower my gun. Nor did I move toward him to arrest him. I should have shot him. He deserved to be dead, like Dane and Bruce and everyone whose life had ended because of his "organization."

I should have shot him and put everyone out of their misery. I should have killed him. My heart pounded against my ribs. My pulse rushed in my ears, drowning everything else out.

The bullets downstairs, the shouting, the tremble in my hands, Tony's voice next to my ear.

My mind snapped back to reality. I glanced to my right and saw Tony staring at me.

"You okay?"

I nodded slowly. "Can you cuff him?"

He nodded and holstered his weapon before walking over to Wellsworth. He cuffed him and then yanked him up to his feet. The world swirled around me, buzzing and blurry.

Tony walked him out of the room. I moved to follow, but my legs buckled, and I collapsed to the ground.

I was so tired.

In the days that followed, Yumi and Desmond made a deal to tell Aisha everything they knew about the organization. I didn't know where Yumi was going after she testified. I thought it better not to ask. Desmond was going to prison but for a lighter sentence and under a different name.

Gage wouldn't speak even with his attorney present. He didn't care about going to prison or any of the threats that were made.

I tried my best to get him and everything else out of my mind. The case was solved. The Ortega and Dale families were killed because they stole money from the organization.

Desmond said even if they could pay it back, they would still have to die. But if either man was willing to pay it back, their families would have been spared.

I tried to stop thinking and wondering about why Mr. Dale and Mr. Ortega didn't try to pay it back to at least save their children.

I couldn't.

But at least it was over. We had put all the pieces of the puzzle together. The Dale and Ortega families had been given justice, we had more information than ever before on the organization, and the entire FBI field office mobilized to work with all sorts of agencies to bring in so many suspects. At this point, it was above our pay grade. And I was glad. Because my part in the case was over, and now I could finally rest.

EPILOGUE

"I can't believe you are hosting a party," said Tony as we walked to my condo.

"It's a New Year's party, and why is that so surprising?"

Aisha chuckled behind him. Apparently, I was right when I thought they had a relationship. It ended because Tony wasn't ready to get married, and she was. Both agreed to give it another try. I wasn't sure if that meant he was ready to get married now or if she was willing to overlook it.

It wasn't my business, so I didn't ask.

In my condo, there was a nice assortment of work friends and condo friends talking and drinking, waiting for the clock to strike midnight.

Harrison sat next to me on the sofa, while Tony and Aisha sat across from us. I watched them. All of them laughing and drinking. Old friends and new friends. A smile kissed my lips.

Usually, I was apprehensive about the start of a new year. Worried about where I was in life and that I wasn't doing enough. Or all the changes I should have made the year before.

But now, as I watched my friends laughing and leaned into my boyfriend, I was content.

Not only content but hopeful for the upcoming year. I thought about all the things I wanted to accomplish during the next year, and I finally felt the confidence that I could do it. I could do anything. I could handle anything that came my way.

And solve any case.

AUTHOR'S NOTE

Thank you so much for reading *Hidden in Paradise*. Did those lingering questions finally find their answers? I hope they did, but fear not – Mia's adventures are far from over! I can't wait for you to join Mia in the next book as she faces unexpected challenges when a fire erupts at the Golden Paradise Inn. With many leads from the nearby residents about the innkeeper's colorful marriage life to her many exes, Mia follows the trail of salacious gossip and evidence. But it's the discovery of a hidden place within the inn that really turns the case on its head, revealing intentional arson and a shocking truth about the inn woman. It's a narrative filled with twists and suspense, and the charm you've come to expect.

As a new indie author, I am incredibly appreciative of your support for this series. Your reviews and word of mouth recommendations fuel my passion for writing and for bringing these stories to life. If you could spare a few moments to leave a review for Hidden in Paradise, it would make a world of difference. Also, by sharing your thoughts, you can become an essential part of my creative process, allowing me to create an even more immersive reading experience for you in the future!

Are you feeling up to another mystery? I've got something perfect in mind for you to dive into – *The Good Marriage,* the thrilling finale of the Glenville Small Town Mystery Thriller series. After Detective Heather Bishop's marriage fell apart, she moved from the big city, longing for a fresh start. She began to heal and face her inner demons with each new case, but her past resurfaces when she's confronted with the case that almost shattered her world - the murders of Katy Graham and Lilly Arnold. As Heather attempts to vindicate her ex-husband, she finds herself in turmoil with questions about her marriage and the life she once knew. And amidst it all, a new romance blooms, but it seems deadly threats find her at every turn. This isn't just another case for Heather - it's an unraveling of her history, a convergence of long-held mysteries, and a cascade of revelations. Even if you haven't followed every twist and turn in the series, this book promises an epic adventure that stands on its own while providing newfound insights into Heather's journey.

Thank you again for your support, and I hope you continue to enjoy my books in the future!

Warm regards,
Cara Kent

P.S. I will be the first one to tell you that I am not perfect, no matter how hard I try to be. And there is plenty that I am still learning about self-publishing. If you come across any typos or have any other issues with this book please don't hesitate to reach out to me at cara@carakent.com, I monitor and read every email personally, and I will do my very best to rectify any issues that I am made aware of.

Get the inside scoop on new releases and get a **FREE BOOK** by me! Visit *https://dl.bookfunnel.com/513mluk159* to claim your **FREE** copy!

Follow me on **Facebook** - *https://www.facebook.com/people/Cara-Kent/100088665803376/*

Follow me on **Instagram** - *https://www.instagram.com/cara.kent_books/*

ALSO BY CARA KENT

Glenville Mystery Thriller

Prequel - The Bachelorette
Book One - The Lady in the Woods
Book Two - The Crash
Book Three - The House on the Lake
Book Four - The Bridesmaids
Book Five - The Lost Girl

Mia Storm FBI Mystery Thriller

Book One - Murder in Paradise
Book Two - Washed Ashore
Book Three - Missing in Paradise
Book Four - Blood in the Water
Book Five - The Case
Book Six - Hidden in Paradise

An Addictive Psychological Thriller with Shocking Twists

Book One - The Woman in the Cottage
Book Two - Mine

Made in United States
Troutdale, OR
03/02/2024

18135913R00159